where are we tomorrow?

TAVI TAYLOR BLACK

Relax. Read. Repeat.

WHERE ARE WE TOMORROW?
By Tavi Taylor Black
Published by TouchPoint Press
Brookland, AR 72417
www.touchpointpress.com

ISBN-13: 978-1-952816-36-9

Editor: Kimberly Coghlan
Cover Design: David Ter-Avanesyan, Ter33Design
Cover images: Bus image provided by Hans Schloesser
Author Photo: Mercedes Cardoza

Visit the author's website at http://www.taviblack.com/

First Edition

Printed in the United States of America.

"Tavi Black brings the reader right onto the bus with an all-access pass to the strange life that is touring. This is a riveting read and beautiful depiction of the ups and downs on the road of life."
—Norah Jones, Grammy Award-winning Singer/Songwriter

"After many tours with Tavi as our tour-manager and experiencing firsthand her humour, her thoughtfulness, her grounded-ness and her observant nature I had no doubt that she would be able to take me into the world behind the scenes of a tour in a way not many people could. If you ever wondered (just like I used to) what really happens behind those dark windows of a tour bus, or during sound-check in an empty theatre or in green rooms—all those dark and confusing alleyways and elevators away from the stage, Tavi will take you there."
—Deva Premal, Singer and Grammy Award Nominee
(*Deva*, Best New Age Album, 2018)

"Every so often, you find a book—against all odds—that changes the way you think. A book that you know you might not have found. *Where Are We Tomorrow?* is just such a book. Tavi Black has written a story about women who are ambitious, who are talented and who are free to their artistry. The main character works backstage in show business: in the dark behind the backdrop, using tools, wearing boots that protect the feet. When I was very young and still startled by the wonders of reading, I found a book that changed my understanding about how women daily contribute to saving society. Valerie Miner's novel about nurses in WWII, a novel that changed me, that I have never forgotten. Books can change your mind about life, about what work you might do, about what kinds of other 'you's might be out there, working in the world. *Where Are We Tomorrow?* will change some readers, especially girls and young women who need the critical reminder that not all women wear heels."
—A.J. Verdelle, Author, *The Good Negress*

"*Where Are We Tomorrow* is the kind of book you sink so deeply into it makes real life seem somehow inauthentic. A gripping, earnest and layered novel about the long and arduous search for a sense of identity—of home— it follows unconventional mid-thirties rock concert electrician Alex Evans as she struggles to overcome her past, family secrets, and the uncertainty of the future. The writing is as musical as the rock concert settings, gorgeous and sublime, but more impressive still is Tavi Black's extraordinary ability to page after page illuminate the truth at the heart of being human: that more often than not, good and bad, right and wrong, are blurred among shades of grey."
—Philip Elliot, Editor, *Into the Void* Magazine,
Author, *Nobody Move*

"This was, hands down, my most beloved novel of the year. I would wait all day to read it, count the minutes until my children were asleep so I could spend time with these women again. Our culture has a particular addiction to fame, and Tavi Black pulls back the curtain on that world and shows us the underbelly as only a woman who has lived on the road can. The lack of a dominant male gaze in this book is striking. I want to press this book into the hands of every woman starting out in music and say, 'Read this. Fame isn't real. But music is, and it's worth it.'"

—Ara Lee James, Singer/Songwriter, Voice Coach

"What starts out as a fascinating foray into the lives of female roadies touring with a megastar becomes something far more profound and lasting. Equal parts *Almost Famous* and *Under the Tuscan Sun, Where Are We Tomorrow?* is a winning novel about grief, trauma, and friendship, and reminds us that it's never too late to become the star of your own life."

—Leland Cheuk, Author, *No Good Very Bad Asian*

"I couldn't put this book down! It's truly an authentic portrayal of touring life for women in the music industry, in both technical and musical roles. The trials and tribulations that women have in such a male-dominated business and the real subtleties of these difficulties—some of which aren't immediately obvious from the outside looking in. Also dealing with the heartbreak of personal loss and grief, past trauma, current abuse, burnout and how it affects the way women have to 'toughen up' to operate under such harsh conditions—which is nothing like most people's perception of a 'glamorous' career! A really honest insight into how touring can affect friendships, relationships, and mental health. Very highly recommended!"

—Sarah Ozelle, Singer/Songwriter.

"Tavi Taylor Black's debut novel offers great writing that draws readers into male-dominated world of toxic masculinity and misogyny to which very few of us have access: the road crew on a concert tour. The book has an "insider" quality that adds an intrigue of its own. The story focuses on four women who are essential to the tour and yet exist on the margins of the boys' club, subjected to "everyday sexism" that, despite their strength and fortitude, they have no easy way to combat. The author seamlessly weaves in the protagonist Alex's miscarriage and subsequent period of grieving and soul-searching. Alex's emotional journey allows Black to show just how deeply inhospitable this workplace is for any woman who is experiencing this difficult loss and yet can't afford to show her vulnerability. Taking readers from New York to Mexico to Tuscany, on the tour bus and behind the scenes of rock concert, with Alex at the centre, the novel presents a literal and figurative exploration of the question: "where are we tomorrow?"

—Tracy Isaacs, Professor of Philosophy at Western University,
Co-Author of *Fit at Mid-Life: A Feminist Fitness Journey*

To Dorsey and Zelda:

We traveled so far, never knowing for sure.

Narrow road, wide road, all of us on it, unhappy,
Unsettled, seven yards short of immortality
And a yard short of not long to live.
Better to sit down in the tall grass
and watch the clouds,
To lift our faces up to the sky,
Considering—for most of us—our lives have been a constant
mistake.

—Charles Wright, *Road Warriors*

It is difficult to know what to do with so much happiness.
With sadness there is something to rub against,
a wound to tend with lotion and cloth.
When the world falls in around you, you have pieces to pick up,
something to hold in your hands, like ticket stubs or change.

—Naomi Shihab Nye, *So Much Happiness*

Chapter 1

INSIDE THE CONCRETE arena, programmed lights whirred and spun in rhythm; eleven thousand fans watched, mesmerized, as vibrant magenta and violet beams sliced through midnight black. On stage, the band regurgitated the same set as the night before, and the night before that. They'd performed the set in Mexico City and Guadalajara. As far south as Santiago and Lima. The road crew for Sadie Estrada's *Home Remedy* tour knew each dip in volume, each drop in the beat. They knew exactly, down to the second, how much time it required to step outside and suck down a Marlboro. These time-zone travelers planned bathroom breaks by the songs' measures; no one missed a cue to mute the stage mics, to hand out room-temp bottled water for set breaks, to pull up house lights.

Behind heavy velvet curtains, separated from the frenzied pace of the show, Alex unscrewed the cover of a moving light to expose the core: circuit boards and capacitors, motors connected to color wheels. Deep bass, feedback, and the fevered pitch of collective voices penetrated the curtain, the familiar, almost comforting reverberations of life on the road. Alex continued her diagnosis, removing the light harness as a mother removes a soiled diaper—routinely, with a touch of tenderness. While she located and replaced the broken part, she kept an ear to the music, alert to the final measure of the set, ready to repack her multi-wheeled toolbox, move on to the next city, set up again.

Alex ran the light through all its functions, testing and retesting once she'd replaced the gobo wheel. The body of the light panned and tilted, working fine. A small victory.

"Sure you know what you're doing, little lady?" Alex turned at the familiar voice of the tour's production manager.

"Funny," she said. "Very original. For that, you get to help me put it away." Alex waited for another barb, one about her not being able to lift the seventy pounds by herself, but Joe simply helped her flip and crate the unit, a harder task for him at 5'2" than it was for Alex, a good five inches taller.

The arena crackled in anticipation of the show's climax. Thousands of voices swelled and surged, a unified congregation. The body of the moving light settled into the carved Styrofoam, and Alex tucked its tail inside the handle. As she slammed the case shut, Joe's laminate got caught inside the box, and he was jerked down by the lanyard around his neck. He freed the latches and yanked it clear, smoothing the wrinkles from the photo of his two young children, a wallet-sized clipping he'd taped behind his backstage pass. Joe caught Alex eyeing the photo.

"When are you gonna give in and pop out a few yourself?" Joe asked.

Alex breathed slowly, letting a brief sadness settle into her body, though her face wore a practiced, blank expression. She gestured into the smothering dark, into the roar of the crowd and sweat-filled air. "And give up all this?"

* * *

On the other side of the curtain, every seat in the arena was sold, but no one was sitting. Fans swayed, shifted, and strained to see the stage. Sadie's devotees knew every word. They echoed her inflections, imitated each expression, every impassioned gesture she made. Alex stepped through the black drapes and checked the digital clock on top of the lighting dimmers. Eleven minutes left. She blocked out spectators who leaned over the railing and gawked, probably wondering what it's like to be her, so close to the performance, within spitting distance of Sadie Estrada.

Center stage, Sadie glistened. Her vibrato soared over the lead guitar. Alex tuned in, recognizing the crescendo. Moving lights—red, amber, cyan—fanned over the audience; patterns changed, strobes flashed, and sparks cascaded across the stage. The production chased the highest heights as the concert keened toward a close.

Sadie and her dancers dropped into position on stage, drenched with sweat, chests heaving. The dancers knelt and crouched into an arc around her, chins up, arms extended. Sadie stood stock still, her left hand poised to punch straight up into the air. She gripped the mic six inches from her lips so she could belt the high C, and BOOM, fist in the air. Choreographed, pure white light streamed through a mist of haze and drew a tight focus on the group center stage, the band behind them lit with just a faint glow of blue.

Confetti cannons burst: cellophane rained over the audience and covered their sweaty heads, stuck to their skin. The crowd couldn't get enough. Some fans, dazed and disoriented, worked up to delirium, opened their mouths, attempting to eat the confetti as if it was communion.

Performers bounded offstage into the wings. Dancers rolled their shoulders, halting here and there to stretch a hamstring or quad. Sound guys took leering gapes at a slender brunette while she bent over, hands on the floor. They'd miss this small freedom, this opportunity to be voyeurs, once they were back home with their wives and girlfriends.

After a break that whipped the audience up into a sufficient frenzy of longing, the band sauntered back onstage, all strut and arrogance, hands in the air, asking for further applause. At the encore song, the bass player nearly forgot the bridge, his lick dissonant and off-beat for a few bars. Thrown, the drummer played too fast on a song they'd performed every night for months. In a domino effect of confusion, the board op missed several lighting cues and left the guitarist in the dark for half his solo until the sound engineer turned around and prodded him to hit the cue. Even Sadie made a rash move with her wireless mic and whacked a dancer fully in the gut.

A collective gasp rang out as Sadie balanced, tips of her boots licking the edge of the stage. The dancer Sadie had struck was doubled over a foot upstage of where they'd collided. For a fraction of a second it seemed Sadie might fall, that she might land on the hard cement of the pit, in the gap between the stage and barricade. Three yellow-shirted security guards rushed to the pit, instinctively hoping to catch her.

Though only a segment of the audience understood what had happened, Alex could see that the musicians were shaken, taking fleeting glances at each other. Only Sadie's voice, once she recovered her balance, pulled the performance out of chaos, her notes clear and tinged with emotion. The band limped through the last few notes while Sadie strapped on a blue Ibanez and strummed an Em7. The band dropped out one by one, until it was just her and her guitar, the stage dark but for a small halo of light. A whispered word, a last soft strum and *voila,* her fans adored her. They'd forgotten, or forgiven, the less-than-perfect performance. The board op hit the blackout cue. Impeccable timing.

Backstage, the crew kept their eyes focused on their gear, taking furtive glimpses up as they detected movement, as sounds grabbed their attention, though every one of them was shrewd enough to avoid Sadie as she stormed off stage. Recognizing rage in her swift exit, in the set of her jaw, they hid their grins until she disappeared down the hallway. Within minutes, the pressure of a quick load-out replaced their amusement. No one except the new production assistant took the time to laugh at the gaffes until trucks were packed, until they were on the tour bus with drinks in hand.

4

"Oh my God," Brooke squealed, clicking up to Alex in her high heels. "Holy shit, did you see Sadie run into that dancer?"

Alex glanced up from coiling a cable, took in Brooke's flowing maroon dress, her lime green scarf that could easily get caught in a running chain motor, a frivolous piece of clothing that had the potential to choke Brooke as if she was Isadora Duncan. "Yeah. That guy's history," Alex said, trying to be nice to the new gal, despite her makeup, her outfit. "He'll probably be fired before we're done loading out."

"Geez, I hope she doesn't fire me before I get out on stage with her," Brooke said.

Kat, the guitar tech, who had been listening in, carefully laid Sadie's Ibanez in its road case and laughed hardily. "What, she's going to ask the PA to come out on stage and—let me guess—iron her dress? Schedule a car?"

"I'll have you know I had a flourishing singing and acting career in Nashville before I foolishly moved to New York," Brooke announced. "And, by the way, Sheryl Crow and Paula Cole both started as back-up singers."

"News flash," Kat said. "If you ain't a star by the time you're pushing thirty-five, odds are against you—but whatever, none of my business." A smack of reality that Brooke promptly ignored.

During load-out, local stagehands took their time, sat in groups and chatted, telling stories until Alex marched up and gave orders. Only one of the eight local guys assigned to Alex gave her any trouble—a young man unwilling to take orders.

"So, tell me," he asked in a thick Brazilian accent, after he'd followed her around making small talk in broken English. "How you get this job?"

Wearing only a tank top and shorts, sweltering in the stuffy arena, Alex coiled up the last of the steel cables used to hang the lighting rig. Thick swipes of grease covered her hands and biceps; her face was streaked black with dirt and grime where she had wiped sweat from her brow. Out of the corner of her eye, she spied Joe, doing an "idiot check" at front-of-house, peering under risers, in dark corners, making sure nothing had been forgotten.

Alex jerked her head towards Joe, keeping a straight face. "Oh," she said. "I slept with him."

The stagehand backed away, hands up in a gesture of defeat, embarrassed for having insinuated.

Fans glanced back over their shoulders as they exited, startled by the sound of chain motors moving. They didn't stop to watch, afraid to break the spell Sadie had cast. They were pleased for the night to envelop them, with beams of headlights cutting through a moonless sky.

In the alleyway just outside *Arena Olimpica*, in view of a row of tan and blue and black tour buses, a couple threw down 200 *real* on a bundle of smack, the only high that might make them forget they'd missed the Sadie Estrada show. Three hours later, they watched enviously as the road crew, free of radios, multi-tools, wrenches, and badges, hopped aboard the buses. They heard the massive rolling metal doors come crashing down behind the last semi-truck, heard the engines rev as drivers pulled out of the bays.

"*Olha, por aqui,*" the tripping woman pleaded, thrilled when the stage manager turned his head. But she had nothing more to say, knew that as the tour moved on, she was unlikely to be remembered.

Watching the city slide by, Alex felt a well-known yank, a mixture of anticipation and dread at going on to the next city. As the crew plopped themselves on the patterned couches, as they opened cans of Bohemia Weiss and tucked away their tools, Alex patted Ethan, her most devoted and loyal (almost puppy-like) electrician, on the leg, a silent gesture of thanks for his work and his allegiance. She laid her head back on the seat and allowed her thoughts to drift fully to her private life, to what was ahead: to life, eventually, off tour.

Chapter 2

ALEX WOULD HAVE turned Connor away after his first approach but for the fact that he made her laugh. He took his time that night at Jazz Alley, watching a couple of other suit-coated men talk to Alex, each rebuffed with a shake of her head and the softest of smiles. He kept looking over his shoulder at her, a single hard-backed chair between them. The glow of a flickering candle on his table threw faint shadows across his day-old stubble.

Connor never smiled at Alex, just gave her a level glance here or there, like he was scouting for bad weather, trying to decide whether he should prepare. The third time he rotated around, his electric blue hipster shirt bright against the muted burgundy of the stage curtains, Alex self-consciously chased the lime in her half-empty gin and tonic with a flimsy bar straw, trying to avoid his gaze. When the backlight, focused too high off the lip of the stage, hit the second row, she noticed his mop of light brown hair had the slightest hint of thinning at the crown.

Sadie's drummer, who'd been tapping out a mad rhythm behind a trap kit on the old, scuffed stage (a side project between legs of Sadie's world tour), headed out to say hello at set break. He performed admirably, driving at the front of the beat, playing with more abandon than he was allowed in Sadie's band. Alex gave the drummer a hug and ordered him a highlands whiskey; the waiter brought a local IPA for Kat, who had talked Alex into coming downtown to catch the show. Kat had picked up this short three-week run as backline tech, though drums and horns weren't her specialty. "I figured any yahoo can put a cymbal on a stand, tighten a snare head and slip in some new reeds," she explained.

After a brief laugh over nude photos of Sadie (questionably her—possibly Photoshopped?) published in the *Enquirer*, Alex relayed a story about Kat's second day on the job, when she spilled milk on the tiled floor in catering. The people behind Kat in line waited for her to wipe up the mess, but Kat just stepped around the milk and announced, "Not my gig."

"Kat left the puddle there for everyone to leap over," Alex explained, still outraged, even though she was used to the touring crew who tended to be vocal about whether a task was theirs.

Kat shrugged unabashedly now at the drummer. "I'm not a janitor."

Their break was almost over; the recorded house music kicked off, giving the signal it was time to start the second act. Her friends downed their drinks. Kat waved her hand in front of her face to ward off smoke from the cigarette burning at the table next to them (from nearly half the tables in the audience). Alex, feeling a sneeze come on, tried to hold it back, but suddenly hiccupped as the sneeze exploded from her nose, the sound loud and strange and echoing into the pre-show-quiet. Rising, the drummer patted Alex on the shoulder before heading backstage, Kat in tow. "Genteel as ever," he said, being from the South and thinking of women in terms of manners and delicate natures.

Connor turned around at the noise, eyebrows raised in surprise. He leaned across the chair between them, his large, surprisingly smooth-skinned hand pressing into the lacquered wood. "I have a friend who always has an insane sneezing session when she's had too much to eat. Like she's under a spell. The sneezes can go on for an hour. I'm afraid to go out to dinner with her," Connor said confidentially.

"Looks like I'd fall into that category too," Alex said, finding herself relaxed with this sort of square-looking, tidy man who must have been at least a decade older than her.

"I'd risk a meal with you," Connor said, lifting the corner of his mouth as if he'd just told her a joke, so she couldn't tell if he was serious. "And just so you don't feel embarrassed at the noise you just made," he said, "I'll tell you about someone I worked with who had a hiccupping problem. He had some strange affliction that made him say 'meep' whenever he hiccupped. So, I'd be typing away in my cubicle and hear him across the room making these random high-pitched 'meep' sounds. Of course, everyone called him 'Meep'."

When Connor smiled, Alex felt an unexpected stir of energy. His bottom tooth was crooked, his eyes glistened when he stared straight at her, as if she was the most interesting person in the room, the way so few people engage. Over the course of the fifteen years Alex had spent meeting new stagehands in every city, she had noticed that most gave a fleeting look in the eyes, then looked away. Some never looked up, but Connor, he was fully engrossed, and it threw her off guard, having grown up with a mother who never looked her in the eye. A therapist she briefly saw hinted that was why she never trusted in love. Mothers, the therapist said, were supposed to give eye contact in those first few months, to help babies feel safe, feel attached.

"That's not a true story," Alex said warily, but Connor swore to the veracity.

Alex couldn't help but laugh when Connor imitated the guy, making a 'meep' sound between songs, ten minutes after he had turned back to the show. Connor 'meeped' a few more times before he finally looked at her again; Alex waved him over to her table.

Under the sweet, delicious notes of the trombonist and the deep resonance of the bass, Alex told Connor about touring, about life in range of a famous person.

"I never think of a woman doing that kind of job," Connor said, eyeing the bright yellow posts of the mezzanine. "I don't mean to be sexist. I've just never thought about road crews before."

Alex bet he was incredibly handsome in his day. Lanky still and classic-featured, as if carved by a late Renaissance artist, he had the confidence of a playboy, though he didn't seem haughty. He almost behaved as if something had humbled him—age, perhaps. Maybe a tragedy.

"Most women probably wouldn't put up with taking three-minute showers in mold-ridden locker rooms in the middle of the night," she said. "But don't get me wrong; there are plenty of perks too: boating trips and river rafting. We've driven cars on the Indie 500 racetrack. Submerged in a shark cage in Oahu. Of course, all those activities are scheduled by promoters during our down time, so you have to choose sleep or adventure."

Connor told Alex that the last big adventure outing he'd taken was nine years ago: walking the *Camino de Santiago* in Spain—much of which turned out to be paved roads, rather than the dirt paths he'd longed for. "There's an excess of pavement in my life. I commute to Bellevue every day through stupid amounts of traffic over the 520 bridge."

He also (amid trying to wrap his complete history into a few pat sentences) admitted quietly that he had a grown daughter, Lucy, whom he hardly knew. "She lives in Virginia, where I'm from." Connor turned his face as he spoke the girl's name, breaking the steady gaze he'd kept while leaning in towards Alex, so she didn't press him for details, though she did wonder how someone could leave their own child.

They talked until the club closed down, until onstage Kat placed each set of chimes in velvet-lined sacks and drumheads in molded plastic cases, until she'd unplugged every mic, folded every stand, closed every road case and packed the trailer out in the back alley, ready to roll on to the next town.

Chapter 3

AT NEARLY ONE A.M., across New York, there was no sign that the party was dying. In clubs on the lower East Side, at galleries in Soho, in lofts uptown and in warehouses downtown, highs were peaking. Eyes dilated; fingernails scratched at prickly skin. Conversations turned to what users thought of as deep, but to the few who were sober—who were there to see art, eat food, or quell the loneliness—those conversations sounded ridiculous and shallow.

Lily watched the posers—Sadie's followers and hangers-on—as they swarmed around and tried to win Sadie's favor with jokes and stories. Lily had noticed that each person in her boss' entourage seemed to host some aspect of Sadie's personality—maybe a trait that she couldn't afford to portray: usually there was a loud, bellicose type; a mousey, studious person; maybe a drunk, or a cackling burn-out.

All night at Sadie's loft in Tribeca, two up-and-coming fashion designers recounted tales of fashion week in Milan, or 'Milano' as they pronounced it, with heavily faked Italian accents. Lily knew where they lived: in Brooklyn.

Lily couldn't engage with any more farce than what she already dealt with nightly—Sadie on stage, Sadie feigning sincerity, Sadie in the throes of distress when she felt snubbed or disrespected, wandering around her apartment swearing in the Chilean Spanish she learned from her father: *'Huevon culiado'* or *'Andate a la chucha'*.

It took weeks for Sadie to finish fretting after she caught a headline in *USA Today*: "SLAM DANCERS: SEXY SADIE POISED OVER THE PIT" with an accompanying photo of her in Rio, balanced on tiptoe near the edge of the stage, while the dancer doubled over from the blow. Time eventually lessened the intensity of Sadie's embarrassment. Shame was easily buried, Lily knew, by proceeding to the next adventure, by surrounding yourself with people who flattered you. Thus, the late-night party.

So, Lily didn't join in the conversations. She pretended she was a waiter and treaded the perimeter with a plastered-on smile, quietly orbiting the couches around the fireplace. Once she established that nobody needed a drink, she sank into an empty brown leather armchair, clutching a lambskin pillow. Only six people still lingered, the vestiges that followed Sadie and Lily home from the back room at Bungalow 8 in Chelsea. An intimate few for a Saturday night. Lily knew how it would go: they'd all refuse to leave until they were forced to, until they were escorted to the foyer, coats pressed into hands, until the elevator door slid closed, and they continued to gaze yearningly over Lily's shoulder for a last glimpse of Sadie.

A Wall Street guy, Kyle, helped himself to another bourbon over at the glass-topped bar. To Lily's eye, he seemed slightly out of place as he treaded across the Turkish carpet, stepping gingerly as if afraid to spill. "Taxis take forever after midnight," he complained.

"So, stay here," Sadie offered. "Jules has already claimed the spare," she said and gestured toward her old friend from boarding school. "Lily won't mind if you use her room."

Lily pictured her old, cramped room in a moldy-smelling railroad apartment in Williamsburg, the last place that felt like her own. Since Sadie always kept Lily near for emergencies—which often came in the middle of the night when Sadie couldn't sleep, or had an idea, or wanted to 'talk' (once, Sadie even called Lily into her bedroom during a thunderstorm, like a child)—Lily gradually moved into Sadie's palatial loft, where she was surrounded by stainless steel appliances and lathered up under dual showerheads in a marble stall.

Of course, there were these other costs. The last time Sadie so casually offered up Lily's room to a guest—to, really, a nobody—Lily was too shocked to respond. She spent the night stewing on the squeaky leather couch in Sadie's den with a piece of lightweight fabric—a 'plush throw'—over her shoulders, surrounded by tall shelving stocked with hard-covered books.

Lily had once asked Sadie, pulling a leather-bound copy of *The Aeneid* off the shelf, if she'd ever read any of the titles. "God no," Sadie said. "The guy who decorated the apartment insisted that it would give the 'otherwise airy décor' some 'well needed gravity'. I think it looks like my father's study, all this musty paper. I should have fired that decorator. No one who comes in here is looking for anything heavy."

"Hear, hear," Lily had said, knowing full well how any sense of dignity seemed to be left at the door during one of Sadie's parties. She'd once found a gal puking into a vintage Hopi pottery bowl in the den; she'd overheard a million conversations about vacations in Bali and Monte Carlo, chatter about new lines of Fendi or Cartier sunglasses. Occasionally Lily's interest had been sparked: one guest tonight cited a new company called Tesla designing electric cars. Of course, not one of the chit-chatters commented about the environmental impact, only that, well, Elon Musk, the founder, was so young and kind of cute and had sooo much money. Not a hint of solemnity around any of Sadie's guests. This time, Lily would not let Sadie roll over her quietly.

"Actually, I think he'd be more comfortable in the den. I have photos spread all over my bed. And I'm still packing. There's your packing to do too, Sadie. Off to Singapore tomorrow night. It's getting late."

"Lily, don't be rude," Sadie said.

"I'm in the middle of a project," Lily protested, a lame attempt to draw a protective circle around her photography. "My room's a mess."

"Go clean it up, then."

The women glared at each other, Lily barely hanging on to her forced smile, until everyone in the room became uncomfortable. People shuffled their feet or took quiet sips of their drinks, the only sound ice tinkling in glasses. "What kind of photos?" Kyle asked.

Before Lily could even answer, Sadie explained. "My assistant is quite the hobbyist, *una aficionada*, taking pictures of all the crew on tour—she's always pointing that camera at stagehands and even at the gear. Imagine that," Sadie said. "Who wants to see a photo of a road case?"

The dig made Lily's jaw clench, though what Sadie said was true; she did take photos of carpenters as they set up the stage, lighting crew who ran cables and climbed way up into the grid. Lily carried with her an old Minolta Maxxum 7000, a relic of the pre-digital age, strapped across her back. Since they'd been off tour, her interest had shifted. Rather than focusing at eye level, she had begun to closely observe what lay at her feet—human beings' connection to the Earth as they moved around and over the ground. Several weeks ago, she began to zoom in on shoes, on toes and heels, leather and canvas.

Earlier tonight, Lily noticed this man Kyle's attempts to engage Sadie, his slightly appealing eyes, his jokes about his own lack of panache. Banter that had clearly worked on the designers who laughed heartily while Sadie gave a lukewarm nod. Lily could have told him that Sadie preferred straight flattery over self-deprecating humor.

She knew this from experience: Lily had put a lot of effort into appeasing Sadie's whims over the years. She ran out minutes before show call in Buenos Aires when Sadie freaked out at her wardrobe options and decided the remedy was the exact pair of flared pants she'd seen at a tango hall the night before.

In Costa Rica, Lily drove Sadie around the jungle to search for a white-headed capuchin ("the kind they had on the show *Friends*," Sadie said excitedly). After three hours of straining their heads out the window of a rented jeep, they spotted the monkey as it swung from the treetops. "Marcel!" Sadie screamed. "*Llegado a mama!*"

Sadie once even asked her to hand-roll sushi, knowing full well that Lily couldn't even cook Sadie's simple Chilean comfort food, *cazuela*, nothing but boiled meat and vegetables. The one time Lily made the stew, Sadie poked at a chunk of corn, wrinkled her nose, and took one nibble before she pushed the bowl away.

"Want to see the photos?" Lily asked Kyle now, surprising herself. "Then you can decide which room suits you better." Lily refused to look over at Sadie, who must have been fuming.

Kyle's tie was loosened at the neck, and his creased suit jacket was worn at the cuffs, though the cut was tailored and the material was a fine, silk blend. His leather soles slapped on travertine tiles. He was slight, though taller than Lily; at his hairline, a few white flakes of dandruff sprinkled his dark, coiffed hair.

Lily opened the door and paused briefly before she flipped on the light, before she let a stranger step into her sanctum. A fleeting acknowledgement rolled over her that she had only invited this man in to spite Sadie, to defy her. And a quieter urge to seek out admiration of her photos, even from a stranger.

On the bed, her most recent project: black and white photos strewn across a quilted beige spread.

"You have a fetish?" Kyle was drunk, she realized, as he approached. The odor of stale bourbon, peaty and sour, seeped through his pores.

Only now did Lily let go, did she relax the stiff, practiced smile that coated her face whenever she dealt with Sadie. "Let's say a fascination." She picked up a photo and studied the rough, calloused heel, the orange tint of rust on a fire escape. Lily didn't always remember who her subjects were, saw mostly the feet, body parts. After she snapped this shot, though, Lily watched the girl, admiring her agility, her lighthearted movements. She had the sweetest angelic face—her cheeks full and round, her lips nearly heart-shaped.

"What are you trying to get at?" Kyle asked.

Lily looked approvingly down at the photo, deciding right then that she would tuck this photo into her suitcase, travel with this dear angelic girl through Asia. "Transitions."

"Like, moving from here to there?" He pointed to a set of photos she'd grouped: a threadbare shoe on a homeless boy next to the spiked heels of a businesswoman. "A story about fortune, good and bad?"

Lily shuffled through the photos. She brushed aside loafers and flats, brown and black, to divine a hint of a story, to reach for narrative. Finally, she chose combat boots at a bus stop and a photo of cross trainers leaping over a puddle. "Inertia versus motion," she said.

His gold watch glinted in the lamplight as he reached across the bed to extract a picture of Italian shoes with squared-off toes. "And what does a pair like this mean?"

Warming to him, Lily peered down at his feet. At least he was trying now, not merely feigning ignorance of art. "Certainly anyone wearing shoes like that is among the fortunate."

"Fortunate, indeed," Kyle agreed as he slid his arms around Lily's waist. He tugged at her, drew her near. "Tell me," he said, "what's it like to live with Sadie Estrada?"

Lily stiffened. There it was: the ultimate question.

For a brief second, before she could react, his mouth touched hers, his breath hot and acerbic, his lips dry. She cried out as he hauled her down onto the bed, into the midst of her photos. Lily wriggled out of his grasp and struggled to her feet.

"Get up," she yelled and yanked on his arm. "Off, off."

He clambered off the bed and brushed photos from his suit. A moment ago, his thin mouth wore a jovial, lopsided grin, but now his jaw hardened. His rheumy, drunken eyes tried to focus as Lily straightened creases on the scattered photos.

"I thought we had a connection," he mumbled.

"I thought you were interested in my work," she said.

His eyes, refocused, displayed an icy mixture of arrogance and hard pride. "You. Your work—whatever."

If she were a different sort of woman—more Brooke-like—Lily might have learned to enjoy the advantages of this life, through the people she has met in Sadie's circles. But she could never live off Sadie's leavings. She couldn't manage to see the good in people when each action was tainted by the desire to be next to fame. The posers were constantly seeking Sadie's attention, her approval, though chances of gaining her attention (forget approval altogether!) were thin. In lieu of eye contact, they'd try just to soak up a little of Sadie's light, ignorant of the fact that most of the shimmer around Sadie was turned on and maintained by a whole crew of technicians. Like addicts, the posers hung around and shared cigarettes on balconies, waiting for just one more taste.

"Explain to Sadie that you've decided to take a cab home." Lily crossed to the door with shaking limbs. "Or I will."

With the defeated posture of a contestant eliminated from a competition, Kyle stepped reluctantly over the threshold. Lily heard him hesitate, anticipating more, as she locked the door behind him. No doubt he was not used to rejection. Finally, his shoes clomped unevenly toward the rest of the guests, away from her. The posers wouldn't miss her, she assumed, out at the party.

* * *

Sadie's eyes followed a couple across the living room—a metrosexual in skinny jeans with an ironic moustache and his girlfriend with jet black hair, death girl bangs. The pair, who held undefined jobs at her record label, had just returned from the

17

bathroom for the fourth time that night—together. Jules sank into the couch next to Sadie and laid his head on her shoulder, a posture they used to take in prep school, while they watched reruns of M*A*S*H in the middle of the night, Jules attempting to stay awake through her bouts of insomnia.

Jules intuited where Sadie's gaze stopped—on the girl's tongue as she licked the last tingling bits of powder from her gums. "Tempted?" he whispered. Even as a young student, Sadie would try any substance that floated across her table. "I mean really—coke? Aren't the kids these days doing ecstasy or crystal?"

"What, now you're on the other side of knowing what people are doing at parties?" Sadie asked. "And more importantly, how are you going to be my opening act on tour if you can't do a little partying?"

"I—and you—play better without it," Jules said.

"For old time's sake? The two of us, all-nighter?" Sadie leaned into him, remembering the tangy nasal drip. "Or won't your girlfriend let you?" she asked sarcastically, almost regretting that she'd agreed to sign Brooke on as the tour production assistant again this tour.

"Can't do it, darlin'," Jules lamented. "And not just because of Brooke. I've got a good thing going now. And so do you, sister. Didn't you say we're going to stay on the straight and narrow this tour with that cutesy little assistant of yours? Granola and kelp and Vitamin D? Where'd she go, anyway?"

Just as he asked the question, Kyle reentered the living room. "Fascinating photographs," he said to no one in particular and helped himself to another whiskey. He loitered awkwardly by the bar, fingers clutched around his glass, as he circled and swirled the ice cubes with one eye on Sadie. The designers had struck up a conversation with the record label people, each holding a drink, jutting hips and tossing glances.

"Stay up with me anyway," Sadie whispered to Jules. "We'll kick these fools out, and you can catch me up on your life. Tell me about some new song you've written that you'll let me sing."

By ones or twos, with some urging, the guests eventually trickled out the door. Before they went, the designers managed to secure a private fitting with Sadie. "Go get Lily—" Sadie said with a wave, "down the hall on the left—and tell her to schedule it." Sadie glanced over at Jules. "She's not off-duty until I say she's off-duty."

The record label duo, cranked up and ready to perform a vigil in the foyer if necessary, finally came out and straight up offered Sadie the coke. "Mother may I?" she pleaded, but Jules rose from the couch and escorted them out. Against the odds, Jules quickly found an on-duty cab in the wee hours and forced Kyle, too, to depart. Sadie waited by the fire, until it was just she and Jules and the memories between them.

* * *

Lily tucked the photo of the girl on the fire escape in the side pocket of her carry-on, bundled up incense, two taper candles, a book on rituals. She dragged a velvet-lined box from under her bed and packed the rest of the photos inside, arranging the project in order, all the while contemplating her disaster of a life, marveling at how complex she found relationships. The last guy she dated, over three months ago, she met at a camera store—he was looking for an underwater camera for a trip to the Bahamas (that should have told her enough right there), so she helped him out, steered him away from the Panasonic towards the Canon G16.

She made the mistake, after their second date, of bringing him back to Sadie's. Lily misjudged him, thought for some reason because he was an adjunct professor of English at NYU that he wouldn't be star-struck. Foolishly, she imagined that he might not even know who Sadie was. Not everyone listened to pop music. He'd talked about Breton and Crevel and Rimbaud all night. They'd even touched on religion—he was a lapsed Jew. She shied away from stories about her upbringing in a Pentecostal church, stuck with her interest in the Celts and their worship of Mother Earth, Father Sky.

In the den, where they sat and sipped prosecco, bodies flushed by the glow from a gas fireplace, Sadie appeared in the doorway under the pretense of looking for her laptop. As if a flashbulb had gone off, Lily felt she ceased to exist. Sadie gobbled up his attention, crossed her legs and flipped her hair in an exaggerated manner that let Lily know Sadie had taken some sort of upper.

So rapt with Sadie's inane story about touching an iguana in Barbados, her date barely nodded as Lily excused herself. In the bathroom, she splashed water on her face and unscrewed the cap to a prescription bottle, downing two Ativan with a sip of water from her palm. She talked herself down from quitting, like she'd done fifty times over the last year. She reminded herself what it was like to live hand to mouth as a yoga teacher, how she scrabbled the rent together through temp jobs, took loans from friends, and paid visits to the bakery outlet store for day-old bread. After several deep breaths to calm her angry pulse, Lily stuck her head back in the den with a forced smile. "I think we should call it a night."

"I'll let him out," Sadie said, straight-faced as a poker player.

That next morning, as Lily prepared Sadie's spirulina shake, as she threw lethicin and spinach and ginger and acai berries into the blender, she sucked up her courage, drew her fury into her mouth, and spit into the mixture. The clear bubble dissolved into the other ingredients. She lidded the glass and struck the pulse button.

When Sadie appeared, hung over and irritable, Lily asked what they possibly could have found to talk about all night long (she had heard the elevator at three a.m.), Sadie blushed—as if she might have had a conscience after all—and said, "He didn't stay the night, if that's what you mean." Lily pushed the shake across the counter to Sadie. "Not exactly."

It felt good, that first time she spit into Sadie's drink: a trivial, yet vile, retribution.

Chapter 4

"ETHAN, THIS IS your first class," Lily said, "so it might seem challenging to you, or foreign, but that's okay."

Ethan unrolled a yoga mat and sat awkwardly in a cross-legged position—his knees stuck up nearly to his ears, and his spine made a hopeless curve. "I haven't felt this out of my element since learning a Mexican folk dance in my high school gym class. I was paired with a cheerleader who refused to look me in the eye. Suzi Markholt. She kept making faces at her friends over my shoulder."

Lily and Alex laughed, imagining Ethan as an awkward, high school A/V nerd. "Everything is welcome here," Lily said. "Any positions, any sounds, any emotions. If you're in pain, you can breathe through it, or you can modify. We leave our judgment about ourselves and about our friends at the door, okay? The yoga room is a safe place to be with our bodies and our minds, to put them in balance."

Ethan nodded and grinned like a boy even younger than his twenty-five years, as if anticipating a gift. He fingered the edge of his mat, rolling and unrolling the pliable material in a small room in the Osaka-Jo Hall.

"Alex, why don't you read what you've brought for us?" Lily said.

Alex hesitated before calling up a poem she had found, her heart jumping at the thought of sharing such intimate words with anyone but Lily, who had been known to tear up at a passage, who had seen Alex at her most emotional as she let out a cry of frustration during

21

bow pose, who had watched Alex push through near-dizzying repetitions of breath of fire.

In some ways, Lily might have come to know Alex more profoundly and honestly than even Alex's own mother—a person that she'd once hoped would share the deepest, most authentic of connections—knew her. In freshman year of college (a time of self-discovery and self-righteous indignation), Alex wrote her mother a long letter asking Estelle to explain why, after the family went ice fishing out on Black River Bay in 1975, all warmth drained from their relationships. Estelle's only response was, "I don't know what you're going on about, Alexandra, dredging up all that nonsense."

Alex's family never visited Watertown, NY again after that bitter, bitter winter. They moved on, to another town, another Army base, another country, her stepfather to another important post in the military-industrial complex of America. But in upstate New York, snow drifted across the frozen stream, cutting like a sandstorm, in wisps that looked innocent enough, but blasted without mercy into any exposed patch of skin. Alex could still clearly see her grandfather in that ice fishing hut, the boards weathered to a bluish gray, crooked and gaping as if the carpenter had been a ten-year-old with a too-large hammer.

She couldn't have been much more than five, her memories fuzzy, but the biting cold was clear: frozen mittens between her chattering teeth, soggy and icy all at once; the taste of dirty snow; icicles broken from the eaves and lying like spikes on top of the unyielding snow.

* * *

Staring at the chipped linoleum flooring in the makeshift yoga room, Alex pulled her thoughts back into the present and said, "Okay, I'll read a couple of lines." Ethan looked interested, his face as encouraging and open as always—an expression so endearing, so

22

trusting of the world, it often made her worry about how easily Ethan could be wounded in this steely touring world.

They sat in a triangle gazing at each other: Alex watching Ethan, Ethan staring at Lily, Lily studying a display of fireworks exploding on the cover of Alex's literary magazine. Alex thumbed through, searching for the Naomi Shihab Nye poem with the line about a world that's hard to live in. An air conditioner kicked on, and an aluminum pipe clattered on the hard cement outside in the hallway. There was a scuffling behind the door, loud voices being shushed to a whisper. In a matter of seconds, before Alex could glean what the disturbance meant, Joe and the head rigger tumbled through the door. "We heard Ethan was taking the class today." Joe grinned. "We want to come, too."

"Of course. Everyone is welcome," Lily said quietly, pointing to a stack of mats, waiting while the men unbuckled tool belts that hit the floor with a thump, the sound nearly as unsettling as fireworks. The room took on a staler smell, full of sweat and feet and male breath underneath the burning incense as the men removed shoes and socks. Lily coaxed them through inhales and exhales, ignoring the odors, pushing through. "Take a deep breath again, into your belly, and hold. Then inhale a little bit more, and a little bit more. And release."

Alex could tell Lily was trying not to catch her eye as she instructed, that she was probably afraid she would roll her eyes or grimace or somehow bond with Alex over the fact that the men had invaded their space. Having to deal with Sadie daily, Lily could unearth insincerity like a security guard locating a laser pointer in an audience of thousands.

She brought them all up to standing, moved into sun salutations. The rigger they called Red, a good ol' boy who'd been touring for twenty years, grunted and clumsily pulled himself up off the mat. He measured about six-foot-five and weighed somewhere close to three hundred pounds. The years had put a stout layer around his middle, full and solid as one of the bunk pillows on the bus, and he wore a turquoise and red bandana over his balding head. A ponytail secured in successive elastic bands ran down his back. Put him in some spandex and he could have passed for a pro wrestler.

Alex alone easily mirrored Lily's movements as she raised her hands to the sky. Ethan fumbled along, shadowing Lily as she lifted her torso, fingertips on the mat, moving into a salutation, warming their bodies up. Joe made the motions, though sloppily and with much noise, his snorts masking the hum of overhead fluorescents. Red, however, stood on his mat without bending, simply waving his arms around in mock repetition.

A candle flickered near the edge of Lily's mat as her arms swept up and past into Namaste. As they returned to standing, Red gave Joe a little shove, sending him off balance and nearly into the cement wall. Lily kept her hands in prayer, took a deep and steadying breath, waiting for the men to stop tittering.

"Let's all share a little bit about why we are here today and what we hope to accomplish from our practice. I'll start." Lily's voice was calm and deep, a teaching tone she learned in a Brentwood studio where she took her instructor training. "I would like to impart some coping mechanisms for handling stress and exhaustion."

Alex tried to emulate Lily in her composure, digging deep to find some compassion for these men whose lives had not been easy—Joe's wife was likely having an affair, and Red, it was rumored, was raised in a trailer park by a stripper mother. A black and white clock on the wall behind Lily ticked steadily. The lights emitted an annoying, steady hum.

"Alex?" Lily suggested, "Why don't you go next? What goals have you set for yourself?"

Alex felt tension creep up her spine, tightening, blocking the free flow of energy. She remembered what Lily previously explained to her, that trauma imprints itself in our bodies, getting stuck, causing aches and pains and subconscious behaviors. She willed her shoulders to relax, but they felt immobile, solidly raised. Alex was prickingly aware of the men beside and behind her. She wished she hadn't worn her thinnest yoga pants that clung to her butt; that felt so revealing with Joe standing a few measly feet away.

"I would like to get this knot out of my back," she said, knowing this was a cop-out, that she was keeping her disclosure physical, rather than the emotional and spiritual bent Lily was going for.

Lily looked hard at Alex, urging her to say more, but Alex was so accustomed to holding back, she couldn't offer anything else. There would be no *sharing* of her feelings with these men who would likely use her words against her. Early on in Alex's career, she made the mistake of telling a male touring mate that she thought the moniker "Babe" was demeaning. For many long weeks, stagehands from cities all over the world (coached by her tour mate) called her "Babe" until the joke grew cold.

"How about you, Ethan?" Lily finally asked. "What brought you here today?"

Ethan looked nervously back at the men behind him, realizing it might have been obvious. Likely everyone in the room *except* Lily knew that he was there to be close to her. Ethan stalled like a musician who needed to tune his instrument (but didn't quite know what to say to the audience while he was tuning.) "Um...well, what brings me here..."

"Women in thongs," Joe said under his breath, to the amusement of Red, who guffawed. The room had grown sweltering with the heat of bodies, with stagnant air. Over their heads, one floor up, a vendor rolled a cart, readying for the rush of audience in a few hours.

Lily looked coolly at Joe, his white Beastie Boys t-shirt tinted ocher by the overhead light. "You have something to share?"

"Nothing." Joe didn't hide his smirk.

Lily wasn't going to let him off easily. Joe had no authority over her, so she wasn't cowed or frightened by him. Only Sadie could hire or fire Lily. "I heard you say 'women in thongs.' What did you mean by that?"

"I was just fooling around, Lily." Joe dropped his voice, using an authoritative pitch, one that worked for him over the phone but sounded forced and ridiculous in that small, cement room, like a sound man doing a mic check. "Go on with your class."

Lily motioned for them all to sit on their mats. She dropped into easy pose, cross legged with hands in *gyan mudra*, thumbs to index fingers. "Let's all take another deep, belly breath. Use your navel, pulling in as you exhale." She let them sit in silence, forming her words. She looked them each in the eye in turn, not allowing for evasion or glib asides. "We are here for honesty, with pure spirit. If you are here to make fun of us or to instigate in any way, that's not going to work."

Alex watched Lily's calm face, no hint of irony or derision.

"Yeah," Red said with his laconic drawl. "I don't think this fancy stuff is gonna work for me. I'm gonna leave you ladies to it." He winked at Ethan and threw a conspiratorial grin at Joe.

Alex turned around, revolted, unable to stand seeing their hairy legs, toenails that needed to be clipped, the puckered skin of their jowls. Joe caught her stare, certainly understanding her resistance to his presence, if not the depth of her disgust. Too many times while she'd showered, a crew mate had knocked, telling her to make it quick; too many times she'd been caught changing out of her pajamas in the back lounge of the bus.

"I'm going to stick with it," Joe said with a grin, though there was a definite hint of insecurity, a weakness that was betrayed by the wavering answer he gave and by the sudden not-so-low tone of his voice (reminiscent of a teenage choir boy.) Joe cleared his throat. "I could use some de-stressing."

The sound of Red's acerbic laughter echoed through the door after he exited, reminding Alex of her first tour with Sadie. Resistant to any woman on a road crew, Red had laughed triumphantly when

Alex couldn't untwist one of the shackle pins during load-in. "This biz is tough," he'd said. "You need a lotta strength." She whacked the pin with another shackle, loosening the threads, and threw it at his feet, swearing that she'd prove him wrong every time.

Alex wondered if she should bail on the yoga class; there was no way she was going to enjoy herself with Joe making grunting sounds and ogling her. Of course, she didn't exactly want to be aligned with Red. Which would make her seem stronger? Sticking it out, holding her ground, in what she considered *her* territory? Or would leaving make more of a point, show Joe that she wouldn't be railroaded? Alex considered her options as Lily guided them into warrior one. Why should Alex give up the only thing that calmed her down on the road? Why should she compromise?

They moved into triangle, hips jutting to the side, gazes turned to the sky—the false ceiling stained by water leaks a poor substitute for "sky"—and Joe let out a loud groan, a long and extended "oohhhh," intentionally rude, clearly faked. "Oh, motherfucker," he said after a dramatic pause.

Alex pulled herself out of the pose by grounding her feet into the mat. She turned her body fully around to look back at Joe, who leaned his forearm on his thigh, resting halfway between triangle and warrior one. He grinned heartily.

"Everything is accepted here," Lily said cautiously, still folded into the pose.

Alex crouched to roll up her mat. "I can't do it," she said. "This is a joke to him." And even as she threw the mat back into Lily's woven basket in the corner of this Japanese room, even as she gathered her socks, her wrench and electrical tape, her sweatshirt, and her watch, Alex had the sinking feeling that she had lost.

Chapter 5

THE ROLL-UP DOOR to the loading dock closed behind three incoming cars; local security, alert and on point, fell back into place while Brooke and Joe and the local promoter lined up to greet Sadie. Black-clad and burly, Sadie's security guard jumped out and offered her a hand down. Sadie reached over, plucked a piece of lint off his shirt, lovingly grooming him, this silent presence who was always with her. She yawned and stretched; her elongated muscles defined through a thin layer of linen.

Band members unfolded from the seats; Lily waited her turn, eventually flipping down the seat herself, climbing out of the far back. Dancers leapt from the van, hyper and corporeal, loudly drawing attention to themselves, to the incredibly fit shape of their bodies. Two of them staged a mock karate battle. Brooke skirted the band and took a stab at penetrating Sadie's inner circle, but she was whisked aside by the massive security guard who escorted Sadie down the hall to her dressing room—the room Brooke had spent a good part of the week prepping, hanging cloth to mask metal lockers, arranging side tables with flowers and notebooks and pens. At the behest of Brooke, Lily once framed some photos she'd taken of the crew—a little personal touch for the décor, but that went over like a nun at a bachelor party. "I don't see enough of these people?" Sadie complained. "Now they're in my dressing room too?"

As Brooke set up the dressing room, she routinely rifled through Sadie's drawer full of jewelry in her wardrobe case—mostly baubles, gifts sent by designers—lifting strings of beads, holding them to the light, trying on earrings. Sadie didn't even know her own inventory; some of the samples she would never try on or wear or even hold.

"What the hell are you doing?" Joe shouted when he caught Brooke sitting at Sadie's dressing room mirror this morning, tracing the curve of her mouth with a brilliant vermilion lipstick and wearing an indigo-colored Jasper Conran dress swiped from Sadie's wardrobe, pretending those accoutrements were hers.

"Excuse me," Brooke said. "Ever heard of knocking?"

"Sadie's room," Joe shouted, holding a vase of overly bright, multi-colored tulips, which he delivered with a clunk onto a laminate-covered particle board side table. Joe pointed to the wardrobe cases. "Sadie's clothes. Sadie's crap. Not yours."

"I'm aware," Brooke said, just as she'd been aware how little was actually hers as a teenager. She spent hours in the South Burlington Almy's fitting room, trying on clothes her family couldn't afford, in the full-length, slimming mirrors, full of glamour. Back at home, her mother stood in front of a thin, cheap mirror before leaving for work at the A&P, tugging at her polyester apron, talking to herself in a mumbling soliloquy. Brooke would cover her ears to block out her mother's self-abasement, her near self-flagellation over her dowdy figure, fueled mainly by her husband's abandonment and the resulting absence of self-worth.

"Why the hell am I carting around flowers like a goddamn delivery boy while you're in here fucking off? I'm the boss! Flowers are your job, Brooke." Joe lowered himself onto the couch slowly, hands first, huffing and puffing as if pregnant. "I'm not going to mention this to Sadie," Joe said, "but if I ever catch you in here again messing with Sadie's clothes, you're gone. Got me?"

"Yes, sir," Brooke said with a calming smile. Joe might actually blow one day and lose it on her if she wasn't vigilant, but no matter, she knew how to defend against tirades, against harsh words. She spent her grade school years ignoring weight-laden nicknames—

Blubbery Brooke, Brooke the Balloon—until her excess weight blossomed into curves, until the boys' attention metamorphosed from taunts to enormous-eyed wonder. The best reaction, she knew, from those early years, was an evocative smile. If the tormenters didn't hook you, they lost their ammunition. She had to take it easy with Joe, her position in Sadie's entourage still too unstable to shield her from one of his outbursts. For now, anyway.

* * *

The beam of Joe's flashlight illuminated darkened corridors. Brooke once brought her own flashlight, but Joe cut that off quick. "There's enough light," he barked. Occasionally a promoter would whip one off his belt, but Joe would let that pass; everyone wanted to be the single source of light, the beacon that Sadie must follow.

"How was your day? Discover a cure for any diseases?" Lily asked when Brooke pulled up beside her.

Brooke frowned, puzzled.

"Did you and Joe make some policy changes that will effect global warming?"

Brooke craned her neck, looking forward, investigating the line.

"Decide what the fate of the union will be?"

"Honey," Brooke finally whispered. "You're such a cutie, but I hardly ever get what you're talking about."

Brooke tried to maneuver around a dancer who'd managed to wedge herself in front of them. Lily quietly watched the daily choreography, the battle for more face time. Often, Brooke would manage to stride alongside Sadie and tell some silly joke (What's worse than having Britney Spears as a mom? Having Amy Winehouse as a nanny!) amusing Sadie. But today Brooke had been blocked from every angle.

Touring crew nodded and stepped aside, lining the corridor like a wedding party, welcoming them in, local stagehands milling around behind, hoping for an incident they could share as an anecdote, an event to elevate this average day.

A young stagehand who had only worked a handful of gigs, who hadn't yet figured out the protocol regarding performers—that you don't bother them, don't try to engage them in any way—paced from the stage to the loading dock like an anxious groom. When the convoy split—Brooke, dancers and band in one direction, Sadie and Lily in the other—the stagehand, knowing that the yellowshirts who would line the corridors and exits during the concert hadn't clocked in yet, made a beeline through the arena, down the vomitory, a connecting hallway that likely got its name because of the propensity for intoxicated fans to lean over from their seats and let loose. His shortcut landed him a few yards from Sadie's dressing room.

As Sadie approached, the stagehand knelt, reaching up with both hands, an offering: a blue and rose-colored string with a tiny lapis slung like a teardrop between chunky beads. "For you," he said with bowed head. "My girlfriend made it."

Like spectators at a ceremony, no one in Sadie's party spoke a word. Sadie gazed at him quizzically while her large security guard lifted the stagehand roughly from the back of his shirt and shoved him to the wall, a motion that reminded Lily of when she was sixteen and thought she was alone in the basement of a rectory as she rummaged for a dish towel, cleaning up after Wednesday night Bible study. The church elder came up behind her, asked if he could help. He placed his hand, large and rough, on the back of her neck. Lily tried to shake him off, but he tightened his grip as she turned. "Let me help you," he said.

As Sadie and her managers moved on in a solemn procession, Lily paused near the startled boy and opened her hand, as if awaiting payment. "I'll take it to her," she said.

"Really?"

Lily nodded, noting the grease under his fingernails, callouses as he placed the necklace in her palm, like a coin into an offering tray. He worked his way up to making some bland expression of gratitude, but he never got out more than a squeak before Sadie beckoned from her dressing room.

"Lily, get in here."

Lily pocketed the necklace without another glance at the kid. Though she'd likely dump the necklace in the next city, she figured this little contribution was the least she could do, helping a stranger keep his illusions alive.

* * *

Sound check was scheduled for four-thirty, but the whole crew bet on a five o'clock start. Only Lily was privy to Sadie's cloistered hours, when Sadie focused and worked some lyric or melody from her songwriters. Today at least wasn't one of those rough days, when minutes ticked by and built up into hours while Sadie stared at a blank wall. After those agonizing minutes, Sadie might startle Lily from her meditation, asking her some inane question: "Did you see that miserable woman in the front row yesterday? Do you think she hated the show?" And Lily might give an unthinking answer: "probably a critic," which would likely set Sadie off, shrieking that the critics loved her, causing Lily to respond: "More likely some hyper-serious grad student doing a paper on pop culture," or to give her some other salve, maybe in pill form. Under Lily's watch, consumption had slowed—she at least curtailed Sadie's serious drug use, warning that any signs of coke or heroin or meth and she was out of there. She'd seen too many friends in art school take a dive into that murky world of drug addiction, only to end up in rehab at their parents' expense.

Lily almost choked on her self-righteous thoughts, barely able to think through her own sedative haze, barely able to see clear of her own rampant emotions. Who was buoying who, she wondered? More to the point, how far down would she sink?

Joe called "places" at four-fifteen, and all departments scrambled to their posts, crowding into the wings like tourists in a cathedral, reverent and focused on their tasks. Locals loitered in the bleachers or lounged in rough plastic chairs, listening to football games with earbuds connected to transistor radios tucked discreetly into pockets.

Lily carted clothes from the wardrobe cases to the quick-change booth, reassuring Sadie with each pass: "You'll be dynamic," she said. "You never disappoint." The same language she used whenever Sadie was jittery, bouncing on her toes, shaking out her limbs like an athlete.

On a pass through the arena, Lily cast an eye down the vomitory, the smell of gasoline pungent from an idling forklift. On the stage, Kat tuned Sadie's guitar one last time. Lily set down Sadie's makeup bag and a straightening iron to snap a series of photos, first of Kat's feet on Sadie's pedals, then zooming out to capture her whole body in stage blacks and combat boots, her silhouette almost lost in the dark of the stage. As the moving lights kicked on, Lily changed the aperture, adjusting to the unexpected streaks and bursts across the lens, feeling like these days she was practicing photography from inside a bubble—and Sadie, squashed in beside her, was sucking out all the air.

As Lily took the time to shoot, she thought about how Sadie kept making more and more demands, like when they were in Tokyo and Sadie decided on a whim to get a tattoo. Before they left the venue, Sadie sent Lily off to gather the women on tour. Brooke joined them, but the others declined, Kat with a curt "no fucking way." Alex considered tagging along, but a new tattoo wasn't a commitment she could make without some deeper reason. She already had a sunflower on her shoulder that she'd rushed to get when she was eighteen. She regretted the placement now; the tattoo, a sweet reminder of the blooming flowers that stretched toward the Tuscan sun, was hidden from her view.

The Japanese promoter, reluctant at first, had driven them to a little hole-in-the-wall, down a busy alleyway; tattoos in Japan, he said, are often associated with yakuza, the mafia. But the translator swore this place had a good reputation; the artists studied for three to five years, he said, before they ever laid pen to skin. "Encouraging," Lily said wryly. "At least they're well-trained criminals."

Mafia aside, Lily had been frightened when she was escorted to a table with a one-handed artist, until he showed his portfolio with a slew of gorgeous, meticulous art. She had him design a cherry blossom branch for her lower back. Sadie, Brooke, and the three posers who had tagged along all followed her lead and got cherry blossoms tattooed on various parts of their bodies. Sadie unsnapped her pants to offer up her tan, shapely hip to the pen; Brooke chose her ankle, which proved to be a surprisingly painful location.

Lily, like Alex, didn't want to get a tattoo without some thought behind it; she realized that a tattoo might be too permanent to acquiesce to Sadie about, but then, because she felt a whirl of complications, the poor one-armed man, the beauty, the exotic locale, the futility of arguing with Sadie, she caved.

The stump of the tattoo artist's missing hand served as his skin-stretching tool. His stump, pulling against the skin of Lily's back, felt eerily like a giant knuckle. A couple of times, ashamedly, she shuddered, feeling keenly where that knuckle touched her. Each time she shivered, the tattoo artist lifted his arms and permitted her to settle back down. "Sorry," she stammered, imagining his stump and ink gun held up in the air, as if he was being arrested.

"Our tattoos will unite us," Sadie said over a cup of chrysanthemum tea while the five of them waited in small plastic chairs for Brooke to finish up, Japanese techno crackling out of a tiny speaker in the corner. Lily never saw the other three people who got "united" again. The tattoos did their unification work, though, for Lily and Sadie: she couldn't argue that point.

Chapter 6

ALEX RAISED HER beer in mock salute. "To living the dream," she said, after popping the bottle cap off with the butt of a lighter. Up at two-thirty in the morning, all eleven crew members on the production bus milled around, impatient and wired, shuffling up and down the hallway lined with bunks. Over half of the crew crowded into the jouncing back lounge of the tour bus, waiting for the border crossing into Mexico. They joked and laughed as mile after mile of pavement disappeared behind them. Freshly showered in a Los Angeles arena locker room, Alex was scrubbed free of motor grease and sweat-sticky grime that had lodged itself under her nails and into the fine creases of her skin during load-out. She sat wedged between Ethan and a video guy on a stiff blue couch, all the while holding a book between her palms, trying to ignore the crude expletives and defecation jokes in a South Park episode on the television in the corner.

Mirrors that hugged all three walls gave the slightly disorienting impression that the small lounge was bigger than a ten-by-ten box; as in a funhouse, the mirrors reflected back upon themselves, ad infinitum. Unlike self-adoring Sadie, none of the crew spent any time staring at their own reflections. A forearm, an elbow, a torso pressed close as a co-worker reached over, into the built-in cooler for a beer, wasn't intentionally physical. Like a large family in a small apartment, they'd all gotten used to being jostled.

Kat and Brooke were up in the front, as usual, avoiding the back smoking lounge, but Alex liked to make the rounds, to check in with the rest of her crew. A year now without a cigarette herself. She sucked at the tobacco-heavy, stifling air, still taking perverse pleasure in the smell. She watched the smoke curl and stream out the cracked window, billowing out behind the bus in a rush of current.

Connor had never smoked. She loved being with a man who hadn't been slave to that kind of addiction, with someone who played sports on the weekends instead of shotgunning beers in the middle of the night after packing five semis to the ceiling, road cases flipped up row after row, wheels to the sky. Besides a two-year stint with a cheating promoter, the only other long-term relationship Alex had was with a booking agent. He was loyal, but he ultimately couldn't tolerate the mystery of how she spent her down time, whom she might be with. He was disinclined to believe that she preferred to wander a new city alone, popping into bookstores, foregoing the hotel bar. He begged her to get off the road, said he could get her a job with a friend of his. In an office. Making phone calls. Moving paper around.

She mentally listed what she loved about Connor: he had never added extra pages to his passport and waved it around like a trophy; he found Hooters tacky and demeaning; he planted kale in the neighborhood pea patch. Once, he got an extra twenty-dollar bill in change from a grocery store and went back in to return it so the cashier wouldn't have to pay.

Alex took a sip of her beer, swallowed automatically, before she remembered. Cracking a beer after load-out had been customary for her for fifteen years—a near ritual for most road crew. Alex patted Ethan's leg and got up to dump her beer in the small bathroom up front, but she was barred in the doorway by Joe, come to warn them all to get their passports ready. "Leave 'em on the dash," he said, hoping the border agents would just take a glance, put faces to names, and let them pass quickly into Mexico.

Holding her beer high, Alex yanked open a side cupboard to

retrieve her passport, but the bus veered sharply and bags tumbled across the floor of the lounge. She stumbled slightly, backing into Joe. Her backpack, the zipper open at the top, spilled its contents under a pile of other bags. In a panic, Alex realized what happened, but she couldn't get there before the other techs who had lunged in with quick hands, fast reflexes. She took a deep breath and looked up from the unopened pregnancy test that sat wedged between a notebook and a truck-pack diagram, to lock eyes with Ethan. He'd seen it too, but bless him, his hand was on top of the box, obscuring the labeling, until he'd shoved it back in her bag.

Alex looked around, trying to guess who might have seen. She didn't even know herself if it was true, if she was actually pregnant, but she had begun to feel swollen and warm. Her confidence, too, had morphed from the normal bravado she put on when dealing with crusty stagehands who didn't know how to react to a woman as head electrician, into a feeling of real power from within, a solidity that she couldn't exactly explain, but had been trying on.

During a slow hour yesterday afternoon in L.A., she ran to the pharmacy and tucked the test in her bag until her next day off. No one else seemed to have seen it, everyone concerned with their own belongings, digging around for passports. Ethan smiled and handed the bag to Alex, a question in his eyes. He wouldn't say anything, she knew, just like when a tampon fell out of her sock during load-in last year—she'd carried it there just like she had in high school, convenient, usually fairly secure. Ethan just deflated the whole embarrassing moment by picking it up right in front of the local stagehands and placing it in her palm like it was some spare change or a mint.

"I owe you," she said quietly, hoping the other guys had shifted their focus back to the screen. But the rigger caught the exchange and wanted to know what the secret was, and how he could be on the receiving end of a favor from Alex. "Keep dreaming, Red," she said with a smirk and went to dump her beer.

Crew from all four tour buses tumbled out onto the paved zone between the U.S. and Mexico, the no-man's land controlled by border patrol agents, an area where the future was completely reliant on the whim of those agents. Dogs on tight leashes, sniffing and searching, in step with their tight-faced and unamused handlers, weaved in between the weary crew, backs to the wall of buses. There was near silence as the drum tech got pulled out of line, frisked, and asked to follow two of the mustachioed agents inside; orange lamps that arced out from the stucco building threw shadows against the feet of those who remained, waiting to be released.

"Dead man walking," someone mumbled, to a chorus of rippling laughter.

Word made it up the line in record speed: they found a nugget of pot in the drum tech's pants, a forgotten little bud, nothing more than a couple of seeds and a stem, dropped from an inverted pocket. Enough of a quantity, however, to prevent the whole band and crew from flying through customs.

The outcome was unclear for the drum tech as they were instructed to retrieve their suitcases from the bays of the bus and move inside, into the stark customs waiting room lined with six or seven gray plastic chairs, stained and scuffed, each bearing the history of those who had passed through, who had crossed over or been turned back. Sadie's crew stood in line on a filthy tiled floor, suitcases at their feet, each waiting his or her turn to throw luggage up onto a long metal table to be opened up, rifled through, inspected. Alex watched the agent sift through Brooke's myriad of cases. He pulled out scarves and shoes, piling and tossing, to the chagrin of a pouty, silk-pajama-clad Brooke.

"Oh, honey, be careful, I've got those arranged by outfit," she said to the agent, but her usually successful feminine wiles met a dead end. The acne-scarred, buzz-cut Mexican simply scowled and told her in sharp, consonant heavy English to keep her hands at her sides.

Standing in formation like a military recruit, exhausted yet full of anticipation, Alex had the deep longing to be at home, in bed with Connor, his strong breath ruffling the back of her hair, his heavy arm wrapped around her waist. She tried to conjure Connor's baby-smooth, white-collar hands running lightly across her skin. The night they met, Alex had kept her hands mostly underneath the table in the club, embarrassed by her own rough, callused, non-manicured fingers.

Though the very tour bus parked outside the bank of high, streaked windows had passed within two miles of her loft in Seattle only a week and a half ago, the distance had piled up. She was over twelve hundred miles from home now and almost felt like her loft and the man who could be there, asleep and warm in her queen size bed, was actually a dream.

When the acned agent finally latched and sent the last of Brooke's cases down the length of metal bench towards the scanner, everyone shuffled forward a step. The reluctant answers of the drum tech who just lost his nugget of pot drifted from a back office. The Mexican agents had escorted him past the checkpoint, down a short dingy hallway, fluorescent tubes flickering overhead like in some dark English detective serial.

Alex was wedged between Joe and Red (God, how did she manage to get between these two?). Very little was said down the line, with the exception of Joe's yapping at the band's lawyer on his flip phone. As he strutted through the security scanner, the beeper went off, and the officer standing guard there backed Joe up and barked at him to put his phone down.

"Hold on," Joe said, threw the phone in the dish and then picked it up again, mid-sentence, on the other side.

Under the hard stare of the agent, Alex swung her suitcase up onto the table. He lifted a few pairs of shorts, fingered aside a tank top, and impassively revealed her underwear. Satisfied, he moved on to her backpack, tearing into each compartment as if convinced she was concealing contraband: drugs, weapons, explosives.

Despite her attempt to hide the pregnancy test between the pages of a book, it looked as if this agent would exhibit every article, holding each up for display. He rotated a pack of gum in the air, snapped the cap off her lip balm. Everyone watched as if her private possessions were up for bid on a gameshow.

Joe, standing on the other side of the scanner, still on the phone, had his eyes on her pack. Behind her, Red stood staring, his arms crossed over his massive chest, hulking and disgruntled, as if this whole inspection was her fault. As the rigger, Red hung thousands of pounds over their heads at every concert. One mistake could have maimed or killed any one of them: trust was essential. But Alex found his brashness a little hard to swallow, particularly in the middle of the night. Alex would never live it down if the agent whipped out that test.

Diversion, she thought. There was Kat, up ahead, already through the line, chatting amiably with a video guy, her muscular physique giving her a no-nonsense posture that commanded respect from local crews, even though female guitar technicians were even scarcer than female electricians.

Kat gave Alex a cool, confident smile, as if she knew exactly what was going through Alex's head. Single, forty-two, and unflustered by any situation, Kat once told Alex a story about how she didn't want the guys on the crew to see her estrogen: "You know, for fucking menopause, just my luck—early onset." ("Use it or lose it," Brooke had piped in.) Kat had mouthed "female hormones" to the border agent, real quietly, who was holding the tube. "He dropped it like it was a packet of Anthrax." Kat laughed. "Every man's weak spot is any perceived threat to their virility."

Brooke, too, had a story. "I once watched a TSA agent pick up my vibrator—he stuck his hand right into the bag, past the zipper, and fondled it. You should have seen his face! Pink as bubblegum lip gloss."

"Oh my God," Kat said. "You actually travel with a vibrator??"

"What? You don't?" Brooke was flabbergasted. "Honey, you are missing out."

Alex considered if she could get away with the same but decided that admitting to estrogen or a vibrator would probably embarrass her more than a pregnancy test, so she turned to Red and pulled out her rigging plot, the small, laminated version she kept with her backstage pass on a lanyard.

"Hey, I was thinking, Red," she said loudly enough to grab everyone's attention. She held up the tiny plot up close to Red's face, obscuring his view of her pack, "you know how the Mexico City riggers have to come down off the grid to get around the beam to the downstage points? I thought maybe you could spare one guy to go down there right away, then we don't have to hold up the whole load in, waiting. Good idea, huh?"

"I like your energy, little mama," Red drawled, "but I don't wanna talk about motor points for..." he checked his watch, "another twenty-six hours, got me?"

"Oh, yeah, sure thing," Alex said, checking over her shoulder while the agent, seemingly interested in their conversation, stuffed her belongings back in the pack. Half of her career had been spent negotiating how she might move heavy objects through time and space, how she could most efficiently pack and unpack, transport and receive boxes, gear, equipment. And not just gear—clothing, too, books and iPods, toiletries and shoes. All of the trappings of modern travel. But in this world of drugs and weapons and silent threats, it had become increasingly difficult to travel with autonomy. All possessions were up for display. There was no privacy. A person's fate—a yes or a no—a smooth ride or a hassle—detection or invisibility—was in the fickle hands of a stranger. Was he having a bad day? Was he distracted or focused? Was a female guard likely to be more understanding, more sympathetic to the plight of another female traveling with a group of men?

"And sweetheart?" Red said, pulling her out of her reverie. "Leave the rigging to me. I gotcha covered."

"Move along," said the agent, before Alex had the wherewithal to react to Red's tone. The agent pushed her bags along the table, and she was waved through the scanner.

Kat greeted her on the other side. "What the fuck did Red just say to you?"

And because she didn't want to get anything started, as she'd done hundreds of times before in her career, reluctant to be the woman who was difficult, who was reactionary, who was "a bitch," she sloughed it off. "It was nothing," she said. "Everybody's tired."

* * *

Hotel rooms usually felt neutral to Alex, like plastic spoons, or beige rugs—each space an afterthought that evoked little emotion. But today, Alex felt a surprising hint of loneliness as she threw her suitcase up on the stand—the smell of recycled air, a trace of a stranger's aftershave.

At the sound of a knock, quick and muffled, Alex peered through the door and there stood Ethan, mugging into the peep hole, gripping a bottle of whiskey and a bucket of ice, as if he was coming for a campout. A computer bag slid off his shoulder, and he caught it in the crook of his arm.

"So," he began when she opened the door, no hello. "That little box I saw—"

"Wasn't mine," she hedged, eyes on the zig-zag pattern of the short-ply rug.

Ethan's dark hair flopped over his forehead as he bent into her field of vision, forcing eye contact. For three years, he'd watched her every move, amazing Alex with how he could read her. He'd bring her coffee if she was tired, Advil if she was PMSing. She couldn't fool him; he knew her too well.

"This is for me, of course." He raised the bottle. "Not for you, in your state," he said with intent.

Alex crossed her arms petulantly, as if he might be easily discouraged, trying to wait him out, in timing, in speech, but Ethan was unflinching, insistent even as a black-clad waiter rolled a cart down the dim hallway and knocked three doors down. Tray in hand, the waiter loudly announced "room service" as the door was answered, the smell of steak wafting strongly down the hall.

How could she explain that when she saw the plus sign just two hours ago, the first words out of her mouth were, "Oh shit," but that her feelings were changing, becoming more complex, like a layered poem?

Ethan's expression remained deadpan until, finally, Alex waved him in. These nights on tour were a rite of passage, hanging strong when one of your pals needed to evade the encroaching gloom. Alex would be tired no matter what time she got to sleep. And Ethan was comforting, familiar. He didn't expect anything from her.

After the whiskey was cracked, after Ethan made a show of sharing a new computer program he'd found, he threw himself across Alex's bed, sprawling comically. "Honey, I'm here for the duration. Not leaving 'til I get a straight answer. I'll close my eyes while we talk; turn the lights off, and I'll listen in the dark. If I'm going to have your back— and believe me, I have your back— I have to know. Give it over. I always share with you," Ethan reminded Alex.

Last year, on an overnight from Regina to Vancouver, Alex and Ethan sat up all night watching the Northern Lights scatter across the plains of upper Saskatchewan while the rest of the crew hit their bunks. Ethan, trying to explain his reluctance to take on new lovers, lifted his shirt to reveal a series of scars along the sides of his ribs, under his armpits, fingers stretching like tributaries over and through the length of his torso. A misdiagnosis of liver disease in his youth, prednisone that caused him to blow up like a water balloon. An eventual heart operation. In the early light of dawn, as a hint of violet shimmered across the silvery sky and the bus rumbled beneath them, Alex reached out and touched his creased skin.

"Begin," he said in the quiet hotel room and pulled her down next to him. She liked his smell—long-faded mouthwash and a lemony detergent—and the feel of his skin against hers. She absorbed his heat where he touched her arm, unsure how to trust this comfortable, but not sexual, feeling, a type of closeness she'd never had, even with her own brother. She suspected that in her early years, before her grandfather's death, before her family became silent and cold, that there had been an intimacy with Junior. Had she and her brother shared a bedroom? Shared toys and hugs and stories?

"Why do you have to be so nosy?" Alex's head thrummed, even though she hadn't touched the whiskey. "I haven't even told Connor yet." A baby had never been in their plans—if you could even say they had plans. But this man! She felt like she might want everything with him! "My whole life is about to change. These last few days, I've had flashes where I can imagine myself with a baby in my arms, rocking in a quiet bedroom, a soft blanket over my shoulder as night ticks away. Totally foreign."

Alex spilled her sudden, strange desire to commit to Connor, to have a family with him. Only now, as she contemplated how her life might change, had details from her childhood begun to come back. Alex knew something happened out on Black River Bay in upstate New York when she was four or five. She remembered the ice fishing excursion. She could still feel the shame of provoking her mother's rage the day before the trip, but the shame was only a feeling, not something she could articulate.

"Maybe I could go back to Plan A," Alex said, steering clear of her disturbing emotions regarding her childhood. "I always thought I'd be designing lights for Broadway. Touring always seemed like a steppingstone, but somehow I stalled out at head electrician."

The night became quiet around them, until Alex heard only the internal resonance of her own voice and Ethan's deep, steady breathing. She asked quietly, "Ethan?"

His breath became shallower. She was sure he'd fallen asleep, until he reached through the dark and took her hand.

Chapter 7

ON LATE WINTER evenings in the Northwest, darkness came down quietly, stealthily, like a velvet curtain over a stage. Squeezed into a red vinyl booth at an Indian restaurant in Pioneer Square, Alex swallowed a mouthful of basmati rice and picked at her naan, as she considered Connor's question about her brother. Connor had never met Junior, nor was he likely to anytime soon. Alex studied a bright blue and gold print of a Hindu deity—half man, half turtle— over Connor's head.

"I doubt he's a good father, he's so self-absorbed," she answered. "You can't tell what the family is really like from the photos on their Christmas card. They always look staged— obligatory happiness."

Connor mimicked a forced smile. "All Christmas cards look that way," he said.

"To be fair, Junior never had a good role model. Our stepfather was pretty uninterested. Our real dad died when Junior was eight. I don't even remember him; I was so young."

When they stepped out onto First Avenue, the light had simply departed, vanished, the sun swallowed under the concrete viaduct by Puget Sound. Connor gently buttoned Alex's coat, pulled the fabric tight around her middle. "You don't think I'm self-absorbed, do you?"

The smell of cumin and cardamom that drifted up from his fingers was pleasant and strong. In the last two and a half months, she had felt changes in her body, in her temperature, in her heightened senses. Weeks ago, Connor's shaving cream proved too much for her delicate nose, so he tucked it away in the medicine cabinet, amused by the random smells that nauseated her: dish soap, reused towels, new magazines.

Alex felt a small pang, remembering a conversation she had with Brooke and Kat as they wandered the streets of Bangkok, how she'd complained that she'd been sending Connor these long, detailed emails about how she missed him, the smell of him, the feel of him. She described everything they'd seen, like a bombed-out house in Hiroshima, a cockfight under the life-size crucified Jesus in the venue in Manila. A "jello in coffee" drink in Tokyo. Then once in every five emails he wrote back to ask how the greater world was taking the U.S.'s steroid-enhanced military presence in the Middle East.

In response, Brooke had given the sage advice: "Men absolutely cannot talk about their feelings. We know it, we expect it, and honestly, I kinda love it. Who wants some skinny jean, vanilla latte drinking, metrosexual boyfriend? No thanks. I prefer a bit of testosterone."

"It's 2005, Brooke," Kat scoffed. "Open your mind. Nothing wrong with a feminine guy."

"Or a masculine woman," Brooke said, staring pointedly at Kat before she winked at Alex. "Doesn't mean I want to sleep with either one of them."

Alex smiled, missing her tour friends. "Maybe in the first year," she said. "When you didn't answer my emails. Maybe then I thought you were self-absorbed."

Connor playfully nudged under her ribs with his elbow.

"Careful," she said. "The baby."

The glow of streetlights glanced off puddles from the afternoon rain and splashed an amber tint across the damp sidewalk. As they walked, arm in arm, she studied his profile: nose like an Irish boxer, high forehead and almost feminine lips—a combined appearance of ruggedness and tenderness. Classic profile, she thought, like the face on a coin. His child would be beautiful.

* * *

Connor laid in bed next to Alex, eyes wide open, staring into the dark. Soft edges of furniture came clearer as he stared: his white bureau with spherical gold handles, a wicker hassock where he threw his clothes. Every few minutes he turned to Alex, who, radiating warmth, wore a faint smile even in sleep; serenity settled over him while he watched the even rhythm of her breathing, until, inevitably, as he thought of the baby, a tremulous panic took over his chest, threatening to spread throughout his body. How was it she slept so soundly now?

These last few months, Connor had listened patiently when Alex brought up the baby, but his own trepidation, he knew, was often thinly veiled. He could feel the muscles in his neck, tight and pronounced as the two of them watched a pregnancy test the second time she tested, waiting for a plus sign to appear like a ghost through the ether. His hesitation was too long when she asked if he thought they should keep the baby.

The mere mention of a child brought him back so strongly to years ago, the summer after his high school graduation—back when he was barely old enough to know his own mind. Under pressure from the girl's parents, he put his plans for college on the back burner and married his teenage girlfriend in a small stone Methodist church.

Connor fought his building resentment as he labored at odd jobs and took computer classes at a community college. He studied late into the night at a wobbly card table in his in-laws' sour-smelling basement. Connor's mother coached him to stay and take responsibility, to love that sweet and simple girl, though his parents

47

never offered up their own home. Connor's father would have none of it, recognizing how this situation—teen fatherhood—would limit his son's opportunities.

Connor's girlfriend—then wife—seemed content to wash baby clothes and hang out in the back yard all day. She couldn't understand Connor's restlessness, his desire to leave Winston, Virginia. Their fights quickly grew from digging remarks at the dinner table to Connor driving off in the middle of the night after their screams woke the baby. His ex-wife's family was relieved when he moved out.

Connor regretted that he'd not been a present father, or a good father, to Lucy, his daughter. He'd moved across the country to accept an entry level IT job when Lucy was only three. He sent birthday gifts. Visited once a year at Christmas. Within two years, his ex-wife remarried. And then, before he knew it, his daughter was just shy of thirty.

Alex was thirty-six.

And now Alex was preparing for their future: she came home yesterday with a tiny little yellow hat, a solid, undeniable symbol of what was ahead. He believed that they were both equally terrified, but it seemed Alex had overcome her fear, that her dread had morphed into anticipation.

Connor took a long, concentrated breath and lifted his legs over the side of the bed with a rocking motion. He wouldn't sleep, he knew, now that he'd remembered those constricted years in the in-laws' basement. He lifted his robe from the closet, took a book from the side table, though it was doubtful he'd be able to concentrate enough to read. Connor wandered out into the hallway and quietly pulled the bedroom door shut behind him. Let her sleep now, he figured, while she could. She wouldn't be sleeping later.

* * *

Sadie took her seat in first class. Shuffling by the lavishly wide seats, fluted mimosas and fresh baked cookies, Lily moved down the aisle to her seat in economy. Watching Lily walk by out of the corner of her eye, Sadie recalled an assistant in the early days of touring who got so used to the privilege of sitting in first class, he became unbearable, condescending to flight attendants, downing drink after drink. Give a person a little bit of money or status and they became idiots, she knew. So Sadie had changed her policy, made everyone but her security guard sit in coach. But there were days when you needed someone beside you.

Lily disappeared into a row about halfway down. Sadie eyed the line of passengers lumbering by; many gawking at her in amazement, scrutinizing, as if she might be an impersonator. Sadie had warned her cheapskate record label that this was the last tour she was flying commercial. More and more the public recognized her, even when she was well-disguised. She pressed the call button above her head, and the flight attendant instantly appeared, leaning in super-close, her white smile smudged with ruby lipstick.

"Is this seat beside me taken?" Sadie asked.

"Let me check." The attendant's eyes sparkled in excitement.

"Well, if the seat's taken, can you reassign them?"

The woman's hand shook on top of the seat back. "I'll do my best, Miss Estrada." The attendant set off down the aisle, but Sadie tapped her hand before she was out of reach.

"I'd like to chat with my assistant." Sadie gestured towards the coach section. "You saw us come in together."

Without the sense to ask where "the assistant" was seated, and too flustered to turn back, the attendant pushed up the aisle searching for anyone fitting the part, someone bubbly and well-dressed. A gay man, maybe, or a young woman in a business suit. She walked past Lily— who was wearing a pageboy cap and long open-knit sweater over a tank-top, flip-flops and jeans—three times, dismissing her outright. The flight attendant looked shocked when the gate agent, delivering a

49

chart of passengers' names, pointed her out. She tapped Lily on the shoulder and pointed her to first class.

Lily left her bags under her seat and walked to the front, against the current. "You beckoned? Need me to adjust your pillow? Rub your toes?"

Sadie ignored her assistant's smart-aleck attitude and patted the faux leather, motioning for Lily to sit down. "Want to ride up here with me?"

Lily shifted her eyes to the front, unanswering. Despite Sadie's ability to track a single audience member's displeasure, she remained (willfully? intentionally?) oblivious to the fact that there were very few moments when Lily wasn't within earshot of her boss.

Sadie gasped. "What? Is it a difficult decision?"

"Sorry. It's just—you've never asked before."

"Fine, dwell in third class."

"Economy," Lily corrected.

Sadie frowned. Nothing was ever simple with Lily. She could find an ulterior motive in an invitation to tea. Once, standing on the stoop of a church before Sadie's cousin's wedding, Lily even accused Sadie of deceiving her—or had she used the word 'betrayal'? "You didn't say it was in a Pentecostal church," Lily hissed and flat-out refused to go in, pouting outside through the whole ceremony, embarrassing Sadie—as if people weren't already staring. It was probably why Lily doesn't have a boyfriend. Who would put up with such behavior, such suspicion? Who was the last man she even saw Lily with?

"Remember that Wall Street guy at the party before fall tour who went to your room—" Sadie began.

"Kyle?"

"He wasn't in there very long." Sadie lowered her voice. "You have a quickie?"

"You're awful." Lily laughed. "What did he say when I kicked him out?"

"He chatted with us for a while and then said he had a morning meeting 'On a Sunday?' I asked. He said 'investments don't take holidays' and flicked his card at me. The nerve. I looked right at him and threw it into the fire. 'I already have a money manager,' I said."

"You did not."

Sadie nodded. "I figured if you blew him off, he wasn't worth anything."

Lily sank into the seat with a childish look of wonder, as if astonished that Sadie would value her opinion.

"I didn't like his aftershave anyway," Sadie continued. "Reminded me of my Uncle Cisco who tried to kiss me on the lips every time he visited from Chile."

"Too much aftershave. A feeling of coercion," Lily said, cryptically. "Every woman has an Uncle Cisco."

Sadie lifted an eyebrow but was interrupted before she could ask what Lily meant. A man in pleated pants and a Yankees ball cap stopped in the aisle and lifted his computer bag into the overhead compartment. His eyes were on Sadie, but he continued to stow his luggage. The people behind him waited, unable to help but stare.

A girl in her late teens pushed forward, squawking, "Oh my God, it's Sadie. Oh my God." She rifled through her carry-on and extracted a purple pen and a notebook with a flowery plastic cover. She shoved it toward Sadie. "Please, please," she mumbled, unable to get any other words out.

The girl's expression reminded Sadie of a statue of a penitent offering himself up to God that sat at in the corner of the small church when she attended *Iglesia de la Vera Cruz* with her grandparents in Chile—an experience remarkable to Sadie. She remembered the rich smell of incense, the Latin phrases (so unfathomable yet calming) chanted in unison, the reverence that each person afforded the priests, the building—all of the things she tried to emulate in her performances, in order to evoke that sense of adulation from her fans. Of course, her lyrics and music were mostly counter to (maybe even the antithesis of) the mores of the Catholic church, but it wasn't conversion she was after; it was the feeling that she tried to summon, the sensation that no other meditation or drugs or parties had conjured—only there, with her grandparents, in that little, red-painted Santiago church, had she experienced true awe.

The man assigned to the seat next to Sadie tapped Lily on the shoulder. "Excuse me," he said. "I believe that's my seat. 4B." He showed his boarding pass.

Sadie took the notebook from the girl. "What's your name, sweetie?"

"Margaret. Maggie. You can write it to Maggie."

"I'll put Margaret. Maggie sounds like an insect."

Lily nodded at the man and started to get up, but Sadie restrained her with the hand that clutched the notebook. "One moment," she insisted. "Call the stewardess."

"Flight attendant," Lily muttered and pushed the light.

Sadie finished the autograph. "Coming to the show in Dublin later this month?" she asked the girl.

"Um, yes?" Maggie said.

The flight attendant charged through the aisle, using her hips to nudge the passengers aside. The boarding line had come to a standstill, and the people in the jetway sighed and transferred their bags from shoulder to shoulder.

"Didn't you get this fellow another seat?" Sadie asked the flight attendant.

"I'm sorry, Miss Estrada; the flight is full. We don't have another first-class assignment."

"Then he can trade with Lily." Sadie smiled up at the man, catching his eye for the first time. "I'm certain he won't mind."

"Um, I don't—" the man voiced, strangely awkward, like an adolescent boy at a junior high school dance

"Rest assured, we will find a solution," the flight attendant said.

Lily stood. "I'll just go back."

Sadie frowned, sensing that she was losing control. "Don't be ridiculous, Lily. It's quite simple. This nice man will help us out." Sadie fluttered her lashes at the man and lowered her voice. "We'll set you up with a couple of front row tickets. Give Lily your information, and she'll sort it out."

The man glanced from one to the other. "Well, alright, I guess." He questioned the flight attendant. "Will I get a refund from the airline?"

"I will arrange everything," the attendant said. "Let me get your things for you." She reached overhead, revealing sweat stains spreading across her blouse.

"See?" Sadie patted Lily's arm. "Always keep something in your back pocket. Have something to offer."

As the plane taxied out to the runway, Sadie reclined her seat and tugged her mask over her eyes. "Goodnight." She'd had two vodka tonics and a Klonopin. And now she had Lily beside her. She'd sleep the whole way there.

* * *

April in the Northwest was a great expansion of gray: at no time in the month did those bright, crisp days appear that could show up in February, surprising everyone who had grown so gloomy over the winter. Days that caused a spike in sunglasses sales, days that got everyone out of their houses and onto the rough, stony beaches. There were a few optimists, of course, who continued to hope that spring would show itself in its full glory at any moment, one of them being Connor's co-worker and soccer buddy who had invited them to a bonfire on Alki Beach, despite the misty April skies.

A few restaurants were still serving along Alki Ave—Blue Moon Burgers and Duke's Chowderhouse. Starbucks, of course, was open way beyond the hour anyone should be drinking coffee. From the beach, the bars looked lively and warm, the lights a yellow glow feathering the street; houses in the neighborhood behind the strip emanated warmth, heaters on, cars parked on side streets for the evening.

Alex removed her shoes, let the sand cool her feet, inching its way between her toes as she and Connor walked hand in hand towards where his friends had lit a fire. Maybe twenty-five people lingered around watching the wind whip up the flames, the ever-present drizzle threatening full rain, though they all knew it was unlikely.

The heat from the flames felt good on Alex's chilled body. Someone handed them each a beer in a thermal cup, and Alex held it in her gloved hand. "I guess none of them know," she whispered to Connor, raising the cup.

Connor was slapped on his shoulder just then, and he turned away, not before offering Alex an apologetic smile.

"Man, I didn't think you two would come," this fellow said, tall and wiry with a shock of yellow hair that looked in the firelight as if it might be dyed, though Alex guessed from his equally pale eyebrows that his odd coloring was natural. "We never see this guy when you're in town," he said to Alex. "Now I see why."

The night passed with greetings and jokes and general chatter as darkness slipped in between bodies, over the vast waters of Puget Sound, out past the peninsula, beyond to the Pacific Ocean. Alex sat on a well-worn log and chatted with the wife of an engineer in Connor's company. She was a teacher at Garfield High School. She talked animatedly without pause about income inequality in Seattle, how students without means, without family members to guide them, had multiple challenges including lack of belief in themselves and lack of confidence throughout their lives.

"It's really hard for those kids to pull themselves out of a cycle of hopelessness," the teacher said, finally taking a breath. "Wow, sorry. I do get going. I haven't even asked you, what do you do? You're Connor's girlfriend, right?"

"I do contract work," Alex said. "Lots of traveling, so I'm gone a fair bit. Honestly, compared to your work—the direct impact of it— my work feels kind of meaningless." Warmed by the fire, Alex removed her sweater and unwrapped the light scarf she'd put on, anticipating a chilly night.

"Cool shirt," the woman said, pointing at Alex's tour logo, a piece of swag from Sadie's London show a couple of years ago. "I love her. Such a strong female role model. And my Latino students, you know, it helps them see there is the possibility of success. Sadie and J. Lo both, not that I'm suggesting pop star as a viable career choice, just that they are self-identifying with her lyrics: '*I'm not gonna take your shame/ I'm not gonna take the blame*'," the teacher sang.

Connor slid up next to Alex, slung his arm around her. "Talking Sadie? Don't we get enough of her?"

The schoolteacher furrowed her brow, trying to track Connor's meaning. "Superfan, huh?" she asked.

"Employee," Connor said. "Though Alex never tells anyone. She's Sadie's head electrician on tour." Connor's voice was full of pride, as if he enjoyed the surprise that moved across people's expressions when they registered her proximity to fame.

"Not anymore," Alex reminded him.

The teacher's eyes grew wide. "What happened? I mean, you actually worked for Sadie Estrada and, what, you got fired? I heard she fires people all the time, like, if you look her in the face, you're out."

Alex laughed. "No, Sadie's not like that. She's a little moody, but she's only ever been sweet to me. She gives me fist bumps on her way to the stage, or when she comes off, she might joke about how she had a wedgie the whole set. She's actually kind of funny."

"That's a relief—you hate to hear that someone who you admire is actually an awful person. So, how'd you get fired?"

"Not fired." Alex checked in with Connor, wondering if she could tell this woman, a new acquaintance, about her pregnancy.

They were almost there, to the twelve-week mark when the doctor said she'd be past the danger point and could start telling people. But no, Connor's face told her he wasn't ready to drop the news so casually. "Sorry," Alex said. "I can't really discuss it yet."

Connor rubbed Alex's arm, a silent thank you. His fingers trailed along her forearm, up to the mottled skin of her triceps that had exploded with acne since her pregnancy. He absentmindedly squeezed one of the pimples between his fingers, wiping away the pus with the side of his hand.

Alex jerked her head down, startled at this bold, intimate, slightly disgusting move. Connor himself looked surprised at his automatic action and he laughed. Then there were only the two of them, recognizing his tenderness and affection. The teacher faded away and whether or not she was a witness to this affirmation was irrelevant. In that moment Alex understood, though the sentiment had not been verbalized, that Connor loved her.

They were quiet on the drive back to Ballard, as if divining the night to come. When they climbed the stairs to Connor's bedroom, his naked feet plodded against the bare treads. In the dead of winter, even, he refused to wear slippers in some sort of punk or revolutionary stance. Under the covers, Alex pressed her body closer to his. She drew her knees in, hugged them to her rounded stomach and soon fell into a fitful sleep. At 12:17, she jolted awake, stricken with cramps.

Alex took six trips to the bathroom and came out shaking each time, unable to speak, unsure whether to wake him. She lay down again on the cool sheets.

At two o'clock, Connor reached over to find her side of the bed empty, then dozed until he realized she had not returned. He grabbed his robe, stepped over an abandoned piece of unfinished wall trim by the bed, and knocked on the bathroom door. "You alright?" he asked when she cracked the door, her face ashen. "Honey?" His brow was wrinkled into channels, eyes beady with concern.

She couldn't put into words the intensity of her pain, how her body hurt more than the broken wrist she suffered while rock climbing, more than the time she sliced her palm open with a Leatherman multi-tool.

He wanted to help, came downstairs with her, and pressed on her lower back, leaned his thumbs into the flesh next to her spine. "Here?" he asked.

She breathed deeply a few times until the pressure became too much. "Enough," she gasped. Connor tried to fold her in his arms, but she was too restless. He read to her from Margaret Atwood.

"What do you think, Lexi?" he finally asked. "Do you need a doctor?"

"Maybe," Alex choked out.

"Emergency room?"

"Not yet."

Hours morphed past, Connor's eyes grew heavier, his body clearly exhausted, strained from his inability to console her. "I've got to get some sleep," he finally said.

Incredulous, she let Connor kiss her on the forehead and tread up the stairs, leaving her on the tan couch in the living room. Alone. For hours, with only Connor's tabby cat as witness, she battled pain and fear and exhaustion.

No one ever talked about the blinding physical pain. The digital clock in the bathroom read 3:21. Three two one, like a countdown. Alex's guts roiled. Three, two, two.

In the downstairs bathroom, doubled over, she waited, whimpered while blood trickled into the bowl below. She thought briefly how this might feel, experiencing this confusion and pain in an emergency room bathroom, but she could only associate hospitals with age and dying, with the sickly-sweet antiseptic smell in the room when she visited her cancer-ridden great aunt. Better to suffer in Connor's house, at least, though even here she had little comfort. On and off the toilet, in and out of the bathroom. She imagined it would be over in a rush of blood—one instant you were fine, the next, the baby was gone. Nearly four hours had passed.

The empty quiet of the night surrounded her. At the foot of the stairs, she leaned to pat the tabby, hoping to hear Connor's footsteps on the floor above. Surely he would come.

A shot of pain rippled, radiated out through her groin, down her thighs as she made for the toilet. She moaned, clenched her jaw, and sweat beaded at her temples. Alex shivered and fought the urge to vomit, forcing a steadier breath. More blood discharged into the bowl, and she wondered, for the fifteenth time tonight, if the child she'd been carrying was gone.

Alex wiped the thick, slimy blood still on her skin, stood to look at what had dropped out of her, to see if her baby, tissue that was supposed to be the size of a lima bean, at just over ten weeks, was there. She'd read that on a baby site— a site for mothers— just two days ago. Blood was clotted in the bowl; four or five chunks drifting, mostly a deep crimson red, mostly splayed like drawings of dendrites, stringy with tendrils. If there was a bean, she could not see it for the blood.

Alex leaned against the bathroom wall, a satiny moss green, a masculine color. She cried weakly for Connor, though she was fully out of earshot. She sank to her knees and flushed. Rested her head on the rim of the seat until she found the strength to rise. She curled into a fetal position on the couch and tugged a scratchy wool blanket up over her shoulders, knees up against her chest, and held her breath at each sharp and steady jab that pulsed through her abdomen.

At four forty-two in the morning, she found her, tiny and pink and more like a comma than a bean, which would have heft, and thickness and strength. Alex stared and then peeled her eyes away, and then looked again—knowing she couldn't flush the baby down the toilet, initiating a torrent that would take her comma child through the city pipes, out to the sewage treatment plant. She searched the counters, the cabinet for some tool to help her, but there was no container, no vessel that a woman's bathroom would certainly contain.

Alex stumbled to the kitchen in a rush, as if afraid to leave the embryo alone, as if she had abandoned her child by looking for a cup to catch the tendrils of her. Dizzy and in a blur, Alex grabbed the handle of a silver ladle as if it was an oar. Like a hospital employee, she marched back to the site of the trauma with a sterile, cold stainless-steel bowl. A roll of paper towels under her arm, ladle and bowl in each hand, Alex fruitlessly and silently willed Connor to come and witness how their lives had changed. The cat—not Connor—descended from the landing of the stairs and wound itself around her feet, perhaps sensing Alex's grief, her need for companionship.

In the bleached-out bowl, the water was tinted pink, and blood was pooled on the floor of the toilet, a dark inky spot, but their little comma still floated at the top. Carefully, Alex sank the ladle in and scooped up the requisite clump of blood and tissue.

Such a tiny little mark. Alex began right then to mourn the loss of a future she'd just begun to imagine, just begun to accept. She didn't know how to dislodge, how to move away from the cold stainless-steel scenario she'd managed to create for herself and her little dream. But she did understand, instinctively, that this part of her journey was over.

Aching from thighs to chest, Alex warmed a sponge and wiped the floor and the toilet seat. She carried the stainless bowl with her into the living room and stared mutely at its contents, at this child she had lost. Eventually, she fell into a fitful sleep, exhausted.

In the early hours of the morning, the door to the upstairs bathroom closed. Connor tapped his toothbrush twice against the sink before the stairs creaked under his feet. When his eyes flickered across the cooking bowl, streaked with mucous-y pink fluid, his face changed. With her eyelids only half-open, Alex watched him absorb what he had missed, saw a flicker of revulsion. Did he think she was crazy for hovering over this tiny piece of tissue, their little bean?

"Was it..." he started to ask.

Alex's voice was hoarse. "I didn't know what to do with—her." She'd assumed all along the baby was a girl.

"I'm so sorry, honey," he whispered, barely getting out the words.

Sorry for what? Sorry for sleeping? Sorry you disappeared when I needed you? Sorry you woke up to this sad scene? She was too incredibly (perhaps eternally?) exhausted to voice her thoughts, to interrogate him, as she felt she rightly should.

"Do you need to go to the hospital?" he asked, lightly touching her, as if she was made of papier-mâché. "Do you want to bury it?"

"What?" escaped from her throat, a near-yelp. Too soon. She hugged the bowl close to her chest.

"We don't have to," Connor said.

She'd prefer a burial some place she felt connected to. Her industrial loft in Georgetown was no home, nor was Connor's house in Ballard—his perennially unfinished remodel—a definite bachelor pad, right down to the nearly empty refrigerator and the absence of any useful container in the downstairs bathroom.

Alex couldn't think of a single place she could truly call home. She'd rarely felt connected anywhere, to any land. Her military stepfather moved them around so much when she was a child that Alex learned not to get attached to the people they met, to the houses they lived in. If there was anywhere she might have loved to settle, it was Tuscany. Her family resided—re-nourished themselves—in Tirrenia for a few months shy of a year. She was eight years old and had just become comfortable with speaking Italian when her stepfather announced that they were leaving again. His mission at Camp Darby was finished. Alex had made a group of girlfriends there—one in particular, Helena, made Alex feel a part of her large, loving family, a family so unlike her own broken and patched-together clan. Rooms filled with rapidly speaking aunts and uncles and neighbors and siblings. Pots that overflowed with tomatoes and onions and peppers and sausage. Laughter. The smell of garlic. The Rizzieris, shouting over each other, dancing around their crowded kitchen, embraced Alex as one of their own.

Alex threw a tantrum when she heard they were leaving Italy. She still remembered the sensation as she thrashed on the carpet, the sun that streaked through high branches of an olive tree she glimpsed through the skylight, the pressure in her chest that made her want to explode with frustration; she felt desperately sure, twisting inside that beam of sunlight, that she was leaving her true family.

Alex couldn't imagine how to transport her tiny speck of a baby, how to wrap her up, or keep her warm, or make any detailed plans. She needed Connor to take over, and of course, he was confused, and seemed not fully awake. She felt strangely nothing more acutely than the need to call Helena, her childhood friend, and to seek comfort in Helena's mother's heavy touch.

"We can't go to my place. There's no yard," she said.

After he sat with her mutely for an amount of time neither one of them could count, Connor guided Alex out into the brisk April day, the grass frigid and still wet from dew. She had slipped her bare feet into dirty sneakers; goose bumps rose on her legs as the chill rushed up under her nightgown, a knee-length blue cotton sleeveless dress she would save forever, though she would never be able to wear it again.

Connor set the bowl on the grass while he selected a spade from the tool shed. Alex sank to her knees as if to protect and guard her baby bean from the elements, though nothing could have possibly done her further harm. The weather could do no worse than her body's ejection, turning her growing baby out, first into unclean water, and now into a casket of a cooking bowl.

"Here?" Connor asked as he dug the tip of the shovel into a soft patch of earth underneath an aging madrone that had grown in this yard for nearly a hundred years, limbs twisting and reaching upward in pursuit of the sun. Its gold trunk shimmered under bark that peeled back like a curled ribbon, as if the tree itself was a gift.

Alex cocked her head to the side, silent, empty, unable to answer. Connor studied her face for a moment, then began to dig.

Chapter 8

FROM CAB TO CURB, across a vast tiled lobby to a chest-high marble check-in desk, Alex lugged her suitcases, biker bag slung across her chest. A bow-tied, jovial young man checked her in and handed her a rooming list. Key card in hand, Alex ducked past the subdued lighting and loud retro music of the bar, aiming for the bank of elevators, not in the mood for socializing with touring crew who were sure to be belly-up, sucking down Irish beer.

"Whoa, hold the elevator," a man said. American accent. His hand jutted between the nearly-closed doors—dirt under the fingers, no wedding band—a crew guy, she guessed. He wore tan cargo shorts and a black t-shirt with a ZZ Top logo. Bingo. The man flashed a grin, open and flirty, and leaned across to press 16, nearly grazing her chest.

The rolled paper he held in his hand, frayed at the corners, pink and blue highlighters soaking through, looked familiar. She recognized her handwriting on the back, a calculation of cable length.

"Is that my lighting plot?" she asked, incredulous.

"Oh," he said. The elevator dinged open on 7 to reveal a blue and tan abstract painting, reminiscent of sand dunes. "You must be Alex. Are you Alex? I'm Tim," he said, twisting around awkwardly to stick out a hand, then added: "New guy."

He had to be close to Connor's age, with deep lines around his eyes and curly chestnut hair streaked with a few strands of gray. He wore it long, nearly chin-level, plied with some gel or product to keep it from frizzing. The polished aluminum elevator suddenly seemed sweltering, claustrophobic.

"How'd you get my plot?" she asked, ignoring his outstretched hand.

"Joe gave it to me." The door shut, and the lift continued to rise. He retracted his hand, wiped his palm on his shorts. "This is fortuitous, running into you here. Shall we meet in the bar later to plan load-in? Say seven?"

Fortuitous? *Fortuitous*? Had she ever heard a road guy use that word before? His formality made her wonder about his history. "Listen, I'm pretty tired," she said defensively, despite her curiosity. Tim was here, she knew, because she turned down the tour at first. *When Connor and I were good,* she thought, her throat constricting.

After two dozen bleary-eyed tromps to the bathroom, after ten days of strained communication with Connor, she stood at the window of her loft as the sun dropped low behind the Olympic Mountains; silhouettes of cranes lowered cargo onto semis in the Port of Seattle. She picked up her phone and begged for her job back.

Joe simply Fed Ex'd her an airline ticket with a note that read: SADIE WANTS YOU BACK. NEW GUY'S COMING TOO.

At her floor, Alex squeezed past Tim. "Let's talk in the morning," she muttered, luggage in tow. "I'll take the paperwork, though." She waited for him to turn over the plot, but the elevator doors slid quick and firm between them.

* * *

The tour bus idled at the entrance to the hotel, the engine drowning out a conversation between a bellman and the concierge, who was craning his neck to catch a glimpse of Sadie (though she happened to still be in bed, lightly snoring, sporting a gel-filled sleep mask that had shifted halfway up her forehead.)

First to check out, Kat jumped aboard and headed straight up the narrow steps of the double-decker bus to grab a middle bunk, away from the smoking lounge. Alex collapsed onto the couch on the first level to wait out the jostling for bunks, reminded of the bustling Rizzieri house in Tuscany, people cycling in and out, trying to claim space and snatch food off plates. Sadie's tour would play Pisa within a few weeks, just outside of Camp Darby where Alex lived as a child. Could Helena's family possibly remember her, nearly thirty years later, one enthralled child who passed so quickly through their energetic lives?

When Kat descended from the mad rush, she looked shocked, almost relieved to see Alex there, clipping a c-wrench onto her belt like it was any other gig day. "Thank God you made it. I wouldn't stand a chance against the boy's club without you; I'd be shutting down porn flicks in the front lounge and stepping over dirty boxers in the hallway. I mean, come on, with only dingbat Brooke and the drunken yogi as my allies?"

Kat wouldn't let Lily off the hook, not since she found her tanked-up, leaning on a Vespa and making out with an Italian outside the hotel in Hong Kong last year. "Some role model," Kat muttered as she passed carrying rickshaw noodles and milk tea back to her room.

As the bus filled, Kat welcomed the video crew chief with a high-five. "What's up, vidiot?" The burly guy took the slam lightly, used to the nickname. Sadie heard Kat use the term years ago and briefly took it up with gusto, shouting, "Hey, vidiots," whenever she climbed onto the stage and once even during a concert (where she was, quite possibly—actually, undeniably *under the influence*,) she spoke into the mic: "Hey, vidiots, can you get the guy on camera one to back off on the super tight shots? The back row doesn't need to see my nose hairs."

Just before the clock turned to seven, Red hollered down from the bunks. "Who we waiting on?"

"Brooke," several people answered in unison.

"One of these days I'm going to oil-spot her," Joe said, threatening to leave her behind, just as the lobby doors opened and Brooke appeared in dark shades, wearing a fifties-style pleated dress, flared out at the hip, three-quarter sleeves, with a wide red scarf over her perfectly coiffed hair.

"Jesus, Brooke," Joe yelled, "step it up."

Brooke let the bellman load her suitcases, dropped her handbag smack-dab in the middle of the aisle and pushed into the booth with Alex. "Sorry we didn't chat last night, sister." She gave Alex's hand a squeeze and launched into a story about her boyfriend. "You know Jules isn't coming over for rehearsals, right? He was thinking about it, but then I did his laundry last week without checking his pockets." She spun a complicated tale that Alex couldn't quite follow about her boyfriend's wet passport, an iron, and a hairdryer.

As the bus pulled out, they all shifted and settled, grasping a counter or cupboard for balance, getting their sea legs under them. Despite countless infuriating, nasty parts of touring, as the bus swayed back and forth in the early morning, the aroma of coffee filling the lounge, Alex decided she'd made the right choice to rejoin the tour. Heading toward the show was what she understood. The anticipation of a new venue, a new local crew, if a bit nerve-wracking, was also reassuring. She was part of an event larger than herself. A loud, purposeful, distraction from her problems.

Through the thin walls of the bathroom on the upper level of the bus, Kat heard the loud southern drawl of Red as he talked to some other guy whose voice she didn't recognize: quiet, almost cheerful. Their chatter reminded her of her southern neighbor in New York whose accent she heard through the wall of her bedroom, along with car horns and clanging trash can lids, percussive in the pre-dawn darkness, sounds she'd awoken to every day—the weeks she was home, at least—since she signed the lease on her rent-controlled apartment in the East Village twenty years ago. The dissonance reminded her that the city was alive and that its pulse beat steadily on. After her mother died a few months ago, when she had the impression that life itself might pause like kids in a game of freeze tag, those noises were her connection to the material world. They dragged her out of her lethargy, reminding her that morning comes.

Kat discarded her used toilet paper in the waste basket, squirted on hand sanitizer, and headed to her chosen bunk. Two new bags with carabiners and backstage passes clipped to the handles were nestled between her backpack and overnight bag. "Whose are these?" she asked.

Red—the only other person in the hallway—shrugged. "Maybe the new fella's."

"My stuff was already here. This is my bunk."

"Ain't nothing to me," Red said. His Tennessean twang was slow and insolent. Kat once spied a Confederate flag taped to the wall at the foot of his bunk, as if Red enjoyed lying there staring at it all night (as if he could even see over that massive belly.)

Kat tossed the black tote into the top "junk bunk" and tromped downstairs with the laptop bag. In her twenty years of touring, she'd only once been stuck with a top bunk, and then only because she'd bothered to dispute a mini-bar charge at check-out and missed the rush for premium beds. Since then, she'd learned to settle her bill at night; the six bucks she'd saved by arguing wasn't worth the month of hefting herself up over the sound guy's bunk every night. Dude was probably psyched to get a good crotch-shot every time she got up to pee.

Joe and a couple of sound techs all relaxed on the couch, shades open behind them to reveal Ha'penny Bridge in the distance, the iron aglow as streetlamps flickered out, the early morning sun creating reflections that stretched out across the River Liffey.

"Someone's bags are in my bunk." Kat raised the laptop as evidence.

All heads turned towards Kat with anticipation. Usually, they were a good week into the tour before Kat laid into someone.

Though she was a knowledgeable—even exceptional—guitar tech, if it were up to Joe, he would have hired someone else to save the headache, but Sadie loved her. So Kat stayed.

"That's Tim's bag," Joe said.

"He can put his crap somewhere else," Kat grumbled. Newbies never got a middle bunk—that's just how it was.

"I told him he could," Joe snapped.

"What kind of bullshit is that?"

"This isn't your bus, Kat. Your bus will be at the venue at ten. You'll travel with backline and video this time."

"The hell I will." Kat and Joe had battled like this before, over space, over timing, over proximity to Sadie. Last year when the monitor guy wanted more real estate and lobbied for Kat to relocate her guitar rig, Kat and Joe threw down, each recruiting players to their side: sound guys vs. backline, managers vs. band. Kat was forced to go to Sadie and explain her spatial needs, how she must have a clear sightline to the stage. She'd go to Sadie now if it meant avoiding traveling on the other bus, with no other women.

"Don't argue with me," Joe ordered.

Kat had a flash of when she first started touring, when she gave up working with horses to be on the road with a young punk rock trio—none of them over twenty-two. The band traveled in a VW van with a faulty starter they'd knock with a ball peen hammer until the engine turned over. Kat took on most of the driving, crossing the country on long stretches of highway. She learned how to back up the van with a trailer attached, learned how to sleep on the cardboard beds of motels with neon vacancy signs in the window and empty cement pools out back.

By the time the band graduated to their first real bus with new management and real techs, Kat felt she'd earned everyone's respect. She'd mothered those boys from bar band to platinum-selling artists, slaving away for no money, loving the edginess, until the new manager came along. She didn't recall why they were fighting, but she remembered his command: "Don't argue with me." He grabbed her arm as if she were a child, dragging her from the green room. Kat, strong from years of working at stables—days of baling hay, controlling spooked horses—broke free from his grip and threw him up against the wall with a hard shove.

She felt as steamed now as she was back then, but these days her impulses were a little more under control. Instead of slugging Joe (though she was tempted), she bent and grabbed a bottle of water from one of the drawers. Eyes on Joe, she uncapped the bottle and took a long, slow swallow. Wiped her mouth with the back of her hand. The only conversations were the bus driver's CB squawking in the front compartment and laughter from the smoking lounge upstairs. Everyone hung on Kat's next move.

"Should I clock him over the head with this water bottle for talking to me like that?" Kat asked as the hush lingered. She widened her legs, steadying herself against any bumps and swerves in the road, fingertips touching lightly on the table behind her. "Stomp on his toes?"

Joe tucked his feet under the lip of his rolling bag, just in case. Kat once chased him down a hallway and threw bags of Dove chocolates at his head while Brooke trailed along behind, picking up the bags, reminding them that the candy was for the production office. "To make people happy!" she scolded. "To bring joy!"

"How about," Kat edged closer to Joe, "I throw this in your face?"

Water sloshed over the side of the bottle, and Joe flinched as laughter filled the cramped lounge.

"Cut the shit, Kat," Joe said, though he shifted in his seat. The morning light revealed fine lines across Kat's forehead, etched into her pale, freckled skin, parched from a combination of air-conditioned hotel rooms and too much sun in her youth.

"I was just messing with you," Kat teased, defusing the tension. "But really," she took another drink, "that's my bunk, so tell what's-his-face he can take the bottom."

"I said no," Joe said, but with less conviction this time.

"We'll see." Kat smirked and raced back up the narrow stairs.

She caught Tim squatting on the carpeted top step, listening in, a look of amusement on his face, as if he wouldn't be easily intimidated. They held each other's gaze for a full breath before he opened the door to the smoking lounge, a plume of smoke escaping into the hallway. "What's with the guitar tech?" Kat heard him ask through the thin door.

"Bitch," said the board op. "But Sadie and the band love her."

"Don't get on her bad side," warned the systems tech.

Tim's flint sparked over and over, as if he was having trouble lighting his cigarette. "Too late."

Chapter 9

HUDDLING IN A bathroom stall was no way to escape heartache; a smoke was cheerless medicine, yet still, Alex lifted a cigarette to her lips. She hesitated before she struck the lighter, working to steady her hand, listening to rigging cases roll off the truck on the other side of the arena. The clack of solid rubber wheels down a metal ramp drowned out the low rumble of the stagehands' chatter as they pushed gear toward the stage.

Alex inhaled, let the smoke fill her lungs like a memory floods a mind. The tobacco, ripe and burning, summoned the memory of her grandfather in the days before he died, how he held her on his knee, fleshy and timeworn.

Alex didn't know her grandfather well; he was visiting for the holidays. They called him Bubbie; he was her mother's stepfather, a boxy man, who smelled like pipe tobacco and talcum powder mixed together. He wore old man high-waisted pants and a pocket protector. His presence seemed to force everyone into a tense, unbearable, and unexplained silence. Where was her grandmother? She had still been alive then, certainly, but Alex can't remember Mema there, couldn't picture her orange lipstick and tight curly hair in their house in New York, an old rambler in a quiet development of army families, four miles inland from the bay.

The day before all of their lives changed, Bubbie had held Alex on his knee and teased that she was too old to be sucking her thumb. The fruity smell of tobacco wafted from his crooked, callused fingers. His teeth were yellowed as he grinned. He played some sort of game with her there on his lap, chasing her thumb with his mouth, pretending he would chomp her.

And then her mother angrily sent her from the room. In the back bedroom, Alex stood confused and frightened while the adults argued. Through a cracked door, she saw Junior, her big brother, frozen in the hallway. He turned to her once, finger to his lips as he listened to the conversation. Junior was not quite eleven, but those few years between them seemed to offer him adult privilege and knowledge within their family, a position that she would never be able to surmount, at any age. She felt it keenly that winter, her exclusion from the secrets that her parents and Junior shared with stoic expressions. Whatever he heard in that hallway, he never explained, no matter how many times Alex asked.

Alex stared at the black scuff marks on the floor and refocused, intentionally pushing back the memory; she searched for a cheerier association, exhaling the smoke through her nose, like the Italians she lived among in Tirrenia, all those years ago.

As a young girl, she watched her friends' mothers with admiration; they seemed so stylish and suave, posturing in headscarves and sunglasses outside the school, chatting while they waited for their sons and daughters to charge from the exits. With a final exhale, the women would throw down their cigarettes and grind the butts under high-heeled shoes, take their children by the hands, and shout "*ciao*" to each other with a casual wave. Such outgoing, boisterous mothers. Alex fell in love, the type of love that little girls have for female role models, the type of awe and quiet respect that causes girls to emulate those women in action and in dress, in accent and in gesture. Alex wanted to be just like her friend Helena's mother so much that she started sneaking lipstick to school in her backpack and bought a pair of cheap sunglasses with her allowance; she even took a puff of a cigarette once, with Helena's older brother Milo, though the smoke made her cough and gag.

The nicotine rushed to her head now, creating a tingly sensation in the back of her mouth, a familiar metallic aftertaste. The last few days she'd managed to convince herself not to light one, but this morning, she couldn't summon a reason.

She smoked the cigarette down to the filter, let the ashes drift onto her pant legs. In the hallway, two men passed, speaking in hearty accents, words that sounded like curses. Tim and Ethan and the rest of her crew would expect her soon, would call on the radio, surprised that she wasn't automatically in place with them, present when the rigging cases were lined up and they were about to crack the doors on the lighting truck.

Alex checked her watch and tried to figure the time difference across the continents. It was ten p.m. back home in Seattle, and Connor would be in for the night, prepping for his early workday, laying out socks and underwear, trying to find a shirt that didn't need to be ironed, paying some bills, and propping the stamped envelopes by the door.

Last night when they talked—a brief and stilted conversation—he was late for a dinner party and cut her off. Their sentences became more clipped from there: "Okay, then." "Talk soon." "Miss you." "Me too."

She chucked the cigarette butt into the toilet, left the stall, lathered up liquid soap, and scrubbed the skin around her mouth and her neck, psyching herself up to join her crew. "Go put that rig up," she said. She'd done it a thousand times.

Alex ambled toward the sound of forged steel ricocheting, chain lifted into the air by the riggers balancing on narrow I-beams overhead, and the thud of motors being dumped out of their cases. She used to love aweing the men by lifting the eighty-five-pound motors onto the deck, yanking 200' of chain faster and faster out of its case, hand over hand, fingers covered in grease. She even felt sexy some days, bathed in sweat and dirt, hair plastered to her forehead.

Tim was downstage, clipping chain bags to the side of each motor and settling the excess chain down into the bags, the exact opposite of where she asked him to begin, opposite of where they normally started load-in. She should have met up with him last night, should have paid more attention this morning as she debriefed the house electrician. As if he'd sensed her thoughts, Tim looked up and caught her eye. He winked.

Something like a switch flipped inside, and her muscles tensed, her spine straightened; though she tried to rein it in, she was aware of her strut, like an officer in uniform. "Did you just wink at me?" she asked.

"Who, me?"

"Don't do that," she said and strode toward dimmer beach, Ethan's domain, where he was setting up power distribution for lighting.

She put the stagehands to work bolting truss, running heavy loomed cables across the stage, top-hanging lights. She inspected the chain bags on the cable bridge herself, making sure the bags weren't tilted or squashed inside the truss. She doublechecked the chain couldn't run out when the truss was lifted overhead, couldn't pour like water out of an overflowing bathtub, hurtling toward the deck, snapping like a whip. A person standing on the deck, hit by a running chain, might be killed instantly.

Tim sidled up, so close that she smelled his sweat, briny and sweet. "I'm on chain bags."

"The bridge is ready to fly," she said. "Get your guys on the cable."

"I realize you used to be boss, Alex." Tim resettled the bag. "But can you save the ordering around for the locals?"

Out at front of house, pushers dropped off consoles and laid out cable snakes that connected the boards to dimmers. At the docks, teamsters began unloading speakers and wedges off the sound trucks. The aroma of bacon floated down the hall from catering, just the faintest hint reaching the stage.

Alex grabbed for the chain bag. "Used to be?"

Tim wrenched the bag free from her hands; the rough canvas scraped Alex's palms. "Yes, as in, formerly. Once upon a time."

The stagehands, used to witnessing arguments between touring crew, watched with detached interest. Ethan, too, watched the exchange, hands on the motor controller, waiting to lift the whole rig, anticipating the go-ahead.

"You think it's easy," Tim asked, "joining a crew that's been together for three years?"

His question took Alex off-guard, even deflated some of her bluster when she remembered how hard it was for her as a child, moving to a new school every few years, trying to fit in and make new friends as kids huddled together in locker-lined hallways, throwing glances her way, always sharing some joke she couldn't understand.

Most groups were like that, insular, hard to penetrate. Right now, in typical road crew style, a couple of the sound guys were playing a prank on the monitor engineer, sawing off a half-inch a day from his bar stool, waiting to see how long until he noticed he could no longer reach the monitor controls. Soon, someone would decide to punk Tim, the newest guy on the tour, too.

"What did Joe tell you," Alex asked, managing to muster a bit of compassion for Tim, "after you found out I was returning?"

"That you'd be my second."

"No. That's not—" Alex started. "No."

Carpenters hung around impatiently and tapped their hammers against the edge of the metal stage legs, waiting for the rig to float so they could build their set on the deck. Fighting the urge to confront Joe right this minute, trained to finish the job, Alex signaled to Ethan instead, circling her forefinger in the air, directing him to lift the truss.

"Rig moving!" Ethan yelled and hit the red control button.

The grid of truss over the stage jerked and rose at once. Riggers and lighting crew all watched for a stuck motor or a running chain and stopped cracking jokes while the rig flew. They paid attention. Stagehands helped guide the fifty feet of cable looms out of their road boxes. All eyes were focused overhead.

A muffled quiet fell over the arena after lunch, after most of the local stagehands were sent home, after sound and video, sets and backline had all been set out, set up, erected. When the last of the floor lights had been plugged, Tim followed Alex to the production office, each hurrying to be the first through the door, as if reaching Joe first would sway his decision.

"Alex won't take orders," Tim blurted immediately.

Joe looked up from his desk, stifled a groan. "Come in." Kat appeared behind them, planning, instinctively, to prepare for battle. Joe cut her off quick. "Out, Kat," Joe barked. "None of your business." He leapt up with surprising swiftness and swept his hand toward the door.

Taken off-guard, Kat sauntered out with a sidelong glance at Tim. "Moron," she said before the door slammed behind her.

"You can't have two head elex," Alex said.

"I agree." Joe sat back down, twirling a pencil between his fingers. A photo of his wife and two kids leaned precariously on the edge of the desk; the children were tackling her in the grass, pushing on her stomach while she laughed, sun reflecting off his wife's gold-flecked hair. Alex wondered if the rumor of his wife having an affair was true. She looked so happy here.

"Tell Alex she's not in charge this tour. She needs to respect my authority," Tim said.

"Respect your authority?" Joe snickered. "Can't you two sort this out yourselves, like adults?"

"I'm still head," Alex said. "It's my rig."

Joe sighed. "Alex, you said 'no' to the tour. I did you a favor when I brought you back. You're gonna to have to suck it up. I hired Tim to do the job."

All of the anxiety she felt when she first started in this business, the need to prove herself, came back in a swarm, the same angst she knew most women felt working in a chauvinistic industry. Even Sadie once confided her insecurity on a trip to Vegas where she hopped buses and playfully squeezed into a bunk with Alex after slamming two jello shots: "I always wonder if my performances are good enough. My papa always thought I was a dumbass, an *ahuevonada*, because I wasn't good in school. He wanted me to be a lawyer, like him. I'm still trying to prove myself."

The muscles tightened in the back of Alex's neck, the first throb of a headache, exacerbated by fluorescent lights overhead flickering on and off. "Tim has no clue what he's doing."

"Untrue," Tim protested.

"Tim's in charge," Joe said. "Deal with it, Alex, or go home."

Alex put a hand on Brooke's desk to steady herself, feeling like the floor might be rolling and bouncing like it did in Madison Square Garden when the crowd got rocking. Never had she cried on the job, but now, exhausted by this old, tiresome fight, a tremor deep inside worked its way through her body. "Don't count on me to bail him out when he fucks up."

In the hallway, Kat waited for her. Together, they moved through the claustrophobic, recycled air of the arena, out onto brick and pavement touched by muted sunshine, a low cloud cover stretching across the expanse of sky. They walked in silence, each fuming over their perception of injustice. They wrestled with their disappointment and inability to change the culture inside their chosen profession. They walked and calmed themselves, breathing in the crisp Dublin air.

After five days, tour gear was dialed in: speakers were balanced, moving lights calibrated, glow tape affixed. Crew from sound, lights, video, rigging, carpenters, and even management, all planned to be near the stage—exhibiting themselves as occupied, diligent workers—at the moment of Sadie's arrival. Whether they'd been with her five days or three years, each one of them wanted to remind

Sadie of their value. Only the catering folks (whose value was obvious to all) continued on in a back room, setting out chafing dishes, lighting Bunsen burners in their erected kitchen, assured that the band, even Sadie, would visit them—she'd even occasionally pull up a stool and watch them chop vegetables, waxing nostalgic: "Cooking reminds me of my *abuela*."

Before Sadie arrived, Brooke broke free of the production office and made a circuit around the building, handing out new tour books for this European run. A calendar inside the book tracked each city and performance space. Each day's page listed the venue name, the capacity, the time sound check started (variable), the time doors opened (usually wrong), curfew (sometimes correct), the hotel name, and bar hours (mostly incorrect). Correct or not on paper, they were waist high in the waters of Europe now: two more days in Dublin and then they were off to Belfast, Glasgow, and Newcastle.

"Book of Lies." Brooke slapped one down on top of Alex's toolbox.

They would live the next few months by these guides, cross each day off as they went, looking for answers they couldn't find: would the drivers manage to maneuver the buses safely through the winding streets of Lisbon? Would stagehands have to push gear through long tunnels in Barcelona? They'd study the pages between the slick covers and memorize the date of the last gig. They'd complain about a six-a.m. load in in Madrid, about the reduced size of the stage in Hamburg.

"Where are we tomorrow?" someone would ask, knowing it didn't really matter, that they'd all be on the bus. Same jobs, same schedule, just in another town.

"FedEx envelopes are in the office in case you want to send a tour book to your sweetie," Brooke said. Alex barely acknowledged her, continued to unscrew a panel on a moving light.

Brooke chatted on. "My guy flew in last night, and we 'splashed out' on a gourmet meal. Five courses. Whole week of *per diems* shot, but whatev. Worth it. At the airport, I hoisted up a sign that said 'Jules Gutenberg, Rock Star' and though he frowned and turned the sign over, I knew he loved it because he's a fame junkie—he's had a little taste, and now he wants more. The sign was a shot in the arm, like B12, like applause after a song," Brooke said. "Anyway, how's your beloved?"

"Connor? Fine. Good."

"In my experience, 'fine' is a synonym for 'there's a wrinkle in the sheets', if you know what I mean." Brooke shifted the stack of tour books to her hip. "I'm on a mission, but first chance, let's gab. By the way, heard you got demoted. Ouch—feeling your pain, honey. How's that been?"

"I feel like a kid again," Alex answered, "in all the worst ways."

Kat leaned over from her toolbox where she'd been feigning interest in a guitar pedal, pretending she wasn't listening in. "I'm going to work on Sadie about this Tim dude getting your job. She won't like it." Kat had already successfully secured her place on the production bus with the other women, thwarting Joe's authority once again, allocating Tim to a bottom bunk.

Alex frowned. "Sadie won't care."

"Are you kidding?" Kat asked. "Sadie told me she worked in a theatre as an usher when she was a teenager—probably the only real job she's ever had—and she was passed over for a promotion. They gave it to a boy because—and they actually told her this: 'young girls tend to be flaky.' She's never forgotten that; this Tim business is exactly the kind of bullshit that burns her. Plus, I'll warn her Joe's targeting the women. If she doesn't take care, next thing she knows she'll have some dude straight off the Metallica tour handing her a guitar."

"Solidarity, sister," Brooke said and handed Kat a tour book. Though Brooke knew Kat hadn't had a partner in years (had Kat ever had a partner, everyone wondered?), Brooke teased her anyway. "Need a second book for anyone?"

Kat turned back to her toolbox and wiped at Sadie's Fender Stratocaster with a soft cloth, changed her mind, and lugged out her pliers and soldering equipment.

"You know her mom just died?" Alex whispered, tapping Brooke on the arm with the handle end of her screwdriver.

"Ooo, hon, right. How are you doing with cleaning out your mother's house and all that?" Brooke asked, without wondering why Alex was whispering.

Kat emptied drawers, pulling out gaff tape and machine screws, wiping up bits of dirt and grease. She waved a hand to ward off any further questions. "Fine. Anger stage." She didn't really know the stages of grief, but she could pretty much guarantee that at every point in "processing," there'd be anger involved. In a bottom drawer, Kat found an abandoned bass string, a broken reverb pedal, and peeled up an old photo.

She studied the details of a pale young woman's round face while Brooke peered over her shoulder. "Who's that?"

Kat turned around sharply. "An old friend."

"Pretty."

Brooke reached for the photo, but Kat yanked it from her hand and tucked it back out of sight, into an out-of-date Behringer manual. "Don't you have someone else to annoy?"

* * *

The board operator radioed to Tim: a lamp hadn't struck on one of the moving lights; the unit panned and tilted but emitted no light. Alex, overhearing the call, flipped the breaker, re-homed the light from the spare desk, lifting her eyes to inspect the grid.

She was not intentionally seditious, had only reacted instinctively to fix the problem, but Tim stepped up behind Alex, unforgiving. "Suit up, madam," he said, "and go change out that lamp."

Alex had scaled the rig just a handful of times in the last few years: only during emergencies, like in Wichita when a storm blew in overnight at an amphitheater; the whole crew went up to cover the lamps with trash bags, watched the geese squawking to each other out on the droppings-covered lawn.

Ethan, tuned in to Alex's fragility, piped up. "I'll do it."

"I said Alex."

"Where's the kid?" Ethan asked, looking for the lampy, the youngest guy on the crew. "Climbing is his job."

"Today, the prize goes to Alex." Tim grinned, as if delivering good news.

"Fine," Alex said between her teeth. She dug her harness out of a bottom drawer, unfolded the stiff and dusty straps, and clipped a lanyard to the D-ring. "I can climb."

* * *

"*Bon Nuit!*" Sadie piped into the mic as cheers soared through the theatre, faces tilted up, arms raised in praise while the bass player thrummed out a steady beat.

"*Pardonnez moi* if I speak in English," Sadie said, convinced they were in France—but what city, she couldn't reliably say. "*Vraiment, c'est horrible, mon Francaise,*" she added coyly. "*Soy una Latina, no Francés.*"

To a tee, each audience member was struck by her talent, by her beauty; they ate her up, drank her in. She transformed the room, transporting them from the drudgery of day-to-day existence to a place where only music mattered, the sound of guitar hum in their ears, the glare of lights in their eyes. Sadie carried her fans along, making them forget their troubles, allowed them to ignore everything outside of their pulsing, sweating bodies. For over two hours, the audience concentrated only on grandeur and art and fun.

"I'm going to tell you a story," Sadie said, a sentence that always enthralled the audience, stroked them. Sadie crouched down at the edge of the stage, this proximity startling to the first few rows—their idol made human, made of flesh. Two young girls in the front row who caught her eye squealed; behind them, their mothers, in ill-chosen clothes from their daughter's wardrobes—shirts with glittery logos, skinny jeans, and rhinestone belts—shook with laughter, barely in possession of their dignity.

"And every word is true," Sadie said off the mic, a secret just for those lucky few. She treaded upstage in her chunky heels, strapped on her Fender, strummed a few chords. "When I was sixteen, I snuck out to go to a Prince concert in Dallas."

The band noodled out a few bars of *Little Red Corvette*, a routine they'd performed about a hundred times, though it was supposed to seem spontaneous.

"I met Prince for the first time that night, years before we collaborated," Sadie said. "I got a backstage pass. And someone... one of *those people*," Sadie gestured toward side stage, toward her crew, "gave me a beer."

A few of the more conservative mothers in the audience who understood English wondered where the story was going.

"I was dehydrated—the sweat, the excitement."

Sadie envisioned her last yoga session with Lily, the stretch of her shoulders in bridge pose, the open sensation in her chest, how Lily suggested there was a block on her heart. The nerve. Her heart was fine.

"*D'accord*," Sadie admitted. "I had three beers. *Trois*."

Kat watched with interest from the wings as Sadie veered off her normal storyline; there had never been beer before.

"When Prince came in, he walked straight up to me like he knew me and put his hands on my hips. I was shaking so hard from excitement." Sadie lowered her lashes, let the memory flood in, feeling compelled to be honest, for no other reason than to show Lily that she was open. This night became, for Sadie, one of those moments she'd rue for weeks, for months even—for as long as she dwelt on any of her behavior. She blurted out truth best kept hidden, a clumsy attempt to prove Lily wrong.

There would be a backlash from mothers—these outraged parents, three of them in the audience that night, would find each other on the web. They'd start a campaign against Sadie as a poor role model for young girls, using the tagline "Home Wrecker," playing off Sadie's *Home Remedy*, a somewhat clever and slightly absurd motto that would only confuse their target audience. They would be no match for the power of Sadie. There wasn't any room for sobriety or sanity in the realm of pop music.

"*Vomite* all over his shirt," Sadie confessed. "All over his ruffles."

The band members checked in with each other, confused. In the usual story, young Sadie met Prince, he pulled her up on stage, and they danced, fueling her lifelong love of performance. End of story. Then Sadie commandeered someone from the front row, taught them a dance step, and passed on the legacy; maybe they too would follow in her footsteps, become a performer.

Two of Sadie's security guards stood on alert by the barricade, ready to escort the young woman up and around. Sadie usually chose someone slightly less pretty than her, a little chunkier, never too tall. Crew members continued to scan the front row; some took bets on who would be selected that night. They didn't see the twenty-two-year-old guy who had scaled the stage right side of the barricade.

Kat saw him, a wiry kid with shaggy brown hair cut into wild jutting tufts, just as his foot hit the stage. She rapidly scanned for the yellow-shirted security guards, but their eyes were on Sadie, waiting for her cue. Kat leapt from her stool and charged up the stairs.

"Prince said, 'Better learn to harness your energy, honey,' and then sauntered out of the room. He was so gracious," Sadie said.

The boy over the barricade posed, both hands raised in the air as if he'd just won an athletic event, until Kat tackled him from the side. The two wrestled for a moment at the edge of the stage before the security guards sprang into action and hauled the guy to his feet. He raised his hands again in victory. A few men in the audience cheered for him, as if he'd done their gender proud.

Barely noticing the scuffle, Sadie nodded at the guitarist, who did a subtle chord change from C,D,G, to D,G,F, from Prince's song into Sadie's.

"This song we worked on together," Sadie told her audience. "Prince and I."

Chapter 10

SOUNDS OF THE ARENA coming to life echoed through the main floor. Vendors readied their booths on the upper tiers: workers pulled frozen hotdogs out of freezers, turned on slushy and ice cream machines, made popcorn and heated salty pretzels. Neon signs flickered to life as food odors, greasy and brackish, wafted through the building.

Alex stood at dimmers, stage right, looking up at the rig. Her pants were damp, and her sneakers were soaked from getting caught in a rainstorm with Kat, a mile from the venue. "Which one?"

"Number 613." Tim pointed mid-stage left to the fixture that was broken, clearly pissed off that he couldn't reach Alex on radio for the last half hour. "There's twenty-five minutes before sound check."

Her legs shook as she climbed the ladder, her body still weak from the miscarriage. At the top, she threw a thigh over the truss and unclipped from the vertical fall protection. How had it come to this, her doing a lampy's job? Alex had trained dozens of newbies herself and had seen any number of them disappear. People whose names she couldn't even remember. People who didn't stay in the business long enough to have reputations, or personalities, or nicknames, or good stories to tell.

"Sixteen minutes," Tim yelled up at her.

At the broken unit, Alex wound her shiv around the truss and dropped one end of the rope to the deck, shouting: "Incoming."

Ethan and the lampy moved clear. Alex's first tour, no one told her what the call meant and she got clocked on the shoulder by a falling rope, to the amusement of her coworkers (who hopefully would have warned her had the falling object been any heavier). She threaded the rope through the handles of the moving light now and tied a bowline at the top, unplugged power and data lines, unclipped the safety chain. Wrapping her damp legs under the back rail, she told Ethan to take weight on the rope, unhooked the clamps, and freed up the fixture.

As they lowered the instrument, Alex flipped upright, level with upper tiers where stark, smooth rails ran the length of the seats to restrain crowds. She, on the other hand, had only a short lanyard tied to a single line of rope to protect her, but she didn't dwell on the danger. Letting yourself worry up in the grid only led to insecurity and insecurity led to fear. Fear led to mistakes.

The new light swung around as Ethan and the lampy heaved the instrument level to the truss. Alex grabbed the handle, lifted the weight the last couple of inches.

"Mine," she said, "good," and tightened the clamps. She hooked the safety, and Tim flipped the breaker at dimmers.

The unit whirred to life as band members joked with each other in the wings. Ethan, always on his toes, tested the pan and tilt, the gobos and color wheels, then gave a thumbs-up. Their teamwork continued, even with the intrusion of Tim's presence. As if he sensed exclusion, Tim loudly ordered her to drop in the line. "The band's here."

"Heads," Alex said and freed the rope. She clipped the shiv to her belt, hurried back to stage right.

Sandwiched between her guitar player and Lily, Sadie approached the center stage mic. "The rug's off center," she said. Lily waited until Sadie stepped off and then jerked the whole rug to the left, nearly toppling the microphone. Kat watched from the wings, her eyes on the guitar pedals. "Too much," Sadie said. Lily inched the rug to the right, causing the pedals to shift, the mic to wobble.

"Should I continue?" Lily asked.

Sadie gave a wry smile, unaware of how she would later completely regret these words. "No, you're done."

Kat rushed over and shoved Lily out of the way, steadying the stand, tugging on the sheepskin to make miniscule changes. "How's that?" she asked.

Sadie kicked off her shoes. "Perfect."

Lily picked up Sadie's shoes, swung her camera to her back, and walked offstage, knowing she was doing Sadie a disservice by continuing to wait on her, knowing that Sadie needed to work through her feelings around assistants, around servitude. Throughout Sadie's youth, a string of young, beautiful men were hired as her mother's assistants. They never lasted more than three months, performing their vague and nonessential duties: shopping, rearranging closets. Sadie's mother, willfully ignoring that half of them were gay, would inevitably come on to each one in a drunken haze. Sadie saw how put-off they were when her mother bent over in front of them, baring appallingly skimpy underwear. Disgusting. At least two of the straight ones were sleeping with Sadie's nanny. Lily figured that Sadie transferred her rage at her mother onto her assistants—and now Lily was bearing the brunt of that rage.

Alex hooked her lanyard to the static line while the guitarists fiddled on their instruments. The drummer tested the tension of his snare, and Sadie rotated her hips, then doubled over in a yogic stretch. Lily, poised in the wings, stealthily lifted and pointed her camera.

The band launched into Billie Holliday's "No More" as Alex began her scramble down. The vertical line snapped over her head, and she heard the distinct sound of a motor chain beginning to run, a high metallic whipping sound. She froze and in a fraction of a second saw a chain mid-stage tip out of its chain bag, dangerously close to where Sadie was doubled over.

"Chain!" Alex yelled over the music.

The couple of techs in the wings looked up, but the musicians (unfamiliar with the warning call) stood immobile without ducking for cover, as any stagehand would do. From stage right, Kat flew onto the stage, eyes on the truss, on a trajectory to tackle Sadie, but she couldn't reach her before the chain whipped to the end of its free fall. The chain rebounded once, and the impact broke the quicklink that held the chain to the chasse. The link bent and released the end of the chain, now twice the length—long enough to reach the deck. Alex gripped the rungs of the ladder and yelled a second time. "Sadie!"

Sadie startled at the sound of her name as the music died out. A solitary bass note echoed into the arena. The chain was on the deck in seconds, hitting the edge of the rug, less than two feet from where Sadie stood, bent over. The chain whipped up next to her, and she screamed and rolled into a ball. Sadie fell to her side just as the end links caught her in the arm, a quick, brutal punch. Sadie screamed out in pain, and the microphone crashed to the ground. Kat swung wide of where the metal thundered in, narrowly missing the chain as she threw her arms around Sadie.

In the wings, Lily lowered her camera, a look of confusion on her face. Band members crowded around Sadie.

"Don't touch me! Don't touch me!" she whimpered as Kat inspected her arm. The flesh had ruptured, though the blood was minimal. Capillaries had burst, and a deep, purple bruise began to form around the cut.

"Can you move your arm?" Kat asked.

Sound, video, and lighting crew all crowded onto the stage, fifteen feet back from where the chain swung in ever-decreasing arcs. Alex rested her head against the cold aluminum, stock still, and tried not to draw attention to herself.

Joe came ripping onto the stage with the tour manager and promoter, one behind the other, like a military envoy. In tow,

Brooke brought up the rear, clipboard in hand, the click of her heels and Sadie's whimpers the only sounds on stage.

"What the fuck?" Joe hollered when he saw the loose chain. "Alex! Tim! Red!"

His face set with grim determination, Tim strode out from stage right. Sadie's eyes were dilated; her whole body shook as Kat and the promoter helped her offstage and called for a medic. The band followed as a quiet awe fell over the arena. Tim flipped his radio to the rigging channel and called for Red while Joe examined the rig.

When Joe's eyes fell on Alex, still dangling from the ladder, his voice was low and controlled. "Get her down here."

Little by little, chatter filled the arena. Stagehands and road crew speculated about what caused the chain to fall now, rather than when the rig was first flown. Alex felt eyes burning into her with silent accusations, piercing her skin. She descended, taking her time, her muscles weary, her feet still damp.

Chapter 11

THE IBIS BUDGET BARCELONA was shabbier than the hotels where Sadie normally put up the crew, the rooms small, with stiff sheets on the bed and solid, utilitarian colors: white and tan and olive green. In a corner suite that overlooked the freeway, Kat and Brooke surfed the internet on Kat's laptop. They checked out houses to rent while drinking a bottle of Chianti in a spirit of anticipation of the two-week break in the tour that Sadie had begrudgingly agreed to—rather than fully canceling—while she recuperated from her "deep contusion" (as the attending medics called her wound).

Last night, frustrated at waiting for a decision about the accident, while other crew members wandered the hallways or stepped outside to have a smoke, Kat gathered the women, even managing to corner Lily for a minute before she returned to Sadie.

"I have a theory," Kat began. "The men are trying to divide the women. I think the boys' club is setting Alex up to take the fall, and that's why the chain fell." Kat looked around and lowered her voice. "It kills Joe when Sadie sides with us. Last week, when Sadie agreed I should ride on the production bus, backing down burned Joe big time. He gives me daggers every time I step onto the bus. Or what about when they booked the women, but not the men, in double rooms in the hotels?"

"I agree, Kat; there's most definitely a boys' club, but no one could have planned that chain falling." Alex fingered the Formica on the cafeteria table where they sat, the metal trim sharp under her nail, and thought of how, in the production office moments ago, all those men stared at her, as if she might have an explanation for why the chain ran.

"I'm positive they'd like to get rid of one of us," Kat said, ignoring Alex's vocalized doubts. "Alex is the obvious choice. Sadie's got no loyalty to her."

"Not true," Lily said quietly. "Sadie thinks Alex is the bomb, mainly because Alex ignores her. Sadie says that she loves me, but she doesn't. She despises me *because* I do her bidding. People don't respect those who obey. They respect the rebels."

"She hardly even notices me," Alex said.

"She even said that if she had to pick one woman to sleep with on the tour—that's a favorite game of hers, pointing out the women she wants to sleep with, though as far as I can tell, she's never been with a woman—" Lily continued, "she said she'd pick Alex."

"I can't believe it," Brooke cried. "What'd she say about me?"

"I don't remember your name coming up."

Brooke was incredulous. "Ever?"

"In this context."

"This is dumb," Kat said. "No one's sleeping with anyone anyway. You're all straight."

Lily's shoulders shook with an almost invisible tremor. "Anyway, I'm sick of how she treats me. I've seen how she talks to you, Kat—with respect. She needs you. I'm replaceable, and she never lets me forget it." Lily took a deep breath. "I'm going on this break whether she likes it or not."

"I'm not hanging out here with the boys' club for a couple of weeks," Kat complained.

"I have nowhere to go. We've sublet our apartment for the next month and a half," Brooke cried. "Besides, Jules has promised himself up to Sadie. Can you believe it? He said he'd stay with her in New York."

Lily looked as if she was weighing every decision she'd ever made and was judging herself harshly. Her head was bowed, her eyes moved back and forth between two invisible spots on the table. "I don't even have a place of my own."

Kat edged close enough on the bench for Alex to smell beef and a slight odor of corn on her breath. The smell reminded Alex of picnics, of humid Midwestern summer days and softball games she attended when she was a teen. The odors are what Alex remembered the most about her childhood. Deep pine forests and sun-soaked seaweed in Maine; salt, exhaust, and asphalt in California; Texas conjured up the sterile scent of denatured alcohol, from an extended stay in a hospital over a broken femur. Indonesia had the durian fruit that smelled like turpentine. And in Africa, there was curry.

The iron-rich smell of the miscarriage and the loamy, earthy odor of her child's grave, she would carry with her always.

"I don't want to go home," she confessed, unsure that there was such a place for her.

"I've got a good idea," Kat announced. "Let's get a place together. Rent a house, just us women."

"I love it," Brooke said. "How about in Paris?"

"Or Vienna?" Lily proposed.

"I know," Alex said, filled with a sudden desire to experience what she did as a child in Italy with the Rizzieri clan—a sense of community, of belonging. "Let's go to Tuscany."

* * *

Lily sat alone at the Hotel Ibis and stared into the dusk, lamps doused, curtains drawn, glad for once not to have to worry about her appearance, about whether she might be photographed with Sadie as she stepped from her room. She pondered the invisible forces that had brought her here, to this sterile room. No sound, no light, no people. The closest mall was ten miles away, the airport over fifteen. There was only television, dial-up internet, and a phone.

One floor up and on the other end of the hotel, Alex picked up the phone several times, listened to the flat tone for a few seconds before she hung up, until this became a pattern. She listened to the sound of the dial tone until the sky grew dark, until it was past six-thirty a.m. in Seattle and Connor had left the house. If she persisted long enough, if she procrastinated, she could just sit here. She replaced the handset in the cradle for the fifth time and wondered what she might say. Traffic rushed by outside; down the hall, the elevator dinged. Finally, her hand dialed, but it wasn't Connor she called.

"Does Helena Rizzieri still live here?" Alex asked when an older woman picked up. *"Posso parlare con Helena?"* she tried again in choppy Italian, hoping that one of the three Rizzieris listed in Tirrenia was the family she knew. *"Sono* Alexandra Evans. From America."

After a stream of answers that Alex couldn't follow, the woman switched to English. *"Si,* I remember you, little Alexandra with pigtails, always putting up her fists. My girl, how I think of you for these years. Helena lives in Radicondoli, *cara.* Maybe 300 kilometers from Tirrenia—you are here? Visiting? I can see?"

"I would love that!" Alex exclaimed, enthusiastically, like a child. "But I don't know if I can."

There was some conversation on the other end until Helena's mother returned to the line. "I would like to hear about your mother, Estelle. About your family."

Her mother? Were they friends, Estelle and Mrs. Rizzieri? She supposed they were, two military wives, though they were so different, one stiff and remote, the other soft and generous.

"Did my mother ever talk to you?" Alex paused. "Did she ever tell you about New York, where we were a few years before we came to Italy? About Fort Drum?"

"Mia cara, you come here and we talk."

"I don't know if I'll get to Tirrenia," Alex said.

"Oh, *dolce* Alexandra, how I would like to have talk with you. I'm carrying truths all this time, wondering about you."

93

"I'll call back when I figure out my plans," Alex said with an uneasy feeling about where she was going in life, about the choices she had made. Alex took down Helena's number and asked Mrs. Rizzieri to spell the name of Helena's town before she said goodbye.

There was no answer at Helena's, no machine, no way to tell if she had dialed correctly. Before she lost courage, Alex punched out the numbers she knew by heart. Her hand pulsed as if ready to cut the line. After four rings, it clicked over to Connor's voicemail, and she left a brief message.

The sky was slate blue, an almost grayish color while the day slid into evening. Alex walked to the window and pressed her nose against the glass. The city was busy, progressive, hopeful. Before she left, she wrote the room number down on a slip of paper and tucked it into her pocket beside the room key, a trick she discovered years ago. Nothing like not knowing where to go at three in the morning, wandering the halls of a hotel when your shoulders hurt and your back was tight. Could make you wish you lived in one place, like normal people.

* * *

Across the ocean, Connor stood in the doorway of his house with car keys in hand, waiting until the message service picked up. He was positive it was Alex on the phone, but he checked his watch, verifying he didn't have time, as if to justify his hesitation.

A neighbor pulled out of his driveway, the garage door lowered, and his car shifted into drive. Connor turned and watched the taillights fade up 49th Avenue. He considered picking up the phone but would only have to cut her off again. He was wary of upsetting her, like the last time she called. From the moment they met, he'd desired only to soothe her—to smooth out all of those rough edges and find the sweet, soft Alex he spied inside her smile.

Connor's cat squeezed through the mudroom door, curled once

around his ankles while his attention was caught, then darted quickly out the open front door. "Radio," Connor hollered at the tabby. "You go out now, you're out all day."

Radio turned in the tall grass along the sides of the driveway, as if he understood completely. He arched his back, bragging that he cared not a whit, then sprung off towards the deeper weeds of his neighbor's back yard.

Connor glanced at the clock. No time for chasing cats. Another five minutes and he'd be late for work. He couldn't answer the phone. Alex's relationship with time was different from his; at first, her freedom from the nine to five grind seemed liberating, but now, often, it simply tired him. He stared through several more rings while he remembered her canned-milk smell in the morning, her low, nearly husky voice. Remembered how, a few days after the jazz club where they met, he ran into her at a bookstore. She wore a plain t-shirt and beat-up old jeans; her hair was up in a ponytail. She stood, legs sturdy and wide, with the confidence of a rock star, holding a volume of Jane Kenyon's poems. He felt overwhelmed by the desire to kiss the bare skin of her neck. Cute and rumpled, as if she'd just rolled out of bed, Alex smelled like the warm, sun-soaked shirts his mother plucked off the clothesline in his early childhood.

Instantly, Connor regretted not answering the phone and crossed the room to pick up the handset on the kitchen counter. But he was too late. He'd missed her.

* * *

Sadie used her good arm and lifted her phone from her lap for the twentieth time to listen for messages. No sound. Yesterday, after the chain fall, all of those people surrounded her and now nobody. Managers and crew members, dancers and promoters wanting to talk to her, wanting to soothe her, but give them a night alone in a posh hotel room, and they all disappeared. She pushed the text message button and typed: WHY WON'T U ANSWR? WHERE R U? and then pressed send. It was seven p.m. Sadie flipped on the television and watched an episode of "What Not to Wear."

The host was making fun of a sloppy, chubby girl's wardrobe. "What a bitch," Sadie said, wishing someone was there to natter back at the TV with her. She could appeal to any number of people, certainly, and they'd be over before she hung up the phone. Of course she could. Sadie muted the television and checked her screen again. Sometimes phones dropped signals. But, no, the phone had three bars. She typed again: I'M NOT MAD. IF U COME BACK NOW, WE WON'T MENTION U WALKING OUT.

The program came back on, and she stared at the screen for a few minutes while she idly picked at her arm bandages. She checked the dial tone on her phone then texted again. DO U WANT ANOTHER RAISE? Send. Wait. Tap her foot. WHAT DO U WANT? Send. Tap tap. Wait. Check for messages. Tap tap tap. NAME YOUR PRICE. Send. Wait. JESUS, LILY, ANSWER ME. Send. I MEAN IT. Send. I'M NOT KIDDING AROUND. Send. THIS IS YOUR LAST CHANCE. Send. Wait. Nothing.

Sadie threw her phone on the couch and paced the room. Lily always made fun of the people on the show with her. They curled up on the couch and drank mugs of tea like college roommates. Sadie lifted her phone again and typed. I'M SORRY, OKAY? Send. Wait. Pace, pace, pace.

I MISS YOU. Send. I MISS YOU. Send.

Chapter 12

THE CITY OF FLORENCE woke like a party girl with a hangover, slowly, to the sound of gulls over the Arno, motorbikes puttering to life. A half hour off the train from Barcelona, Kat pounded on the aged wooden door of the car rental shop, pricking her clenched knuckle on a jutting splinter of wood. A Florentine turned the lock, wondering who could be getting up so ridiculously early. The conversation between Kat and the Florentine was only half clear. Kat blithely proffered a credit card, and then almost joyfully grabbed the keys, informing her friends that she'd drive. Unsteady and exhausted, Lily breathed a visible sigh of relief as she eyed traffic that had begun to maneuver down the cramped side street.

To Kat, the pace of cars that zipped and wound around each other seemed like Italy at its most legendary. She was ready to rip. Pedestrians took their lives into their hands to cross the street. The Italians moved laconically, as if daring cars to hit them. Foreigners, especially Americans, were easy to pinpoint by their baseball caps and khaki pants, by their knee socks and sun visors. The tourists seemed harried and even offended by the notorious Italian traffic. No crosswalks in the heart of Florence. No stoplights, only round-abouts and barely-acknowledged yield signs.

Kat cursed along with the native drivers, made gestures out the window and shouted at Alex for directions. Stone buildings flew by as they circled the narrow streets. In the distance stood a vaulted bridge, a hint of water. Kat drove as if she'd been trained in a racing camp, steering in and out, swerving far too quickly between other cars. Brooke grimaced in the back seat and gripped the door handle. Lily rode with her eyes squeezed shut, her thin fingers fondling her camera. Even Alex was unnerved, looking sharply over her shoulder after Kat nearly grazed another car's bumper. Kat slammed on the brakes and then gave something close to an apology. "This is the Italian way of driving. You have to get into the flow or you'll never get around," Kat said, nudging the accelerator again. "What street do we want?"

Alex answered, reaching for the map. "I thought the rental guy said take the second left. We just passed the second left."

"*Viale Spartaco Lavagnini*," Brooke said with an exaggerated accent.

"Yeah, that's right," Alex agreed. "Go around again."

Frustrated with everyone's lack of focus, with no sensitivity to Alex's tour worries, no time for Alex's distress at being blamed for Sadie's accident, Kat shot her a look. "You're supposed to be the navigator."

Kat focused on the traffic patterns several yards out. She kept to the middle of the roundabout fed from five radiating streets. She was in a zone, super-aware.

Two streets up, a woman took a tentative step off the curb. She was blond, stocky, and Kat caught a spray of freckles on her face as they zoomed past. As Kat checked the rearview again, her stomach dropped, and she wondered if it was possible as she lost sight of the woman.

"That street's coming up again," Brooke said.

"On it," Kat said and veered right. Then, in a fit of bravery or foolhardiness or some jolt of nerve, she turned sharply and headed into traffic again, daring fate to show its hand, as if the universe was a great jokester. The blond woman, fully crossed-over, headed away from the roundabout. Her hair swooshed slick against a black raincoat.

"Hey," Brooke shouted. "You missed it again."

Kat, inside her own head, inside a memory, yanked on the steering wheel and turned down the side street. She pulled the car over abruptly and double-parked. Kat was even more certain now, as she caught a second glimpse of the woman's profile, pert nose, sharp chin. It was her—Jessica. All these years later, all these miles away. Kat's vision narrowed to a fine tunnel. Her thoughts twisted into a vortex. She was in the past, standing in a field with the sun tucked behind a cirrus cloud, wispy and full. Back then she shivered, looked up, and Jessica was there.

On the streets of Florence, the woman strolled on without noticing the car. Her leather boots landed softly on the sidewalk. Around them, drivers laid on their horns. Kat leapt out.

"What are you doing?" Alex called after her.

Car keys dangled from the idling engine as Kat ran after the woman and grabbed at the black fabric. Startled, the blond woman yanked her arm free.

Brooke leaned forward into the front seat, asked whether Kat had gone insane. "You can't be repressed for that long and not have some negative consequences."

"Not nice," Alex warned with amused affection, sounding motherly.

Lily rested her head on the back of the car seat, lacking the energy to be concerned. "Must be someone she knows."

For a brief second, Kat actually believed it was Jessica, that time had made unpredictable changes to her face. Then the woman spoke. Only one word. "*Perdono?*" Her lips moved in a way Jessica's mouth never did. She cocked her head at an angle and suddenly looked nothing like Jessica. Kat stared at her so strangely that the woman tried English. "Can I help you?" She had a sharp Scandinavian accent.

Brought back to reality, Kat almost stuttered, "I'm sorry, I thought—" Her words caught in her throat.

The woman put her hand on Kat's arm. "I'm not who you think," she said, softly, even kindly, before she stepped away.

Kat watched the sway of the woman's long hair across her back, following that rhythm until she was lost in the crowd. Bowing her head, Kat studied the sidewalk, remembering the feeling of Jessica's wispy hair tickling her cheek.

To a symphony of shouts and horns, Alex crawled out of the car and approached Kat. Traffic rushed and flooded around and past. People ambled and ran and sauntered and dashed and meandered. Strangers walked around them. Energy flowed. Memories faded as Kat stood there disappointed. And time refused, stubbornly, to halt.

Alex wrapped her arm around Kat's shoulder and steered her back to the car. "I can drive."

"No," Kat protested. "I got it." She climbed behind the wheel and wiped her forehead with the back of her hand. She breathed in and out in staggered patterns and maneuvered the sedan out into the traffic stream, through the roundabout again. Kat said nothing, although she could scarcely believe that she thought Jessica might be walking these streets.

Kat watched the road as it was swallowed up by tires, as it passed under the hood of the car. She pressed harder on the accelerator. The speedometer quivered and rose. Kilometers had little meaning anyway.

"Take it easy," Alex said.

Kat blinked, flipped on the radio, turned the volume up. Scanned through accordion music, pop, talk radio and finally turned it off in disgust. No one said a word as the Italian hills and valleys passed by in a blur of muted color.

They stopped for groceries in a small town along *Superstrada Firenze-Siena,* and Lily stayed with the car. She had never liked shopping, stemming back to the days when she and her sister were expected to help her mother with groceries and dishes while their brothers went off to Royal Rangers meetings for future "Christlike men" (sculpting boys into servant-leaders).

"Shop away." Lily handed Alex a fist full of euros, threw a foot up on top of a rear tire, toes gripping the edge, and leaned forward in a stretch. "See if they have some mint tea."

Floorboards in the old store creaked with each step; a bell chimed as they pushed past the screen door off the porch. An old man in wader boots lingered at the counter chatting, while a trio of local matrons eyed Alex, Brooke, and Kat, as if wondering where they came from, or what they were doing in this little, local store. The rich scent of parmesan filled the air; a thick aroma of olive oil wafted from behind the counter. Alex pressed a fingertip to the still-warm crust of a baguette, piled, wrapperless, in a basket. Her hands were not freshly clean, but this was how Italians bought bread, and perhaps, the casually-shared germs kept them hardy.

The shopkeeper grinned when they approached the counter, arms full. His moustache hid a heavy upper lip that crowned a thinner, shallow bottom of the mouth. It appeared his moustache might topple onto his pointy chin. The man nodded affably and commented on their purchases, using a sloppy mix of Italian and English: "Yes, *linguine, sono molto buone, molto gustose.*" He waved the handmade pasta. "People like."

Lily doubled over outside the car, taking the time to practice yoga, not caring—in fact, unaware of—how she looked. She lifted her chest, eyes closed to the sky, bent, lifted, breathed, the rush of oxygen to her blood a natural stimulant. As she reached forward into downward dog, her phone fell from her pocket into a patch of grass. She left it there and took a deep breath. Was Sadie suffering right now? Did she struggle at all with her absence? When Lily evoked an image of Sadie, she saw a carved, wooden heart in the middle of Sadie's chest, rather than flesh and muscle. She pictured Sadie parading the heart around, showing off and chatting up the intricate carving. There was a lesson in this vision, but Lily could barely follow her thoughts that far. She couldn't sort out what was provable or not, what was the truth from her sensory perceptions.

101

Lily squatted next to the phone and pushed the power button, grass prickling her thighs. Sixty-four messages. Over her head, fine clouds strung out into oblivion. She closed her eyes again, willing herself not to fall back into Sadie's suffocating grasp.

Less than thirty-six hours ago, Sadie's dressing room that was cast in a yellow-green glow from recessed lighting had emptied out by the time Lily returned from pow-wowing with the other women. Sadie paced across the short-pile carpet and checked her arm every couple of passes.

"Alex and Brooke and Kat are going to Tuscany together," Lily began. "They're renting a house."

"How nice for them," Sadie said distractedly. "Off on a holiday while I nurse my injury."

Lily stared at her, silent, leaving space for possibility. On the counter, a facial steamer sent out draughts of cloudy mist, awaiting clogged pores to open, to cleanse.

"What?" Sadie said, a quick dismissal. A lack of permission implied. "You have a job to do."

"I haven't had a break in two years," Lily said.

Sadie sat at her make-up mirror and removed her jewelry. Oblivious. "Here, put these away." As Lily reached forward, her own necklace flapped out in front of her, level to Sadie's chin. "Where'd you get that?" Sadie asked.

Lily pulled herself erect and fondled the gem around her neck. "That stagehand who approached you last tour. He tried to give it to you."

"You're wearing a gift meant for me?"

Lily raised her eyebrows, surprised that Sadie seemed to be lodging a complaint; Sadie famously ignored her countless fans. Moreover, Lily once witnessed Sadie grabbing a fistful of donated jewelry and chucking it in a dressing room garbage can. The metal ricochet as the jewelry settled was as resounding as a running chain.

"You weren't interested," Lily said.

"So how is it you have it on now?" Sadie demanded.

"I offered to play messenger."

"So, give it to me." Sadie thrust out her hand. Lily stared directly into Sadie's eyes, examining her pupils for the wide-eyed frenzy of Adderall.

"Seriously?" Lily asked. The jewelry was a simple, cheap, beaded necklace. Maybe the lapis was worth a few dollars, but just a few. "It's not your style at all."

"Have you been stealing from me?" Sadie asked. "I haven't seen my green silk scarf all tour. I keep missing things."

"What do you mean?"

"Give me the necklace," Sadie snapped.

As Sadie stood and reached for the clasp, Lily put her hand up, clutching the stone to her chest, as if Sadie might strangle her with the beads. In a fury, Sadie put both hands to Lily's neck and wrenched it free.

In that instant, Lily remembered the man in the rectory basement when she was sixteen. He pulled her roughly toward him and pressed her body into his—his mustard-colored polyester shirt scratchy against her forearm. She tried to push away, to struggle out of his grip, but he encircled her and held his hand over her mouth. He was not rushed, not hectic; he behaved as if this was ordinary. The smell of burnt coffee and stale lemon cake rose up from the garbage. Lily turned her face to the low basement windows.

She heard voices outside—two men, a younger woman—and she tried to call to them. The elder, easily twice her size, and nearly three times her age, forced her to the floor, calmly stifling any scream. She bit his hand, and he slapped her face, stunning her to silence. "Don't say a word," he hissed and yanked her head to the side, grasped at her hair. The man's Listerine-tinged breath came hot and putrid on her cheek as he unbuckled his old-man trousers. Lily cried in muffled sobs and twisted under his weight as he forced himself into her. Footsteps overhead, sun hiding behind a cloud as her thin teenage body was rocked and shaken, battered in a brutal rhythm. By the time he ejaculated, Lily had stopped fighting. She lay still, shocked, disassociating. He pulled his penis out, slick with the blood of her ripped hymen, and breathed, "This is our secret."

The man stood up with the vigor of a teen and wiped his penis with a paper towel. He tucked himself into his pants and slicked back his wavy white hair.

"Remember, child, your duty is to serve the needs of others." He looked back at her only once. "Clean yourself," he said and headed up the stairs, unlocked the door.

"Put it on me," Sadie commanded.

Lily took the necklace and swept Sadie's hair out of the way, a gentle motion that caused goose bumps to rise on Sadie's neck.

"I'm sure it looks better on me," Sadie said, spinning until she was right in Lily's face, close enough to spit on her, or to kiss her.

As Lily stood, deciding, a clearer, redeeming vision came to her: a white ladder appeared, the type used on a speed boat, short and metal. Lily knew then that she had to grab onto that ladder, and lift herself out of there, as if Sadie was an electric eel or a hungry shark in the water.

"Please, Sadie," Lily tried again. "Let me take a break with the rest of the women. They've arranged everything. All I have to do is go along. I'm teetering here."

Sadie caught Lily's eye in the mirror. "I said no."

They stared hard at each other until Sadie went back to undressing, the cheap necklace conspicuous and unbefitting. Lily's heart pounded in her ears, in her chest as the memory of the rape flashed strong and insistent. Lily came around to look at Sadie directly. She felt shaky and thought she might throw up or perhaps even faint. She thought briefly of the box of photographs underneath her bed in Sadie's apartment. All that work. Could she let it go?

Lily gripped the table, leaned closer until she could smell the jojoba oil in Sadie's dark hair. "I'm not sure you understand," she whispered.

"Oh no?" Sadie glanced up, one eyebrow raised.

Lily set her mouth in a firm line. "I need to go."

Sadie snorted, cynically, deliberately, as if Lily was a ridiculous child. Without another word, Lily picked up her bag and headed toward the door. She knew the risk she took with every step, guessed that Sadie might throw away her box of photos.

Sadie shouted at her back. "You'll be fired."

Though she flinched at those words, at the finality compressed within them, Lily left Sadie's dressing room buoyed, as if a lead vest used for x-rays had been lifted off her chest.

"You'll be fired," echoed out into the hallway a second time.

Lily whispered feebly, "I've already thought of that."

Lily stood by the side of the road with the overloaded phone in hand, overwhelmed by thoughts of how she had been fettered to Sadie, chained to her every whim. She remembered every dig Sadie had made, about Lily's seriousness, about her rigidity, about her quest for higher consciousness. When Lily had trouble sleeping, when there were circles under her eyes and she started to lose weight, Sadie didn't give her even one day off. She sent Lily to her doctor to get a prescription. What a joke, them naming the tour *Home Remedy*. As if any healthy ingredients that Lily blended up for Sadie would be helpful. Life with Sadie had made Lily weak and vulnerable, as if even her bones had been ground down to a fine powder. She understood now the futility of spitting into Sadie's tea that first morning, and every time since. The satisfaction she felt was brief, too fleeting. And then, quickly, her willful action turned into self-deprecating thoughts. How could she give in to such a base human urge for revenge? Lily wished, now, that she had confessed to Sadie, or better yet, had spit right in front of her.

She pressed the text button and typed out one last message: I SPIT IN YOUR TEA. *Send*. Pulling her arm back, Lily hesitated for only a second before she let go—of the phone, and of her photos under the bed. The phone revolved and fell and plunged through the air. She lost sight of the glinting metal amid a tall patch of grass. The phone made a dull thud when it hit the ground. Lily squinted into the distance until she could no longer detect or imagine where the phone landed. She glanced up and down the road, then finally pulled her bag out of the back seat and rummaged for her prescription bottle. Each pill swallowed filled her with shame. But the need to suppress her racing thoughts exacted a greater pull. She wanted to sleep, and she would.

Kat and Alex wandered out, chatting, their arms laden. Brooke stayed inside the store and plied the shopkeeper with questions about the area and local wines. "What happened back there?" Alex asked. "The crazy car chase? That woman?"

Kat tried to conceal her embarrassment, though her flushed skin gave her away. They waited as a few cars passed, and Kat pretended to check her pockets for keys. She started to cross, but Alex, behaving motherly again, threw her arm out in front of Kat and blocked her.

"Talk to me," Alex said.

The image of Jessica's face floated easily across Kat's vision. What was happening? She had kept Jessica out of her mind for fifteen years. All those feelings, a jumble of ages and people. But now they resurfaced, clear and powerful.

At seven years old, Kat convinced her best friend to kiss her on the mouth. The girl's mother walked in the room as they lay on the bed, Kat sprawled on top of her friend. The woman screamed and pulled them apart. Kat's mother was called. A hot, whispered argument escalated in the cramped apartment hallway when she arrived. Kat's mother, on their short walk home, growled, "Maybe you don't know how a lady should act, Katrina. Your brothers are teaching you to behave like a boy? Is that it?" Kat shook her head in fear, though her mother wasn't looking for a denial. She wanted a deeper answer, an explanation that Kat was too young to give.

Although certain people might label her a rough woman, with cigarette-addled skin wrinkled like parchment, Kat's mother had great, high cheekbones. Thick auburn hair that grayed early. Hints of former beauty, before her husband had died.

Kat's dad, a spirited guitar and fiddle player, taught Kat how to string a guitar when she was nine, one of the few solid memories she had of him. A carpenter in Local 608, he died when she was only twelve. The day of the funeral, her mother cowered in a corner chair in their living room, surrounded by sisters and cousins while she clutched Kat's father's bathrobe in her hands and wailed. The next day her mother was up and running the kitchen like it was any other day. Not once did she bring up his fall from the scaffolding on his worksite. After his death, the family never played music together again.

Mrs. McMillan had a wicked sense of humor and not one of her children was spared a tease or crack when she'd had enough whiskey to set her off. When Kat's mother felt mean, a silence fell over the house. "Don't you ever touch another girl that way, you hear me?" she'd said on that walk home. "I'm gonna pray to the Virgin Mary the whole neighborhood don't start talking about you."

Kat found a gap in the traffic and stepped out onto the road, leaving Alex to trail along after, to follow her as they tucked groceries around their bags, into crevices in the trunk.

After five minutes, Kat tapped the keys on the hood of the car. "Dammit, Brooke could delay the start of summer, and no one would say a word to her."

"Looks like we're only about an hour away from Radicondoli," Alex said, having turned her attention to the maps.

Lily aimed her camera at a wooden ladder leaning up against the roofline of an old church. "No schedules, no demands," she spoke softly, reminding them to take it easy, wanting to keep still in this kind of purgatory for as long as possible.

"We'll have trouble finding the house if we don't get to the village by dark," Kat reasoned.

Brooke sauntered out with four bags of groceries, two of which, behind her, the shopkeeper carried. He set the bags on the trunk and pointed down the road, off toward low-lying green hills.

"I tell," he insisted excitedly, "*Sorgenti calde.*"

"There are some hot springs near here," Brooke announced, gnawing on a string of black licorice.

"Groovy," Lily said.

Kat shook her head and rattled the keys, an outright refusal that she hoped would establish her authority. She was the driver.

"Let's just stick a leg in." Brooke locked her hands together and semi-knelt in front of Kat.

Kat turned to Alex, anticipating an ally. Practicality was called for.

"It can't hurt," Alex said.

Kat slumped into the driver's seat and rolled down the window. She shook her head as if Alex had somehow betrayed her. "Fine. We'll look, but we need to get where we're going before dark. We could fall off a mountainside out here."

The women piled in. The shopkeeper waved after them, becoming smaller and smaller until finally, he disappeared.

There was no notation of hot springs on the map, so they pulled over twice to ask for directions. Brooke got out each time and made friends with locals. Through wild gestures and a mix of French and Italian and English, they made their way. As they approached the entrance, vehicles lined the road past an old stone restroom. The day was brisk, but the sun warmed each surface it touched: the metallic blue roof of the car, the broken asphalt, their skin. Lily, groggy, flopped back in her seat while Brooke cheerfully opened the trunk and rifled through her luggage.

"Wonder if they wear suits here," Alex said. "No one does at hot springs in the Northwest."

"I'm not going to be naked in front of a bunch of strangers," Kat exclaimed, horrified.

A boy wearing an arrowhead pendant around his neck stepped out of a parked camper with a dreadlocked girl. They wore bathing suits and carried threadbare towels. The couple headed down a path through sparse woods, the boy's hand across the small of the girl's back, half covering a Chinese character tattoo.

Lily, watching, winced and considered the cherry blossom on her lower back, how meaningless, how false—and how permanent.

"Looks like your dignity can remain intact," Brooke teased Kat.

They changed in the car one by one, cramped legs wiggling into dry suits.

"We can't dawdle," Kat warned as they followed a gravel path down to the pools.

Alex wrapped her arm around Kat's stiff, unyielding shoulders. "Take it easy," she said, as Kat leaned awkwardly into her, making a weak attempt to loosen up.

When they emerged from the trees, the land spread out into a handful of rocky pools where a dozen people lounged. In a wide lower pool, the young couple and an elderly man had plenty of space between them. The smooth, white rock lifted and sprawled. Three upper pools had been carved out, some shallow, some deep. Water cascaded down from rocks more than ten feet above the pools. The falls made a low roaring sound that reminded them they were in another country; they had left the claustrophobia of arenas. Beyond the pools rolled a lazy stream, its rocky bottom visible for the first ten or so feet, until the water became deep and inky blue. Twenty yards downstream, an arched stone bridge passed over; the stream widened at that point into a little river.

It was past three by the time they dipped their toes into the first pool. The sun worked hard to penetrate the spring air, but a cutting breeze cooled its rays before they reached the earth. Lily shivered before she sank her body into the warm water. Sulfur had streaked the rocks orange, though the smell was milder now.

Lily closed her eyes and reclined into the curve of the rock to warm her body, feeling like something inside her had broken during her years with Sadie, an essential trait for preserving her stability. Even yoga hadn't been able to mend the shattered part. But for the moment, the silky water felt healing; Lily lowered herself further as the water soaked through her bathing suit and onto her skin.

The voices of other bathers rolled over her. She sank her head down into the pool of warmth until water rushed into her ear canals, filling her head with a stopped-up sound. So dissimilar from being submerged under a spirit of weight and obligation. Lily dunked her whole head, pretended this was a holy dip. When her air was almost gone, she resurfaced and took a deep breath. In the distance, a baby cried, a sound Lily thought she might have imagined.

In the shallow part of the stream, a mother supported a baby wrapped in a sling. The woman swayed back and forth and tried to comfort the child, but he wouldn't be quieted. Finally, the mother offered her breast to the baby, who greedily took the nipple into his mouth.

"Ever heard of modesty?" Kat muttered.

Though she was lightheaded from the pills and the heat, Lily reached for her camera. She kept the lens low and inconspicuous as she bent and shifted for the ideal angle and snapped photos of the nursing mother.

Alex didn't watch the woman; she stared downriver, her face red and sweat-streaked.

"It's kind of gross," Brooke said, "the thought of some little creature yanking on your tit. Hard to separate from the sexual."

"Breastfeeding is natural," Lily said from behind the lens, imagining herself a mother, what that would be like, how your focus would change. "You'd feel differently if the baby was yours."

Brooke grimaced as she watched the mother squat on the edge of the bank. "It's icky, especially with boy babies," Brooke added. "Oedipus and all that."

"That's ridiculous," Lily said.

Brooke held up her palm, done trying to convince. "I'm just saying."

The sun had retreated. Lily lifted her chin to the sky and set her camera down. Through half-closed eyes, she observed her friends, these women, all between thirty and fifty, who had no children. Oddballs, each of them, unusual females employed in an industry that encouraged them to be neutral, even neutered, to not cultivate their feminine sides. The road had no room for babies, or for husbands, or for personal relationships.

Alex, silent until now, stood up in a sudden rush, all full of urgency, nearly panicked. "I need to get out of here."

The air rose goose bumps on her skin, and she hesitated, shivering. She bent a knee and was poised to step out of the pool when Lily warned her: "Ah, Alex?"

"What?"

"Oops, honey." Brooke tugged on her arm. "Sit down."

"Why?"

"Seems 'your little friend', as my mom used to say, is visiting," Lily told her.

A streak of blood ran down Alex's leg, and she wiped at the smear with her hand. The older man across from them averted his eyes and stepped out of the pool into the next level, while the dreadlocked couple looked on with interest. Alex's face went white, and she sank down into the water.

"Oh God, people saw," she moaned.

"Ew," Brooke whined. "We're stewing in your menstrual blood."

"The hot water kills bacteria," Kat said. "Besides, there are probably a lot worse things in here than Alex's blood. What about people who haven't showered in days? Shit they haven't cleaned out of their asses, etc. Just relax, and soak. We've got a half hour."

"That is absolutely disgusting," Brooke cried, and jumped out of the water. "Way to ruin it, Kat." She peered around helplessly. "We don't have any towels."

"Give me my pants," Alex said.

Alex rubbed her thighs under the water one last time. She jumped out and put her jeans on over the wet suit. The fabric stuck awkwardly to her skin, took a painfully long minute to drag over her thigh. The dreadlocked girl gave an empathetic smile; every woman had dealt with this embarrassment.

The women gathered their bags and clothes, aware of how many people followed their progress. Brooke and Kat hurried up the path, one behind the other. Their bathing suits dripped water in streams that puddled into their shoes.

"This will all make for a good story someday," Lily assured Alex as they headed back to the car.

Alex gave Lily an unconvincing smile—a practiced, even smile that hid Alex's strong, straight teeth.

Chapter 13

RADICONDOLI WAS A little village in the Tuscan countryside that graced the top of a massive hill—not quite a mountain, but impressively high. A winding road switched back on itself so frequently and tightly that you could get dizzy, driving. At one point, Brooke asked Kat to pull over so she could pee, but Kat ignored her.

"I guess that's a no," Brooke said with a frown. "No worries, Kat, I'll just hold it. Not a problem at all."

The rental house sat two hundred feet beyond a tall stone wall and looked like a place where even the most tightly wound show tech could rest. The driveway curved, and a patently Italian terracotta roof sloped up to reveal just a hint of chimney. Online, photos were posted of the sprawling lawn next to a swimming pool, but with this wind, and this altitude, at this time of year, they probably wouldn't be swimming. Dusk settled in over the picturesque brick buildings in the village, spreading blue light over cobblestone streets.

Kat and Alex climbed out of the car and tested the gate, but it was locked. They looked up and down the street, deciding. In the backseat, Lily dozed, her head thrown back, her mouth open. She emitted little rhythmic puffs of air, as if she was practicing breath control in her sleep.

"Check-in at four o'clock," Alex said, having verified as much on the paperwork.

Kat checked her watch. "It's close to six. I told you we shouldn't have stopped. And now maybe we've missed the person who was going to let us in."

"Don't get excited," Alex answered, almost enchanted by the little town. The evening was cool, and they weren't at a venue. They'd escaped! Alex went to the car for a sweatshirt. Careful not to wake Lily, she whispered to Brooke, "Can you find her cell phone?"

Brooke gingerly wrenched Lily's cloth bag from underneath her feet, a patchwork of green and maroon striped fabric woven with gilded thread, so completely Lily, reminding Alex of clothing at a Renaissance fair she attended back in her theatrical days. Brooke unbuttoned the bag and carefully, quietly, rifled through. At the bottom, next to a packet of slippery elm, Brooke grasped and held up a pill bottle and a photograph. One bare foot on a fire escape. A prescription, undoubtedly responsible for Lily's snoring.

"Behold." Brooke displayed the container. Alex motioned for her to put it back.

"What's going on?" Kat yelled.

"Shhhh." Alex glared at Kat, annoyed as a mother whose baby sleeps.

Brooke shook the bottle lightly and whispered, "Did you have any idea?"

"None of our business," Alex said.

Brooke let out a mischievous, tinkling laugh, and Lily stirred; Alex couldn't help but smile as Brooke animatedly threw the pills back in and tossed the bag on the floor of the car.

Kat stuck her head in the window, no hesitancy, no pussyfooting around. "Hey, Lily, wake up. Where's your phone?"

"Very kind of you," Brooke said. "Such calm and gentle treatment for our exhausted friend, who is trying to get some rest after her extremely trying week."

Lily's eyes fluttered open, and she blinked a few times, her expression vague. "Battery's dead," she mumbled, shut her eyes, and turned to sleep again.

The sun retreated completely behind the western hills, glanced over treetops, and faded pink off the low clouds as a night chill took hold. All across Tuscany people reached for sweaters, started fires, kicked up the heat. Electric lights flickered across the hillside like glowing embers on a charred log.

Kat charged around the car and grabbed Alex's arm, almost roughly, as if she was a child in need of discipline. "Stay here," Kat told Brooke. "We'll be right back."

The narrow cobblestone street was free of cars; Kat and Alex walked down the center toward a small brick facade, softly lit, a business that might still have been open. They peered under stone arches and past shallow stairs, down shadowy alleys where bicycles leaned in doorways. Music drifted out from a tavern across the street, and they moved toward the din.

Two elderly men sat at the bar that ran the length of the north wall. At a table in the back, a couple considered each other intensely, silently, as if they'd had an argument. An old transistor radio played music that sounded Slavic, maybe Hungarian.

"*Buonasera*," Alex said.

"You the Americans?" the bartender asked, his accent very heavy. He seemed welcoming, though, and wore a brown fedora-style hat half a size too small for his head.

"*The* Americans?" Kat asked defensively, illogically. Alex wanted to shush her, but the bartender went on.

"Renting the Serra house?" he asked.

"Yeah," Kat answered. "We don't have the key."

"I go get Valencia, in charge of house," he offered. But then he stopped to chat with a patron, as if he had all the time in the world, with the same jovial, laconic manner as all the locals they'd come in contact with here in Italy: the rental car agent, the storekeeper, the men Brooke asked for directions.

Kat and Alex stood in the middle of the room, anxious, more hurried than was seemly in a bar high up in the Tuscan hills. The bartender gestured toward bottles that lined the shelves behind him.

"*Si*," Alex said.

He flipped one short, clear glass over and poured a tawny liquid over ice, and then slid the drink across the bar. Alex sniffed at the liquor and put twenty euro on the bar before she held the glass under Kat's nose—the aromas themselves were intoxicating: anise and whiskey, tobacco and earth. Kat turned her head away, and the old men snickered under their breath. They tried this trick with all of the tourists. Alex took a mouthful, finished half of the drink. Her face reddened, and her eyes watered, but she managed to hold it together without sneezing or coughing, without letting anything go.

The oldest man in the bar, ancient-seeming with time and sun-wrinkled skin, said, "*Grappa!*" The men tittered.

"*Brava*," the bartender complimented Alex, giving her a nod.

"*Scusami.*" She leaned into the bartender. "*Tu sai* Helena Rizzieri *lei vive qui*?" using the tiny bit of Italian she remembered, trying to ask if he knew Helena.

The bartender pursed his lips. "Helena Amatteis?" he asked.

"Maybe. I guess she's married? *Lei sposare?* Dark hair? Bubbly?" Alex pantomimed her energetic eight-year-old friend, struggled to remember the Italian words. "*Energico?*"

The bartender nodded his head enthusiastically. "*Ma lei non e qui*," he said with a shrug. "*En Firenze.* Few days, she come back. *Dopo la vacanza.*" He wandered off down the bar.

"Shoot," Alex said. "I was really hoping I was going to get to see Helena. It felt like a monumental decision when I thought of coming here, like I was almost compelled, as if reconnecting with her was important. Seems kind of silly now, considering I've never kept in touch with the Rizzieris. Funny how memories sometimes just rear up out of nowhere. How they can hit you so hard, make you change your direction."

"Memories." Kat said as she fiddled with a saltshaker. "Yeah, weird. Been happening to me too on this trip." She grabbed the pepper, touching glass against glass, a small clinking sound.

Alex reached over and stilled Kat's hand. "What's going on with you today? You're so nervous. I've never seen you act like this before."

Kat looked up into Alex's eyes, so startlingly blue. Blue like Jessica's.

"Why don't you tell me what happened with that woman you chased after?"

Kat wondered if she dared tell Alex about that summer. She hadn't allowed herself to say Jessica's name, hadn't conjured up her image for years now—until she found the picture in the bottom of her toolbox the other day. In the photo, Jessica stared out beyond the camera and focused on the roan horse Kat had just dismounted.

Whenever Kat was on break from touring, she rode the horse in the photo every chance she could, out at a stable on Long Island. A groom at the ranch, Jessica was only twenty-one. She reminded Kat so much of herself at that age—so self-assured with her work, so good at what she did, ambitious.

Kat was totally surprised by Jessica's advances. She felt her own sexual inexperience acutely and resisted at first, mostly because she'd never been with a woman. But she had imagined over and over what a woman's touch might feel like on her skin. When the opportunity arose, Kat could not admit that she'd dreamed of exactly what Jessica was suggesting.

Throughout her teen years, Kat rarely had the same urges as the other girls in her class: she didn't draw hearts around boys' names or participate in giggly whispering about boys in gym shorts.

In the group of kids that Kat hung out with, black-haired, perfect-skinned, willowy Julia was the accepted leader. During half-time of a basketball game, in the bathroom of the South Street Middle School, Julia laughed as a fan from the away team entered. The plump girl had a boyish haircut, wore thick glasses, baseball cap and boy jeans. "Um, this is the girls' room," Julia said to a chorus of twittering laughs. "Kat, tell this person he needs to go to the boys' room."

"That's not funny," Kat mumbled. Cruel, powerful Julia turned with a smirk. "Or maybe it's just what I thought: you're rooting for the other team? What do you think, girls?"

One of her entourage, confused by the question, answered, "Yeah, maybe Kat's a Hicksville Comet."

Julia, her face twisted in disgust, clarified: "What I mean is: Do you think Katrina's a lesbo?"

Julia's loyal sidekick, a petite little blond, laughed and chanted "lesbo, lesbo."

Kat reacted with the only defense she had; she gave the girl closest to her a shove as she picked up the chant. "Cut it out."

The boyish Hicksville Comet slipped out while Julia's focus turned to Kat. "What's poor Mrs. McMillan going to say when she finds out?" Kat and Julia's mothers were good friends, had thrown the girls together in playdates, in family outings since infanthood. They attended the same Catechism classes, were members of the same Girl Scout troop, and had both attended the Thomas School of Horsemanship summer day camp (with the motto "Let Horses Bring Out the Best in You") for the past three years.

"Her only daughter," Julia continued. "So pathetic. Too bad you're such a freak, Kat."

By the next day, the girls in that gang acted like the teasing was all in good fun, but those chants, the threat that Julia might say something to her mother, stayed with Kat. As time passed and she found other friends, less cruel, Kat still dreaded discussions of sex; even the word 'penis' repulsed her, with its tiny little 'e' sound, its whiny 'iss.' There was no one she could confide in about her feelings for women—everyone around her seemed relaxed and easy; they all wanted the same things.

Before she met Jessica at the stables, Kat only ever had sex once—with a dry-lipped teenage boy her senior year of high school. Drunk, flattered by the attentions of this basketball player, she'd consented. Those good Catholic girls—some of the same girls who had called her names in middle school—reminded Kat that she was the only one of them still a virgin. The boy pushed her down on top of coats piled in a bedroom at a party. Within seconds it seemed, his penis tore into her with blunt thrusts; the condom chafed, rubbing painfully against her labia. The basketball player buried his face in her neck and made a dog-like ruff as he came.

That night, Kat ran home and showered. She hid her bloody underwear from her mother, lowered her eyes the next day as she said good morning, imagining her mother could see into her very soul. Over the years, she went on a few dates with men her brothers knew, but she never let another man bark into her neck. And though she moved into the city, where she spied pockets of every sexual orientation imaginable, where she witnessed a sickening display in the bathroom of a lesbian bar, she never knew how to penetrate her early shaming— the accepted opinion that she was wrong to love women.

Jessica was bold, so bold it made Kat blush even now to recall it. She wore Kat down over the month she was home, keeping pace beside Kat whenever she went out on her horse. Jessica brought Kat coffee in a steaming mug, made her a necklace out of hemp and beads. Jessica wrote notes that suggested what she might do to Kat in private; she left the risqué letters in Kat's saddle bag, unsigned, but in big, loopy letters no man could have written. Hearts over the 'i's like those girls had drawn in junior high.

When Kat finally gave in, Jessica's kiss was sweet and soft, unlike any kiss she had even envisaged, and Kat lost herself in it, savoring the flood of warmth through her body. For the first time in her life, as their bodies pressed together under a maple tree, Kat forgot about decency or caution. She abandoned herself to a shaking desire she'd never experienced before or since. Her hands ran across the soft skin of Jessica's belly and up onto her chest, and Kat came close to passing out from the pleasure of her scent, the cut-grass smell of Jessica's sweat.

They were together for three weeks that felt as full and as fraught as a long-term relationship. They bickered about dinner arrangements: Jessica wanted to go out; Kat wanted to stay in. They made love in waves that calmed and then crested once again. Jessica talked about the future. They fought, intensely. Kat insisted on keeping their relationship a secret—her friends and family were everywhere in Manorville, people she grew up with. Decent, family people. When one of Jessica's co-workers got suspicious, he joked, "What's up, Jess? Get yourself a little kitty Kat to play with? I heard that you like pussies." Kat, mortified, protested loudly.

That night, after she showered in silence, Jessica stepped out, dripping wet. "Coward," she said, looking as beautiful as Kat ever saw her. When Kat turned away to finger a gold crucifix around her neck, Jessica told her she was an insult to the gay rights movement. "What we're doing is not wrong," Jessica insisted, though she covered her breasts with a towel as she spoke, as if, while her body was naked, her words might lose their power.

"I've got to get out of here," were Kat's last words to Jessica. She left on tour a few days later. Though Kat intended to call, or write, in the end, she couldn't face what they did, what she felt. The tour was out for three months. Kat threw herself into her job: she moved sound gear, fixed and tinkered, anything to keep her body in motion, her mind occupied.

When Kat finally returned to Long Island, she heard that Jessica had moved to New Mexico. At the time, Kat thought it was for the best. Now, as she remembered Jessica's sweet face, the memory rushed back and Kat hung her head, afraid of tears. She should have written.

* * *

"She arrives," shouted Lily from a second-story window when Alex finally joined them. "Come on up, Alex; let's choose rooms."

Brooke sauntered out from beside the house, a bouquet of daisies in hand, and took Alex's arm; they walked through the living room and den to a spacious bedroom with a private bath that was tucked in the far corner of the main floor. Across from the master was a second large bedroom. The others had already sacrificed the master suite with a door that opened onto the pool to Brooke, the aesthete, the enthusiast. They assigned the second main floor room to Kat.

Alex agreed to a room upstairs with two double beds and a dormer window with a view of the expansive countryside. She breathed in the muted umbers and faded greens of the hills and fields, steaming off the winter season. As she settled in, she heard the rustle of paper bags in the other room, footsteps in the street. Across town, an engine gunned. In the quiet of the country, there was so much more to hear. Amplified music had gone mute, and Alex could not be happier about that. She rubbed her hands together to encourage her circulation, to dissipate the cold in her fingers. Connor's hands always emanated heat, warming her belly while the two of them lazed in bed, shielding her body from Seattle's winter chill.

Alex allowed herself deep distraction, conjuring Connor's smell: straw and warm clay, like a potter's ovens. She loved how his stubble grew out so fast, some days he shaved twice. He ate like a starving soldier. He would have liked this house, all the stark, cold tiles—no wall to wall carpeting. He had an opinion on all kinds of subjects ranging from the breeding of purebred dogs to the state of the government in Somalia. When he was tired, he murmured sweet romantic phrases, as if he was saying what was important before sleep took him away. Around his friends, he acted cool but still kept his hand on the small of her back. When they made love, he was attentive and aggressive. They could have made love in this house.

"I miss you," Alex said, to the countryside, to the universe—to Connor who was not there, to Connor whom she willingly chose not to go home to. She pictured him in Seattle, his cat perched on the windowsill. She imagined Connor as he stared out at the streetlight that haloed the sidewalk. Two thousand miles away from him, she rested her forehead against the windowpane and realized why she did not go home: she wanted an apology for that night, for his sleeping through her miscarriage. She required, at the very least, an acknowledgment that he let her down.

Bundled up in sweaters and jackets, the women moved one by one into the brisk spring evening, each of them rejoicing, in her own way, in this unexpected freedom from schedules, from Sadie's demands. Their voices echoed out into the night as if there were no other people on earth, as if they had the hills and the sky to themselves.

"I kind of miss the tour," Kat admitted once they'd all settled at the table, after they'd parceled out slices of cheese and dollops of jam. "Most of my life's been spent on the road. With bands, with horses. I do better when I'm mobile."

"It always takes a few weeks to come down off any tour, to ease the show-biz itch," Alex said. "I usually spend a few days by myself. Cleaning my loft, unpacking. I sweep and dust, do laundry. Chores bring me back down to regular, solid everyday life," she said.

Brooke frowned. "Bubble baths are more like it."

"I haven't felt grounded for a long time now," Lily said and wrapped her sweater tightly around her thin frame.

"How'd you manage to talk Sadie into letting you come with us, Lily?" Brooke asked, fishing.

Lily gazed off into the gray of the distant hills. Beams from occasional headlights wound around roads that seemed far away, illuminating steep inclines, and then falling into shade. Lily picked up her bag without answering the question. "I want to start our break with a ritual to mark the occasion—a gratitude ceremony. I hope you'll join me."

She glided over the lawn and removed equipment that Alex barely knew she had: incense and candles and a couple of crystals taped to sticks. Lily deliberately set out her props in four different directions.

"North?" Lily looked from one corner of the lawn to the hills again, as if unsure which direction was which. Finally, she knelt to set out a bowl of salt, then moved to the right and lit a piece of incense, sticking it into the ground toward the east. Facing west, she placed water and to the south, candles. When she was finished, Lily motioned to her friends to come forward, invited them to step inside. "I'm raising a circle."

"What kind of ritual?" Alex asked. "Hindu?"

"I'm invoking the gods to ask for guidance. It's based in the Celtic tradition."

"Hell no," Kat swore and crossed herself. "Count me out."

Brooke whooped. "But Kat, those are your people! Pagan worshipers. White magic, with spells and potions." Brooke reached for Alex, tried to yank her to standing. "Come on, sounds like fun."

Alex pulled her hand free and inspected an ant who wandered down the side of the tablecloth. "I'll just watch."

Lily orbited the perimeter of the circle she'd just defined and pointed a wand cobbled together from a crystal and a pine branch. "I solemnly create this circle in goodness. I form this circle with love and intention." She addressed each direction, wand up in the air, carving out space. "Goddess of the North, we welcome your cold; we offer you this salt as a symbol of the earth. You have come to teach us about change. Welcome."

Kat looked on in amazement. Alex thought of the pills they found in Lily's purse and wondered if Lily might be completely wasted. She also considered that Lily might have been practicing this "magic" the whole time they'd known her, that maybe, despite their close traveling quarters, she really didn't know Lily at all. It was doubtful that Brooke, on the other hand, who sat openly laughing, had any such secret practices.

"Goddess of the East," Lily continued, "Provider of the dawn sun, Goddess of birth and of spring, we welcome you. We offer incense. Come teach us to be born anew." Lily chanted and lifted up offerings.

After she saluted each of the four corners, Lily invoked gods and goddesses, summoned Father Sun and Mother Earth, outlined a globe with her wand.

"May nothing but truth and love enter this sacred space; may nothing but truth and love leave." With a flourish, she flicked the wand, circling the tip three times before tucking the stick away in her striped bag. "It is done."

Lily came to the edge of the circle, bent low and etched a rectangle into the air.

"Now there's a door," she said to the other women, opening her hands to her friends, her colleagues, "so if you decide to enter, you can."

She began to move clockwise, heel to toe, each step slow, intentional.

"I ask that my path lead to truth, to humility." She spoke in a clear, loud voice and invited them into the ritual. "I ask for Happiness, elusive as she may be, to touch her hand to me."

Alex rose, concerned for Lily, yet somehow captivated by the circle, the rhythm of her stride. Alex advanced forward, propelled by the memory of the night she paced, so aware of her humanity, so wired with pain and fear when she was losing her child. The sky was still and quiet, and Alex hearkened back to wet grass at dawn, to the sound of Connor's shovel piercing dirt.

Lily produced what sounded like a soft moan at first but was actually the start of a song. She sang with no precision or authority yet carried a decent tune. Her dry throat cracked as she continued, unashamed.

"I'm coming in," Brooke announced and mimed opening the door with a knob.

Lily paused mid-verse. "Sing with me."

"Always." Brooke fell into the dance. She trilled over Lily's melody, though she strained to catch the words: *Isis, Astarte, Diana, Hecate, Demeter, Kali, Inanna.*

"Really?" Kat asked. "You can't be serious."

Brooke twirled and whooped at Kat, taunting her. She motioned to the moon, breathed in the air. They finished the song, and Lily slowed her pace. "Let's dance *wittershins*, backwards, asking to get rid of the negative."

"Will Kat disappear?" Brooke joked.

Lily slowed to a halt. She put her hands on Brooke's waist and guided her. "Stepping backwards, have faith. You've already seen what's behind you."

Brooke kicked off her heels and followed Lily backwards. Checking over her shoulder, Brooke stumbled, laughed.

"I ask to get rid of my attachments," Lily prayed.

"Not me," Brooke said. "I'd like to get rid of twenty pounds."

Lily continued. "I ask to be liberated from my fear of failure."

Alex took a tentative step forward. She hesitated at the place where Lily carved a door, feeling silly as she considered joining in. But she wasn't on tour; she didn't have to act with cool level-headedness. And she wasn't with her family, who quelled any attempt to talk about emotion, about relationships.

Lily opened her arms wide and motioned Alex forward, into the circle, into the healing ritual.

"Alex?" Kat asked, incredulously. Alex couldn't listen, or she would have lost her nerve, embarrassed under Kat's scrutiny—Kat who had been her ally in their fight against the boys' club. Kat, ever solid and rational.

Alex walked backwards into the circle, looking up, overhead, where stars flickered behind passing clouds. "I'd like to get rid of the pain," she prayed, low, to herself. Strands of Alex's hair broke free of her ponytail. "I want this emptiness to go away," Alex said, louder this time. "And I don't want to be mad at Connor. I want to forgive him for leaving me alone when I was in the worst pain."

"Excellent, Alex; keep going," Lily coached.

It felt good to confess, and so Alex continued, reaching for the truth, for the root of her recent confusion. "I want to forgive my family for being so distant. For keeping secrets from me."

Brooke hummed, providing music of her own invention under their requests. "This is all I've got in the new-agey hippy realm," she said before she broke into *Aquarius*, from *Hair*. She performed the song as if standing on a stage, arms reaching wide, gesticulating into the air while she danced.

Feeling aligned with Lily, with her reach for a new perspective, Alex loosened up her neck and shoulders and continued without a backwards glance, without checking for divots or sticks or anything else that might trip her up. They danced until Brooke hit the final notes of her chosen Broadway tune, belting it out with full diaphragm, tipping her hand about her real aspirations. Her voice carried down the hill, through an open apartment window where an elderly man listened to the distant song, its tune familiar, the words incomprehensible.

"I ask for release from the desire to please Sadie," Lily insisted when the song was over. "Emancipation."

Brooke fanned her arms. The southern candle flickered out. Alex wondered if that had any meaning, if they were asking for too much and the gods had said 'no'.

Brooke asked bluntly. "Did you quit, Lily?"

Lily slowly stopped moving and tilted her head as if recalling her own words: *May nothing but truth and love enter this sacred space; may nothing but truth and love leave.* Into the quiet space that waited, Lily breathed. "Yes, I quit." At the picnic table, Kat gasped, shocked and almost disbelieving. "I barely recognize myself anymore," Lily said. "There's hardly anything left of me."

Alex took a deep breath, feeling warmed by Lily's courage. Even though the night had grown colder, Alex absorbed a sense of calm and protection, as if the circle had its own energy field, separate from the place where Kat sat gawking and questioning, and refusing to participate. Like an athlete warming up, Alex shook her shoulders, her head, her body.

Empowered by Lily's confession, she spoke aloud: "I lost a baby." Alex cleared her throat. "I was pregnant. That's why I turned down the tour. And then I had a miscarriage."

Immediately, her friends started speaking all at once. They moved toward her. Their platitudes falling over her like so much rain, like humidity she wasn't prepared for. She wiped at her eyes and searched for tissue in her pockets, but they were empty.

"That's why you were bleeding in the hot springs," Lily said, putting it together. "You must be so sad."

"I am." Alex sank to her knees in the grass, prickly and cool on her fingertips. "I am sad. But it's not just that. When I was in yoga one day, Lily, even before I buried her, all of these memories I wasn't expecting rose up like fog. From when I was little, when my grandfather died. After the day we lost my grandfather, my family seemed to change overnight. I never felt like I had a home after that day. Until I came here, to Italy when I was eight. I don't know; maybe I'm being foolish, but I think there's something here for me. That's why I wanted to come to Tuscany, to find my childhood friends."

Alex buried her face in her hands and began to sob. Hot and disheveled, totally unsettled, Alex looked up to see that Kat had entered the circle, had marched over the threshold of the door.

"Let it out," Kat said, in her best attempt at empathy. "Tell us the story."

* * *

By dinner time on the day Alex had sat on her grandfather's knee, tempers had settled down. They all ate silently, passing

127

around roast lamb, boiled potatoes, and brussels sprouts. No one seemed to notice as Alex fed her vegetables to their cocker spaniel under the table. Dan Rather droned on in the background. Americans were trapped, being held hostage. Alex understood trapped, but nothing else.

Alex watched the choking silence between Bubbie and her mother, the anxious scrutiny of Junior as they unenthusiastically planned an ice fishing trip for the morning. Estelle tried to back out, but Alex's stepfather—the only father she had ever known—wouldn't hear a word of it.

"Lt. Fischer set it up for your father as a favor to me, so we're damn well going out there," Clive barked, his voice like a megaphone.

Estelle immediately set about finding thermoses and woolen mufflers, her mouth drawn into a tight, disapproving line.

Junior woke Alex pre-dawn, shoving her roughly with stockinged feet. "Rise and shine, T-Lex," Junior yelled, using the nickname he'd used since her birth, which happened to be at the height of his dinosaur infatuation. "Time for a happy family outing."

Alex rode between her parents in the front seat of their Buick, fingers wrapped around a thermos of hot chocolate. Their headlights swept across the frozen river, which looked ominous, a sheet of dark ice, as they parked at the river's edge. Alex's cheeks stung as the car door let in the cutting wind. They trudged across packed snow, dressed to battle the weather, wearing lined winter boots, thick wool socks. Her stepfather Clive led their formation, carrying the ice drill. Estelle brought up the rear, toting the food basket as their boots crunched loudly in the snow. Alex inspected the ice for cracks, feeling almost presciently that they were marching towards a funeral.

In the shack, a draft sliced through the boards with a high whine. There was one bench. Alex trudged over to sit on the icy plank, dutifully getting out of the way as her stepfather cranked the auger.

Shavings of ice flew out and Clive shouted, "Watch out!" She swung her legs back and forth to keep warm, her job to hold on to the rods while Bubbie baited hooks, his heavy fingers squishing up the worms.

At one point in the morning, still well before sunrise, Alex and her stepfather marched back to the car and returned to the house. Something forgotten—some piece of gear? The ice hole was open when they left, lines submerged. Over time, Alex has wondered what more they could have needed. At the time, Alex was happy to get out of the cold. She stayed in the car listening to "Tie a Yellow Ribbon," broken up with static, playing on the FM radio. Her stepfather came to the kitchen window at one point, gesturing to the phone set in his hand. And then they were moving again, their tires loud on snow-packed roads, heading toward the bay.

Her brother was there, standing halfway between the shack and the riverbank, staring as if he was an actor caught unprepared in a spotlight. He gave a miniscule head shake, as if warning them off.

Clive popped out of the car. "What is it, son?" Junior looked to his left, just a quick, frightened nod, a son making brave for his stepfather, a man he alternately hated and wanted to impress.

"What's going on?" Alex asked, but she was ignored. At the door of the shack, Estelle turned and stared, wide-eyed, shaken. Looking at her mother, Alex could tell, even from that distance, that something was horribly wrong.

"Stay here," her stepfather ordered and shut Alex in the car with the engine running. She reached out angrily and punched the radio knob, sitting in silence, alone.

Estelle yelled something Alex could not understand. Her mother gestured into the distance, over near where a copse of trees came down to the edge of the bank. Her parents met in the middle where Junior stood, and they huddled around him, conversing, deciding. Alex felt forcefully excluded from the rest of her family, intentionally left out. Hot tears streamed over her cheeks. She wiped them away with rainbow-colored mittens.

The gear was left in the shack, forgotten. The food, too, abandoned as her family returned to the car. "Where is Bubbie?" Alex asked. "Is he still fishing?"

"Shut up," Junior said, getting in the back with Estelle. Her parents didn't correct him, just let him talk to her that way.

A few hours would pass before Alex would understand that suddenly, inexplicably, her grandfather no longer existed.

Kat and Brooke and Lily sat in a circle on the grass listening to Alex pull up all that she could remember, all that she felt. A sense of relief came—unlike Alex had ever felt. Sitting there on the Tuscan ground had begun to unearth what she had spent a lifetime tamping down. The night closed down around them, stars burning themselves out far above their heads, almost blind to the naked eye.

Chapter 14

ALONG WITH A ROBUST spring breeze, the morning brought with it a sense of calm determination for Alex. She knew what she had to do, and for once, she wasn't inclined to back away from her family. Alex purchased a calling card at the small market up the street, using choppy Italian, gesturing to an old rotary telephone on the wall as reference. In the front room of the rental house, she held her breath and then dialed.

"Mom."

"Yes? Who is it?"

"It's Alex, mom. Your only daughter."

"I know who my daughter is. I just couldn't hear you well. You sound far away. So where are you, Alexandra. How is the baby?"

Alex gripped the phone tighter. She had the impulse to tell her mother about the wild cycle of conflicting emotions she'd felt these past months: fear, elation, relief, despair.

But then she imagined what Estelle would say. She'd make one of her typical, cutting remarks, as if voicing her displeasure might somehow have changed the course of Alex's life: "Well, you are almost forty." Or: "It's no wonder, with your lifestyle."

Telling her about the pregnancy had been difficult enough. She'd had to squeeze the news in between reports of her brother's successes, about his new speedboat he'd christened *Estelle*.

"I'm in Italy. I have to ask you a question, about when we lived in Watertown, at Fort Drum."

"Why in the world would you want to talk about that? Good Lord, that was so long ago."

"Mom, I just need you to tell me the truth here. I'm trying to figure out why, after that winter..." she trailed off. "Bubbie fell through the ice, right? When we were ice fishing? That's how he died?"

There was a slight choking sound on the other end of the line, and Estelle cleared her throat. "For God's sake, Alexandra, why would you bring that up?"

"You were fighting with him. And the next day we went ice fishing. I remember Dad and I returned to the house, and when we came back, Bubbie wasn't there." Alex paused for only a second, full in it now. "We all left without him. Why would we do that? And why wouldn't you tell me what happened?"

"What do you mean?" Estelle raised her voice, sounding angry, almost barking. "You know what happened. He went out to relieve himself, and he fell in. End of story. I just don't understand why you keep asking about it."

"Keep asking? We have never talked about it. Not once."

"Back then, I mean. You wouldn't stop. You kept asking. I'm going to give you a piece of advice, Alexandra: some things are better left alone. There is no sense dwelling on his horrible death. Leave it in the past and move on with your life."

"Yes, that's what you've always taught me," Alex said, gritting her teeth.

"Even as a child, you were prone to dramatics." Her mother laughed, sounding inappropriate and false. "Now, what you are doing in Italy while you are pregnant? Don't tell me you are working."

"No, I'm not working." There was no point in asking further questions. And there was no point in blurting the truth about the baby. Estelle wasn't interested in truths.

Another calling card, another set of questions for her brother and her stepfather, but neither of them was talking either. Junior—

military, all business, answered in the same constant, stoic tone he'd had since they were kids. Never could she faze him.

Once, at eighteen, he walked into Alex's room while their parents were away, catching her and her boyfriend half dressed. Junior didn't shrink away or scream or delicately excuse himself; he stood with arms crossed, watching, until the boy grabbed his clothes and scooted down the hallway, until Alex threw a shoe at him.

Junior wouldn't say a word about her grandfather's plunge into the ice, as if somehow that knowledge was not for her ears. As if she was still somehow too young. How she wished she had asked her grandmother, who might have been more honest. Mema died when Alex was sixteen, before Alex left home and took too long to look back.

"I know you're hiding something from me!" she finally yelled at Junior, who wouldn't have cared.

Brooke watched from the hallway as Alex slammed down the phone. "You gotta butter them up, hon, before you take a bite," Brooke suggested. "No one likes to be interrogated."

Alex crossed her arms and paced the room, knowing Brooke was right. She had never known how to speak to people sweetly, not even her own family. Regardless, she wouldn't be deterred by their continued deflection. Now that these memories had surfaced, their presence weighed on her like a heavy harness. She had to get herself free of the past.

There was one more person she could talk to.

* * *

Alex, hung-over and drained, her throat dry as an air-conditioned motel room for the second morning in a row, downed a glass of water, and then put a pot of coffee on to boil. At the table, Lily slouched and yawned, still wearing her pajamas. Brooke, tidy and fresh in a summer dress, returned from the bakery down the street with a dozen fragrant amaretti cookies, the almond scent wafting through a thin cardboard box. Crisp air followed her in the back door, past where sun struck the picnic table, revealing shades of yellow and purple in the weathered boards.

Brooke plopped herself down on a kitchen chair and opened the lid of the box to reveal her offering, "*Voilà*, or should I say '*Prego*'?"

"I think *prego* means 'you're welcome' or 'don't mention it,'" Alex corrected, but Brooke ignored her and reached into the box, drew out two oblong cookies, and bit through the crisp crust into the soft insides. The powdered sugar stuck to her fingers, coated the corners of her mouth. "*Manga*," she said.

Kat placed small plates in front of each of the women before sitting herself, artlessly dipping a cookie into her coffee.

"Damn, but my head hurt when I woke up," Brooke said. "I didn't think I drank that much last night. How about you all?"

Alex offered a tentative nod, her neck too stiff for a larger movement, her heart too tender to emote any further.

"Still pounding, huh?"

"Mmmhmm."

Brooke recommended they all go for a swim. "I went in soon as I woke up, and now I'm ship shape. In my opinion, the only cure for a hangover is an icy dip in water," she said, then remarked on the irony that here on vacation she was the first one out and about, whereas on tour she was usually the last.

"I've been awake for hours," Kat said. "I took a walk through town already. I've been back in my bedroom since eight o'clock."

Brooke handed her a cookie. "Why didn't you come swimming?"

"Too cold," Kat said. "Hey, were you naked out there?"

"Yes indeedy, why do you ask?" She winked at Alex. "Were you spying on me? It wouldn't be the first time a woman admired me."

Lily watched the conversation and sipped her tea, subtly ignoring the offered cookies.

"Jesus, Brooke, we have neighbors," Kat scolded. "You two shouldn't have drunk so much last night."

"Thank you very much, mother." Brooke scowled. "And anyway, what Alex has is an *emotional* hangover. When you're ready, Alex, we can gab. Even if you're not keen on rehashing that other business and just want to bitch about your man, I'm here. I, too, have a guy that gives me a load of trouble."

In fact, they'd all wondered how Brooke and Jules managed to stay together.

"Jules is most definitely in the doghouse," Brooke continued. "I can't even reach him now that he's in New York. God only knows what he and Sadie are up to. My gut tells me that I made a mistake in coming here. The two of them get all cozy, and I get, what? Pushed out of the picture? Not that I don't enjoy bumming around with my gal pals."

Outside, the day was Italy-vacation beautiful, and Alex's head was throbbing. It was past eleven already. Last night, after they'd all had too much to drink, after Lily had found a ladder, climbed onto the roof of the house, and thrown her camera crashing down in a fit of emotion, Alex had begged Kat to drive to Tirrenia, to find Mrs. Rizzieri.

"I don't need two of you acting like idiots," Kat replied, "First Lily's destroying property, and now you want to drive off blindly into the Tuscan hillside? Not a chance."

Kat had an announcement to make now.

"Sadie's ready to rock." She'd been to the library and checked email. Joe sent a notice that they were scheduled for a show in a week. They were to be back in Paris by Tuesday, rehearsal Wednesday.

Alex leaned back into her chair and waved an amaretti in the air, bits of powdered sugar flinging in all directions. "Oh, good. I've really missed climbing the grid." She tossed the cookie onto her dish and took a gulp of coffee instead. "And here's my favorite part of touring: when a stagehand—some guy I've never met before—tries to wipe grease off my face."

Sun angled further into the kitchen, warming the floor tiles. The surrounding valleys gave all indication that a ripe, sweltering summer was on its way, the olive trees in full blossom, grass on their lawn already a high summer green. At a certain hour of the afternoon, pollen hovered in the air.

"Okay," Brooke said. "We're all going swimming."

Lily blinked, instantly alert. "Yes. A voluntary cold plunge. I'll fetch towels, my queens."

"You too, Kat. You may not be hung over, but you could use a float; a little buoyancy wouldn't hurt you," Brooke insisted.

"What does that mean?"

"Don't start," Brooke instructed. "Just move."

Through a barrage of protests, Brooke hurried them all past the door and into the yard. She led them around the corner, to the swimming pool. Dark blue tiles lined the brilliant-white painted cement. Alex dipped her toe in to nudge a stray leaf that glided on the surface. Hastily, she yanked her foot out of the icy pool. Lily joined them with towels and began to undress, and by the time she was down to her bra and underwear, they could see she was a mere skeleton. Kat and Alex exchanged looks, though Alex saw that Kat's expression bordered more on repulsion than worry.

"I'm not going in without a bathing suit," Kat declared.

"Oh, yes, you are," Brooke said through her teeth. She pointed a finger and ordered her: "Strip." To everyone's surprise, Kat did.

When they were all naked at the edge of the pool, Brooke insisted they take each other's hands. Wedging between Alex and Lily, she swung their arms back and forth. Kat lightly grasped Alex's other hand and waved her other arm around the yard as if to ward off intruders.

"We'll all go in together, okay?" Brooke announced. "On my count. *Uno, due, tre, andiamo!*"

Alex gasped when she hit the frigid water. Her fingers fumbled around as Kat's hand slipped away. Her eyes were closed, and liquid crept into her crevices, trickled over her shoulders and onto her neck. The icy water felt nearly cold enough to stop her heart. A shiver seized her spine, almost paralyzing her. Alex curled into a ball, as the image of the fetus that had grown inside her enveloped her thoughts. The child had floated for over two months, her senses just forming, no direction. Nothing to do but be kept safe and warm.

Alex unfurled after she hit the bottom, fluttered her arms to rise up. She intuited the other bodies around her as they sliced through the pool. Alex broke into the air with a burst and gasped for breath. She choked and sputtered, coaxing her nearly frozen lungs to life. Thought of her grandfather and his last moments on the frigid Black River Bay.

Brooke screamed and whooped beside her, fully embracing the exhilaration of having done something (twice now today!) daring and on the edge of foolish. A light spring wind raised goosebumps on their skin. Kat wrapped her arm around Alex's shoulder, her skin radiating heat in the frigid water, the smell of her body doused with chlorine.

"I can't believe I let you talk me into that," Kat yelled to Brooke, though she grinned heartily.

Brooke swung her arms around in the pool. Her breasts rocked back and forth, in and out of the pool. Lily hugged her arms around her body and waded quickly into the shallow end. Kat and Alex jumped up and down being playful, pushing away unwanted memories, laughing through chattering teeth like little girls.

* * *

Alex and Lily walked leisurely toward the park behind their rental house, no mention of their call back to duty, though it was on both of their minds. They doubled back down a path that ran along the east side of the property and then curved around to the south, past a vineyard. Here, the land dropped off unexpectedly, as a roofline appeared suspended in the air before the embankment sloped down and leveled off.

This morning, Helena Rizzieri, on holiday in Bergamo, called the rental house. "What a surprise," Helena exclaimed. "I have not talked to you in over twenty years, but I remember you so vividly. How disappointed I was when you stopped writing, when my letters were returned."

"Me too, I remember all of you!" Alex answered. "We moved so much back then, I kept losing touch with everyone. Hey, how did you know I was here?" Alex asked, confounded.

"Small town," Helena answered. "Big family. Stay put, my friend. I want to see you. Remember my brother Milo? He's coming too—he may beat me there."

Helena promised she would be back in Radicondoli before Alex left, probably Sunday. "Don't cut your vacation short for me," Alex said.

"Are you kidding?" Helena answered in perfect English. "I can come to Bergamo any time. You and me, we have twenty-five years to catch up on."

A lightly wooded section of the park disseminated light between cypress and live oaks. The low scrub-brush branch of a parasol pine scraped at Alex's shoulder as she passed. The park was silent, as if the land waited for an event. A large gray squirrel jumped out from the brush and crossed just in front of them. He glanced back over his shoulder briefly, then kept his back to the women while he scratched at the ground.

When the copse thinned out, the women passed into a clearing. Alex's eyes adjusted to the light across a scraggly meadow of untended lavender and gorse. Past a glade where the dirt path curved into a gentle S, a view of the valley was blocked by a high chain link fence, fifty feet wide, and beyond that, a radio tower blinking red lights.

"What a shame," Lily said.

Alex agreed. "But they have to put the towers somewhere. Otherwise, people can't communicate."

Water trickled and ran somewhere close, though no stream or river was visible. The park was little-used, the grass knee-high beyond an old wooden park bench whose paint had been stripped down to raw wood. Alex picked up a few beer bottles strewn through the weeds, threw them into an unlined metal trashcan. She wiped her hands on her jeans; the grime made a dark streak across the fabric.

Alex and Lily rested on the bench for a few moments, Lily looking at the white ladder on the tower that ascended to a platform, forty feet high. "I have some photos for you," Lily said. "I don't think I can get them developed for you here, though."

"What are they?" Alex asked. A hazy layer of low clouds had burnt off, but the air was still cool, and Alex wished she'd thought to wear warmer clothing. She pointed to a loose thread on Lily's sweater. Lily pulled on the string, and the gray yarn loosened the last row of knitting.

"You up in the truss." Lily continued to yank.

She distractedly glanced back up at the tower while continuing to unravel her sweater. Alex, too, followed Lily's gaze up just as a solitary bird dipped and flew directly into the fence. The bird bounced off the metal mesh and fell to the ground. A few of the dark feathers stuck to the grating.

"An illusion or real?" Lily asked.

Alex took a moment to respond. "Real," she said and they both rose. Lily let go of the thread, and they crossed the clearing, the length of yarn trailing behind. By the fence, the bird lay on its back, unmoving, legs straight up in the air.

Alex poked at it with her toe. "It's dead, I think."

"Suicide?" Lily asked.

Alex looked at her sideways. "What?"

Lily knelt and gently stroked the black feathers on the crown as she hunted for signs of life. The murmur of water was louder here, and Alex searched the horizon for the source. On the other side of the fence, pines swayed. Lily burrowed her hands in the grass beneath the bird and cradled the tiny body in her palms. There was no breath, no pulse, no more life.

"We should bury it," Lily said.

"We don't have a shovel," Alex choked out, transported to Connor's back yard, to the awful intimacy.

When Connor broke ground on that cold April morning, Alex couldn't think. She was barely aware, petrified in her nightgown and slip-on sneakers. The digging took forever. Alex listened to the crunch and scratch as metal hit stone. She closed her eyes against the glare of the sun. Low rays glinted off stainless steel and sparkled on the dewy grass. Too bright, too cheerful. Connor seemed to work in slow motion; his sluggish pace aggravated Alex, killed her with time itself, the lack of progress. She climbed to her knees and grabbed the spade from Connor. "I'll do it."

Connor sprang back, alarmed by her force, ceding the space to her needs. Blisters formed and broke while she dug. Alex welcomed the sting, a pain separate from the ache of her loss. She dug deeper and wider than the grave needed to be. She hoped to bury it so far no one could ever find a trace. She wanted the moment over, but she also could not bear to let go. Tears streamed down her face as she thrashed furiously at the earth. She stabbed at roots, threw rocks at the fence.

Finally, Connor put his hand on her arm. "That's enough, Lexi," he said. "You're shaking."

Sweat trickled down Alex's temples. Her torso trembled as she tossed the spade to the side and buried her head in Connor's chest. She had remembered, too, in that moment, the sound of a fistful of dirt hitting her grandfather's coffin. Her mother had thrown that first clod like a basketball, like a piece of unwanted garbage.

Together, Connor and Alex set the bowl at the bottom of the hole, their arms fully extended as they leaned over. Lying on her belly, Alex forced herself to take one last view of the tiny piece of flesh in its round silver coffin. A sob wracked her body, and she turned her head away, her cheek flattened against the earth. Connor threw a handful of dirt on top of the bowl and she listened to the ping and thud and wished she had the strength to see with clear eyes, head on, her near-child buried.

"Here," Lily suggested. She set the bird back down on the grass, lifted a long flat stone and began to gouge at the earth. With both hands, Lily scraped and dug until there was a shallow hole. "Help me?" she asked, but Alex froze, immobile. "There's a message here: this bird diving to his death right in front of us," Lily said. "It's our job to listen."

Alex took in the sounds of the park: a few high chirps of a chipmunk and the wind as it rustled through leaves in the canopy. What exactly should I hear? she wondered. Did Lily really imagine the universe sent dead birds as messengers?

When the hole was more than a tail feather long, Lily placed the bird tenderly into the grave. Dirt lined the curves of her fingernails, coated her skin. "We thank this little fellow for giving its life so that we may learn. So be it."

Lily threw a clump of dirt onto the little bird's belly and asked again if Alex would join in the burial. Alex had woven her fingers through the fence and leaned with her nose to the mesh, looking across the expanse of field under the tower. Lily stacked dirt on the grave until it was completely filled in, a small mound of fresh earth the only sign of disturbance.

"So be it," she repeated and joined Alex at the fence. They stared off together.

So be it? Alex wondered silently, then said aloud, "What do you mean by that?"

Lily looked at Alex strangely, as if confounded by the question. "So be it? 'This is the way things must be.' Accepting whatever comes as part of the cycle. There is no changing what has been decided."

"*Que sera sera*?" Alex said, contemplating the idea that there was no free will. "The problem with that philosophy, though, is that it removes any culpability for the choices we make. Sort of takes the burden off us."

"But maybe that's what we need," said Lily. "Some of our burden lifted."

"Wouldn't that be something?" Alex said. She thought it over, wondering what it would hurt to bend to Lily's whims, what she might be able to release. "Why not?" she asked and then added with a smile. "So be it."

Chapter 15

THE NIGHT WAS eerily quiet. Alex peered out the window of her second-story bedroom. The trees, lit by a three-quarter moon, bowed and swayed in a silent breeze. An unsteady olive sapling nearly scraped the ground, back bending like a yogi. It occurred to Alex that Lily had given up yoga since they'd been in Tuscany. Such a surprise, considering Lily's yoga practice seemed as central to her personality as her feathery earrings and her hemp-made clothing.

Alex opened the shutters, and like a furtive teenager, she leaned out the window to light a cigarette. Smoke curled up against a black sky and dispersed over the rooftop, out into the atmosphere. Alex couldn't imagine going back to tour either, at least not without a side trip to Tirrenia first. Maybe she should take the car in the morning, drive by herself. Or should she wait for Helena, hoping she actually showed up, hoping she could help Alex make some sense out of her childhood?

Alex settled herself as best she could on the window ledge to enjoy the solitude and the night view. She heard a grinding noise in the distance, which sent a shiver up her arms. She squinted at the clock on the bedside table: it was already after two a.m. Everyone else must have been asleep by now, so Alex stubbed out her cigarette and wandered through the house, finally peering out into the yard to see that the front gate was open. She stepped outside and looked around for a big stick or a rock or a planter she could lift, for protection, just in case; there was nothing to grab but long stalks of jasmine that crept up the side of the house. The scent of the flower almost made her feel like there couldn't be any danger, but she wasn't native to the Italian countryside; it was instinct for her to be on guard.

As Alex took the steps and crossed to the gate, she heard the rustle of light, quick footsteps. She checked back over her shoulder at the quiet house. Lights from the stairway glowed inside. Overhead, the moon lit the yard a peculiar blue. Alex rushed to close and lock the gate then hurriedly retreated into the house.

When she reached the foyer, she heard a high-pitched, ethereal moan, almost like a loon—a bird song she heard over and over at summer camp in Maine; she was twelve then. Loon calls pulled at your heart, made you crave security—something you couldn't really appreciate or even name at that young age. But this was not a loon; this sound had a human behind it, like the moans Lily encouraged during yoga classes. The sound came again, mournful and further away this time.

Alex tiptoed upstairs and leaned her ear against the door of Lily's room, but she didn't hear a sound. When she rapped lightly on the door, there was no answer. Alex gently opened Lily's door and half expected to see Lily staring at her, awake and silent. Moonlight illuminated empty white sheets. Covers had been thrown back, and a pillow had fallen off the bed. Lily was gone. Alex returned to the first floor and called for Lily, in case she was in the kitchen making a cup of tea or reading or playing solitaire.

She checked under the doors of Brooke's and Kat's rooms for lights, for some sign of life. The night was so quiet, and no one was awake—except maybe Lily, out looning, somewhere. Alex paced up and down, scared to explore the town alone, at this hour.

When Alex knocked, Kat tumbled out of bed in a hurry, practiced at the tour-skill of waking in a rush to roll off the bus and get going. It took Kat a moment to understand that the disturbance wasn't work-related.

"If Lily's that dim-witted to walk out there by herself in the middle of the night, I say have at it," Kat grumbled, once Alex had explained.

"I know there's something wrong," Alex said.

Grudgingly, Kat threw on boots and a jacket over her flannel sleepwear and strode purposefully out into the night with Alex. Neither of them considered waking Brooke. They passed through the gate noiselessly, scanned both directions of the main street, and saw nothing; they peered uncertainly out into the fields and vineyards beyond.

"Looks different out here in the middle of the night," Kat said, sounding strangely uneasy. "Pretty. Beautiful, actually."

Alex gave her a sidelong glance but didn't remark on Kat's unusually quixotic observation. They ambled through the still and vacant town. Yellow pools of light from overhead lamps contrasted with the sweeping blue moonlight. They fell into their regular fast-paced rhythm as they searched for any sign of Lily. When they'd circled back around on the main street, stripes of moonlight casting indigo shadows at their feet, Alex heard the baleful cry again, coming from the distant direction of the park.

At every rustle in the bushes, every crunch of gravel, Alex tensed. The hairs on her arms rose. Kat trekked along beside her, the hint of a grin at the corner of her mouth, as if the two of them were out for a midnight pleasure stroll. When they came out of the trees, the moon lit the low bushes and long grasses as broadly and as evenly as sunlight. Alex grabbed at Kat's arm when she saw a shadow and strained to make out whether the figure far on the other side of the clearing might be Lily.

The loon-like sound filled the meadow, and Alex was sure that it was Lily who cried so sorrowfully. Alex dragged Kat across the grass, over near the radio tower. The silhouette of a man inside the enclosure darkened the base of the tower as they peered through the fence. The sound came, louder this time and from up above, as the shadowy form turned. In the same instant in which they made eye contact, Alex saw movement on the tower, far up.

"Lily?" Kat asked. "What the hell is she doing all the way up there? And who's she singing to?"

* * *

A hint of sunlight glowed just beyond the eastern horizon as if to promise a golden day ahead. Lily stood on the middle platform of the tower looking totally chaotic, twitchy, over forty feet up, high as a lighting grid. Lily wore her exercise clothes, scant coverage for the cool air. Her hair was stringy and damp. On her feet were old canvas sneakers with no socks, her calves and ankles bare. One strap of her tank top fell over her right shoulder.

A stocky and dark-haired man, Italian-looking, walked out of the shadow of the tower toward them.

"Your friend," he said in English. "She is in trouble."

"What are you doing with her?" Kat barked.

He held a hand up in protest and looked over his shoulder at Lily, who continued to wail. He wore a tan vest with pockets, what looked like safari gear, over a long-sleeve white shirt streaked with dirt. The man introduced himself as Milo Rizzieri, a wildlife photographer.

"Milo?" Alex asked. She remembered running barefoot into the Rizzieri's kitchen, grabbing anise cookies from a jar. An image came clear of Helena's big brother as he swatted her with a dish towel. "Helena's brother?"

"*Si*. Yes. You must be Alexandra? I did not expect to meet you quite this way. You talked to my mother last week, *si*? She asked me to come to Radicondoli and find you, to tell you Helena is on her way back—tonight, tomorrow at the latest."

Milo rushed to explain that he heard Lily and followed the sound to the tower.

"My tripod is set up just over the hill. I came to photograph the Striped Crake this morning—very rare in Tuscany."

When Milo reached the tower, he called to Lily, but she wouldn't answer, as if she couldn't hear him, as if she was in another world. Lily continued to chant, to mumble about a ladder. Finally, he had hopped the fence. Milo presented a ripped sleeve as evidence.

Alex wound her fingers through the fencing. "Shouldn't we go get her?"

Milo nodded his head in agreement. He strode away and sped up the metal rungs, grasping firmly at the small round crosspieces. He was gone before they could make a plan, before the women could talk him out of climbing. Milo took a single glance over his shoulder as both women easily scaled the fence—quickly and adeptly, wishing they'd beat him to the tower.

"Lily, honey," Alex yelled from under the ladder. "We're here now. We can help, but you need to climb down."

"Hey Lily!" Kat yelled. "Are you high on acid?"

Lily, seeming not to hear, began a chant in a language none of them could understand, though Alex had heard pieces of Sanskrit and Hindi in yoga class: *Gajaananam bhootaganaadisevitam, Kapittha jamboophala saara bhakshitam.* Her wispy voice sounded sad and hollow.

Milo edged up to Lily as she leaned on the waist-high rail and hailed the brightening sky. He inched his feet across the metal grate. The soles of his boots scratched on the rough surface as he murmured, talking to Lily in a mix of halting English and fluid, whispering Italian. The day was just dawning; light crested the far hills. Milo reached out to touch her with a steady, gentle hand, and she flinched. Rebounding, she squinted down over the rail and whimpered, "No no no no no."

Milo whispered to Lily, a tiny, chirping woman the size of a girl. "*Bella e facile. Nessun problema,*" he said softly to this underdressed, distraught woman on the top of a radio tower. He chanted the words over and over, as if he too repeated a mantra, the syllables cadenced and steady. He stepped cautiously, one tiny motion at a time.

Lily slumped against the railing until Milo drew near and spoke in English this time. "Nice and easy. No problem. Come with me, please," he added, "I will take care. I will help."

Lily turned to him with an inquisitive look. He continued his soothing tone and dropped again to a whisper. Lily listened intently until she finally broke into a radiant smile. The wind ruffled her short hair, and Milo reached to tuck it behind her ear, gently, as he would have petted a child. Lily's whole body seemed to sigh.

Milo held out his arms to offer an embrace, no force, no insistence. Lily walked timidly toward him, her body stiff and erect, until her chest and forehead contacted Milo's vest. He wrapped his arms gently around her, and she tilted her head ever so slightly to rest her cheek on his chest. Milo looked over her shoulder, down at the other women. No one spoke.

The sun was just above the tree line, the birds fully atwitter. Milo and Lily together turned and descended the ladder, Milo leading the way.

Morning sun made its best effort to creep into the house, under doors and around blinds. The rays highlighted Lily's wan cheeks and sunken mouth. A blanket was tucked up to her chin, and her eyes were closed. Alex wondered when Lily began to age so dramatically. Lily had such a youthful manner at the beginning, had such a breezy way that she moved around backstage, not plodding or determined like the rest of the crew. Lily (and Brooke, of course) were always the exceptions, a lighter, airier presence amid the daily gravity. That first tour, when Lily had just come to them from the ethereal world of yoga studios, before she'd been exposed to the misogyny of stagehands, she would walk right through the arena in tight yoga clothes, the top of her G-string underwear visible, ignorant of the comments and ogling. Now, even as Lily skated close to sleep, Alex sensed the tension in Lily's muscles, the immensity of her burdens, and the frailty of her bones, trying to hold firm under all that weight.

She observed the slight lift and fall of Lily's chest under the blanket, saw her hands clenched at her sides. Lily's tennis shoes, once white, were now stained by hundreds of streets, dozens of arenas, and tonight, the grass of an Italian field. The canvas was wet and dark; water soaked up the sides. Alex brushed a speck of dust off Lily's face. Lily groaned, and her eyes fluttered open for a second and then swiftly shut.

Milo had helped bring Lily back to the house. He supported her under her arms until, frustrated at the pace, he finally picked her up and carried her as if from a burning building. After Lily was settled in the parlor, they rallied Brooke; she was grumpy, annoyed to have missed the drama, to be awakened after the whole ordeal had relocated back to the house. The women circled round the table in the white-painted kitchen, cabinets thick with paint and age, while Milo listened. What happened if they all returned to tour in a couple of days? They couldn't leave Lily alone here. There must be someone: family? Lily had a couple of siblings, though Alex knew they weren't close. What about a good friend? An old boyfriend? Alex thought they should enlist Joe: the tour was responsible for Lily; Sadie (or her employees) needed to make sure Lily got home. But where would they even send her? Lily had been living with Sadie.

"Do you think she maybe took something?" Milo guessed.

Brooke perked up. "I found some pills in her purse." She ran to Lily's room, dug through her bag, and returned with the bottle. "Ativan. What's that?"

"Sedative, I think." Alex said. "Should we send for a doctor?"

"And who pays the bill?" Kat asked gruffly.

"She'll need some care," Milo added tactfully. "She felt so delicate, as if I was cradling a baby bird."

"What did you say to her up there?" Alex asked.

He'd babbled to her about the Striped Crake. As he calmed Lily, he went on about the beauty of the bird's wings and about the dawn. "Sentimental things," he admitted.

"Dreamy," Brooke whispered to Alex. "Where'd you dig him up?"

Milo rose to leave. "My sister will be at 35 Via Sedice when your day settles down. Please, do not be shy." They all shook his hand and thanked him. "*Buonanotte*, ladies."

Kat's and Brooke's voices rippled down the hallway as they bickered in the kitchen. Alex stood in the chilly front room where they'd tucked Lily in under a pile of blankets on a stiff, cream-colored couch, excited that, after all these years, after weeks of waiting, she was about to see her friend Helena again. Maybe Lily was right about signs from the universe; maybe the accident on the truss was meant to happen, to shake up the routine of bus, truck, venue, to jolt them all into a different sort of action: less physical, more contemplative. Maybe she was meant to come here. As she watched Lily doze, Alex smiled at how much she'd opened up to Lily's mystical ideas.

Alex bent at the waist and took a few deep breaths, fingertips spreading across the cool floor. She moved slowly, stiffly into a sun salutation, one of the series of poses Lily promoted and demonstrated and encouraged. Alex's muscles contracted at the cold, protested against the tiles as she eyed wood stacked against the unlit fireplace. She did cat and cow, child's pose.

As she moved into cobra, she allowed herself to be swallowed by her memories: she and Helena as they peered in the back window of the barracks at Camp Darby, giggling, though they saw only empty bunks, metal lockers and brown wool blankets folded with precision. The two of them when they made Christmas ornaments in Tirrenia's tiny town library, covered Styrofoam angels with beads and sequins— the praise, the approval from Helena's thick-waisted, honey-voiced mother. Alex remembered her as an iconic Italian matriarch, warm and embracing, always beckoning the girls into the kitchen. Wearing an apron smeared with batter or grease or spices, Helena's mother would motion for Alex and Helena to climb up on high stools next to her, eye to eye, as she rolled out pastry dough. She would ask about their day as if she was truly interested, as if she might learn something from their stories. Alex loved Helena's mother intensely for those few months. When Alex returned to her own house in the evening, she would lie in bed and fantasize that Helena's family was hers. That Helena's mother was her mother.

Alex settled back into *savasana*. She stretched out parallel to Lily, arms by her side, palms to the ceiling, her whole body relaxed in memory. The draft from the entryway stole across the floor and caused goose bumps to form on her neck, down the curve of her shoulders. A shiver rolled up her spine as the force of the wind slammed the French door shut.

Lily's eyes flickered open and adjusted to the light. She pushed her palms against the sofa until she was semi-seated. "What time is it?"

"Almost noon." Alex rolled onto her side. "You okay? Do you remember what happened?"

"Where is he?" Lily asked.

"Who?" Alex responded.

"The man. Was he real?"

Alex studied Lily. "You mean Milo? Helena's brother, the photographer?"

Lily started. "Yes, of course, a photographer. Because I lost my camera." Lily sat up on the couch, pulled at the pillow behind her. "Milo," she mouthed softly. "Milo."

* * *

Connor answered the phone on the second ring. Water ran behind him, a pounding shower. A low female voice droned on in the background. Most likely talk radio. The sound cut out seconds after he picked up the phone. His voice sounded raspy, as if he hadn't yet said a word, hadn't exercised his vocal cords. It was Monday morning.

"Alex," he answered.

"How did you know?"

"No one else calls me at this hour."

Alex imagined him draped in a towel, quickly shaving before work, maybe nicking the soft skin of his neck. Moisture hanging in the air of the unfinished upstairs bathroom because Connor forgot to turn on the fan. He'd have been forced to wipe the condensation from the mirror to shave. The trim that should finish the room, which would one day wrap around the base of the tile, still stacked in the garage.

He spoke quietly into the phone. "I've been worried."

Where in the house had Connor shifted to now, she wondered? Sitting on the edge of his California king, the incredibly comfortable bed that took up a good third of his bedroom?

"I didn't mean to worry you," she said.

She heard a grating sound, as if he'd pulled out a chair. So, she was wrong—there was no chair in the bedroom: he'd walked, still in his towel, down the bare treads of the staircase, the walls painted a neutral tan. Alex wondered if the stairwell still smelled of fresh paint, the powerful scent of latex that emanated from the walls. She felt a kick in her gut when she realized she hadn't noticed the smell the last time she was there, in Connor's house. The night of her miscarriage.

"It's been pretty hard, Lexi, not hearing from you." Connor had moved into the area that doubled as a dining room and an office, the only room with wooden chairs. She imagined that he leaned his elbows on the faded edge of his grandmother's mahogany table, a beautifully preserved, carved oval Victorian piece. An equally ancient roll-top desk sat in the corner of the room, piled with bills and paperwork. Beside the desk, a computer sat on a cheap particle board stand in glaring contrast to the solid piece of history. "Come home, so we can be together," Connor said. "Like a couple. I miss you, Lexi."

Outside, beyond the dining room window, traffic was just picking up on 49th Street. The nine-to-fivers of Ballard, the ones who had to commute across the city, were unlocking their cars or walking to the bus stop. Though Alex liked the location and layout of Connor's craftsman house, in the slightly industrial, ever expanding borough of Seattle, she wondered if she could ever call his house home—the space was so fully his, so continually under construction. She hated to trip over piles of flooring, to bump into ladders in the kitchen.

"I'm such a mess. I thought it would be better to get some breathing room." Alex cleared her throat. The conversation had gotten off track immediately. She wanted to tell him about Helena and Milo, about the first rush of excitement she'd felt in weeks.

"I told you touring in your shape was a bad idea. Maybe I should come get you."

"Come get me?" Alex bristled. "Like I'm a package to collect?"

"You're off living some exotic life, renting a house in Tuscany, for God's sake, and in my life, there's a whole lot of negative space." There was a shuffle on the other end of the line and Alex imagined Connor getting dressed. She heard him scrape some coins off the dresser and pour them into his pocket. "I've got to go," he said. "I'm going to be late. Can we talk this evening? I tried to reach you on Lily's cell. I left a message."

"I think she lost her phone." Alex strained her ears for some other background noise, something to keep her connected. "I'll call you with a number."

"Okay," he said, sounding defeated. "Don't forget."

"I won't," she promised, reluctant, now that she'd got him on the line, to let him go. "*Ciao.*"

* * *

Lily sat hunched over her teacup in the jam-packed kitchen next to Alex and Brooke. Crusts of bread, cloves of garlic and ramekins of olive oil were strewn across the counter. Lily's face grew dreamy and she explained what Alex already had seen: how the path just outside their gate wound down past the vineyards, how the trail opened up into a field framed by cypress trees on the west side and to the east an open vista of rolling countryside. No sign of human life, but there were plenty of birds. Plenty.

"You can predict the weather by how swallows behave." Lily mumbled, and the other women leaned in. "If they fly low, then rain is on its way. That's what I heard, anyway."

"Did you leave the house to see birds?" Brooke asked.

Lily stood up, still shaking. She took slow, measured steps across the room. "Images," she said and opened the refrigerator door to gather jars and bottles. She supported a tube of ketchup in the crook of her arm, picked up mustard and mayonnaise, bottles that must have been there before the women arrived. Lily placed jars on the table and went to the counter to add balsamic vinegar to the mix. She found a spatula in a drawer and threw a dishtowel over her shoulder.

Lily squirted daubs of condiments in a line across the table, along the silver rim where she was seated; a muted palette of earth tones, varying textures. Lily dotted the spatula with ketchup and drew a straight line up the center of the table. She worked quietly and used her fingers to blend and erase areas, to retain the white of the table. Brooke scooted her chair back while Alex quietly took in Lily's process.

Within minutes, a blend of mustard and ketchup, short bold lines of balsamic and highlighted rungs of mayonnaise began to emerge. Lily was drawing the tower, an abstract, painterly impression, but still obvious. Lily's breathing became measured as she worked, her face stern. Her eyes blinked in rapid succession. The painting was surprisingly beautiful, unexpectedly precise.

Finally, Lily replaced the spatula on the counter and shuffled back over to the table, her steps undefined, so unlike the sharp, almost prancing gait she used to have. Alex had once seen a stagehand mimicking Lily's walk; those men would deride any type of joy. Lily pointed to the ladder and tapped on the table as if commanding the women to pay attention.

"Gorgeous," Brooke sighed.

Lily spoke in a whisper. "Even the beauty of the ascension didn't heal me." They all allowed the sentence to hover around in the kitchen. The words hung just below the globe of the light fixture, making space between them.

Finally, Alex responded. "Heal you from what?"

"Can you see it, the tower? The ladder?" she pointed at the painting, as if the other women would miraculously understand why she had created this condiment art. "Every sign pointed here, to the ladder. The photo I took, the vision." Lily began to cry. "I thought the universe was giving me direction, sending me a photographer. But he's not here now. He's gone."

"Who's gone?" Brooke asked, a look of confusion on her brow.

"Why would he appear and then disappear, all of a sudden, just like a baby?" Lily continued to engage in an interior conversation the other women couldn't follow. She traced the platform where she and Milo stood, her finger coated, brilliant red, with ketchup. "Maybe because I've made bad choices."

"Maybe you've never had anyone to help you make better ones," Alex said, thinking of her own family, thinking, in turn, of the Rizzieri's sweet home. "Mrs. Rizzieri used to tell Milo and Helena every time they left the house: '*Fare le scelte giuste.*' 'Make good choices.'"

"I could have used that advice." Lily blinked, her eyelashes wet with tears as she veered off into a memory.

"Me too," Alex said, thinking of all her unsuccessful relationships, her lack of direction regarding her career, her inability to settle down.

"You didn't mean to lose your baby," Lily said. "It wasn't your fault."

Alex moved back, as if struck. "I know that."

"But I did," Lily said. "I did it on purpose."

Chapter 16

THE DAY BROKE BRIGHT and warm, offering a taste of what summer might feel like in Radicondoli. Down the cobblestone street from the rental house, the mercantile owner arranged display baskets outside her shop, carefully stacking pears and plums in neat rows. The baker waved to Alex as if she was a good friend; she offered him an enthusiastic grin as a warm, neighborly feeling spread through her. She could imagine herself living here, so different from Seattle—the slow pace, the beautiful stone buildings that looked to be on the edge of crumbling, as if one small earthquake or another hundred years might topple half the town. A place so intimate that everyone knew your history within two days of your arrival, where you might be surprised by an old friend at dawn in a remote and floriated park.

Alex laughed at her own idealism. Small communities had their fair share of issues, she was sure, but the high Tuscan town was beautiful and fortifying, especially this morning. She was sorry that she couldn't stay in Radicondoli, that she couldn't carve out a home, fall in love anew, learn to tell jokes in a musical rush of Italian words.

When Alex made her way groggily down the stairs at seven-thirty this morning, Brooke and Kat were already rifling through the refrigerator, sorting food into paper bags and cramming the trash can full. The condiment painting of the tower that Lily had made was wiped off the table. Traces of mustard stuck stubbornly under the aluminum trim.

Alex reached for the coffee pot while Brooke sampled from wedges of cheese and a jar of jam, tsking about having to leave so much behind. Well before mid-day, they would have to be cleared out of their rooms, stuffed back into the rental car, and on the move again—just as Alex had found her old friend, just as she was reconnecting with her past in a tangible, solid manner. Finally, instead of trying to make sense of fuzzy memories on her own, she might have had a friend to talk to.

"We could cook a killer breakfast with all this," Brooke lamented.

"No time," Kat said, her head in the fridge.

"I'm going to visit Helena and Milo," Alex announced. Her old friend had called the house phone the night before, as the vacationers sadly polished off their last bottle of local wine. The sense of relief she felt talking to Helena surprised her. Alex had been tossing and turning since the crack of dawn, wishing Helena had been more specific about timing on her return, wondering exactly how early was too early to pay a visit to someone you hadn't seen in nearly three decades.

"Better giddy up. This train's leaving the station at nine o'clock sharp," Kat said.

"I hear you," Alex said, dodging an argument.

"You've got about an hour," Kat warned as Alex headed for the door.

* * *

Alex stopped at the florist's and bought a small bouquet of narcissus. The flowers were early spring pale yellow and equally delicate, the buds just opening as if they'd curled up and slept through the night. The florist tied the stems with a white ribbon and wished Alex a good day. Italian enthusiasm for mornings instilled wonder in Alex; she felt a lust for life, a hope both fragile and pale, like the flowers in her hand.

35 Via Sedice was easy to find. The small town was laid out in a fairly rectangular pattern, though most streets eventually curved to accommodate sharp inclines on the hills. Very few cars coursed the narrow streets. Alex could cross the whole town on foot in about fifteen minutes.

Helena's house was an old stone building with a crumbling front stoop, though the deck was swept immaculately clean. House numbers in black enameled metal tilted unevenly to the right of a red wooden door. Not one person roamed the street this early, though curtains had been sucked outside the open window of a neighboring apartment, their hems unraveling at the edges.

Behind Helena's door someone shuffled but then retreated, hearing Alex's firm knock. It was a show-business rap on the door: signifying that it was time to hustle, to hurry—even though that's not what Alex meant. She forgot about being gentle sometimes, far too often really. Finally, the door opened a crack until Alex saw a hint of a young girl's nose, one eye and part of her mouth. A suspicious little voice asked a question in Italian.

"Hi," Alex bent her neck for a better view. "Does Helena live here?"

The girl didn't answer, only pulled nervously on a strand of unkempt, shoulder-length hair. Footsteps sounded behind the child, and the door swung wider.

The early morning sun cast her childhood friend in full light, and Alex started, reaching out her hands; a sob nearly ruined her composure. Helena's features were the same: eyes the color of dark chocolate, a slim, delicate nose that came to a sassy point, the opposite of Alex's own chunky, asymmetrical tip. Helena's long, wavy, nearly-black hair fell past her shoulders. But there was now a scar from eyebrow to chin on Helena's right cheek. Faded, but clear enough that Alex could still make it out under Helena's heavily-applied base.

"My friend!" Helena cried, reaching up to wrap her arms around Alex's shoulders, nearly crushing the flowers. Helena had to stand on her toes to plant a kiss on each of Alex's cheeks. "You look exactly the same. Many feet taller. Many feet, but the same strapping shoulders." Helena patted Alex roughly, exploring her body like a blind person. "Same golden hair. Dishwater color, your mother used to call it. Same beautiful teeth." Helena reached up and past Alex's lips to tap on a front tooth. "You were missing that one right there last time I saw you. And even then, I was jealous of your teeth."

Helena pulled Alex inside the apartment, through to the kitchen where the young girl reached into a canister on the tiled counter, a dusting of raw sugar pinched between her fingers.

"This is Martina," Helena said and batted the girl's hand until she dropped the sugar. Helena placed the flowers into an empty tin can, torn pieces of label still stuck to the sides.

"She looks just like you," Alex said.

There was a rustling down the hallway, and shortly Milo appeared, his hair shooting out in all directions, a section plastered across the left side of his head. Milo patted the girl's head and removed a bottle of orange juice from the fridge. He took a long swig before he replaced the cap. "It's early," he said.

"Half the town's up," Alex said, sarcasm teasing her voice, a reflex from childhood, from when she first knew Milo.

Helena nodded toward the percolator and coffee cups, casually offering them up to Alex, as if they were still the best of friends, no formality. After she got Alex settled with a cup and a tiny pitcher of cream, Helena busied herself with Martina's hair, combed the dark strands back into a ponytail. Alex watched hungrily, observing the details of this household, where she was known and not known at once.

"I was taking photos until five a.m." Milo pulled a chair out, plopped down, and turned toward Alex, inviting her to settle in the moment. "Let's celebrate our reunion with some American drink: Mimosas? Bloody Marys?"

"I wish, Milo, but I had to plead to come here for just the briefest get-together. We're heading back to Paris today," Alex said, almost unable to stop grinning, hesitant to take in the child and Milo even, wanting only to giggle and laugh now that she'd found her old friend. Helena moved about the kitchen, but also gleefully took Alex in: they were twenty-nine years older, but they were forever joined by their youth.

The young girl who answered the door ate her oatmeal ultra-slowly, busy watching the relationships that seemed to have taken on a familiarity she was surprised to see. The four of them had leaned into a remarkably comfortable silence, as if Alex, too, was part of the family starting another regular day.

Martina bent over the table and spoke in a childlike voice, but comfortably in two languages, to Milo: "*La donna é bellissima, é la tipica donna americana.* She is kind of... *vecchia,* but I like her for you."

Alex understood perhaps more than Martina expected. The sound of certain Italian words wrapped her in a comfortable nostalgia.

"Martina!" Helena scolded, not quite playfully. She turned to Alex, and half-explained, half-asked forgiveness. "Don't mind her. She can be feisty."

Milo reached around the end of the table and tried to lightly spank the girl—maybe a show for Alex, or maybe they were accustomed to trying to quiet her blunt honesty around adults. Martina dodged Milo by rising quickly from the table. She shrieked and made her way to the sink, where she washed her dish and spoon.

"No worries," Alex said, aware of just how Northwest she sounded with that single statement, how crass compared to the ringing-bell-like sound of Italian. "Actually, she acts just like you used to, Helena. A little carbon copy. You were always bold, not a hint of shyness in you."

Helena smiled, like a proud mother, but rushed to return the conversation to what was real and urgent—Alex's visit. "Last night, after Milo explained how he had found your—" Helena hesitated, "troubled friend—I hope you do not mind that he told me about your friend Lily and how she was making sounds up on the tower? Of course, I had a million questions about you, but he was only able to tell me the little bit he managed to find out. You're traveling around? With a band? You're not a musician, but an electrician? How did you learn such a job? Is it dangerous? What a surprise. Life does not shortchange us with surprises! I dug out some old pictures." Helena offered a few photos for Alex to see. Helena's nails were painted metallic blue and seemed cut too short for such deliberate adornment. "Look what little imps we were."

Alex couldn't help but think about how organized Helena must be, that she was able to produce these old pictures on such short notice. Alex leaned on the counter and rifled through the stack. The two of them wearing identical white t-shirts with rainbows across the front; wearing flared jeans and leaning back against each other's gravity, holding hands; posing in front of the tower of Pisa. Another: both of them on horseback in front of a field of sunflowers, Alex's hair bluntly chopped at ear-level, an eight-year-old's idea of self-styling. In each of the pictures, Helena's face was smooth, without the scar that now marred her face. In the third photo, the eight-year-olds wore bikini tops over nonexistent breasts. Alex remembered collecting shells on the beach, the sun—seeming brighter and more jovial in Italy—setting bright and orange behind them. The girls looked at each other rather than at the photographer. Perhaps they shared some small, forgotten secret.

Peering at herself, Alex realized she wore a smile more open and genuine than she'd allowed herself in eons—since she'd grown up, really. The sight of her own mirth and contentment caused a tug of sadness, a longing for easy, happy days. When had she become so serious, so somber? Was it only after the miscarriage, or was it a slow creep throughout her life, from teenage years into adulthood? Was it possible to recapture that kind of warmth and happiness?

In the last photo, Helena's grandpa held them both—one on each knee. He wore a Santa suit, his big white beard grown out for the Christmas season. Alex turned the print over looking for a date or an annotation, but she found neither. Helena had come over to stand beside her, and she looked at the picture of the Santa grandfather along with Alex. Her nearby heat reminded Alex of where she was and who she was with. Alex reached out, hugging Helena loosely around the waist. "I remember being a little bit scared of his transformation, back then," Alex said.

"Yes, but everyone insisted we get this picture," Helena said, "and look, here we hold this picture in our hands, thirty years later."

Alex recalled trying to pull away from Helena's grandpa, but her anxiety did not get caught by the lens. She had reason to avoid the laps of old men. Even as she stood at Helena's counter, in the middle of this reunion, Alex could remember the feel of sitting on Bubbie's lap, her mother's scream.

"We had such dreams then," Helena said. "I wanted to be a famous clothing designer. Do you remember that I made those shirts with rainbows? I used puff paint. Praise God that that was a passing fad. And you—you loved the idea of mechanics, electronics—you planned to be an engineer. I guess maybe you're doing something like that now. And husbands! We were very specific. You wanted to marry an archeologist, just like Indiana Jones. I wanted a musician—like the man in Aerosmith."

"Steven Tyler," Alex said.

"You were going to have five children," Helena continued. "Remember, I said I wanted a round dozen, like my great-grandmother? How would we have found the time?" Helena laughed. "Do you have an adventurer husband? Do you have five children?"

Alex has answered these kinds of questions over the years, negatively, and usually with proud independence. But today, after being reminded of her childhood dreams, she felt saddened, somehow deficient. "Nope."

"Well, neither do I," Helena answered congenially. "It is not too late, I think. Of course, I'm the same as I was as a girl, forever an optimist. I always think there is still time."

The kettle on the stove whistled as if on cue. This nostalgia needed interrupting. "We've hardly had a chance to talk," Alex said summarily, "but I've got to go. We're supposed to be out of our house this morning."

"What about Lily?" Milo asked.

"I guess she'll just come back to Paris with us. We don't really have a choice."

Milo studied Alex for an uncomfortable minute, riveted. He chomped loudly and didn't appear to know or care that he sounded like a cow chewing his cud. His unembarrassed examination of her made her feel especially feminine, and particularly unkempt. She should have at least combed her hair before she left the house; Alex hadn't looked in a mirror with any seriousness or intention since the last hotel.

Milo kicked out the chair in front of him, an invitation. "She can stay here."

Alex plopped into the chair, ungracefully and without sufficient concern, surprised by the offer.

"Certainly, we can house her for a few days," Helena agreed. "I can tell, Milo wants her to. He's my brother and I, for some reason, keep accommodating him. You stay too. We will have fun." Her eyes shone, and her body vibrated with excitement as she gathered food for Martina's lunch.

"Lily's in pretty bad shape." A jumbled series of questions whirled across Alex's thoughts. Why would they offer to take in a complete stranger on the edge of sanity? What had brought Lily to this fragile state? Was Alex herself any less fragile, after losing a child, than Lily was? Alex's thoughts turned, then, to motherhood, to the complexity and uncertainty. How did you know, as a parent, how your children would turn out, given your own shortcomings?

"And I can't stay," Alex finally added. "I have to get back to work."

Helena sighed and turned from the sink to look at Alex. The sky was now a full blue, and the trill of a late bird echoed through the windowpane. "I thought that might be the case. I must tell you something, my friend. I spoke to *Mamma* yesterday, and she made me promise. Last week she sent a letter in the post. I received it when I got home. The letter is for you. But of course, my mother wrote in Italian. Her English is not strong enough for prose. I did not want to do this today, but, it is important, I think. You must hear what *Mamma* wrote to you before you go."

Milo rose from the table and escorted Martina from the room, speaking to his sister in rapid Italian before they went. "*Ciao, bambina,*" Helena shouted after Martina.

Alex set her half-full cup next to a trio of cobalt blue bowls in the porcelain sink that was scarred and stained by coffee grounds and copper pots. A braid of garlic hung next to a row of dried chili peppers, just as in Helena's mother's kitchen, so similar: well-used, regularly cooked-in.

Alex burst into that kitchen the day her stepfather announced the family was leaving Tirrenia. She fell into Helena's mother's arms, the strong scent of onions and oregano emanating from Mrs. Rizzieri's apron, stinging Alex's already wet eyes. "*Io non ti lascerò,*" Alex said, over and over to the whole Rizzieri family. I won't leave you. I won't leave you.

In the end, of course, she had not been given the choice.

"Why would she send me a letter?" Alex asked now.

Helena laid her hand on Alex's shoulder. "It is about your mother. Estelle confided in my mother while she was here, and *Mamma* has felt the burden all these years of keeping quiet. She believes it is time for you to know."

Alex stared hard, her expression revealing a combination of dread and relief, a look that echoed the hard knot in her stomach. Helena might actually hold in her hand, at this very moment, answers Alex had been searching for.

"Your mother was afraid to tell you the truth," Helena said. "But *Mamma*, she always worried for you. My mother watched you closely when you were here; she saw how your family hurt you with their silence. 'Secrets will bury you alive,' she always says. She is talking to me, too, in that statement. She insists that I tell you about your mother, that you have a right to know.

"Honest, Alex, I have warned her that it is none of her business, but she is, well, you remember what *mia madre* is like? She thinks of you as a daughter. Do you know she tried to find you after you left? She wrote you letters, but I don't know if you received them, ever."

Alex leaned back onto the counter for support. "No," she said weakly, "I never."

"Well," Helena began. "I will tell you what she says. In the end, I always do as my mother asks. Here we go."

Chapter 17

MY DEAREST ALEXANDRA,

I remember you as if you were here last week only, with your pale, long-leg body and big smile (when we could get it from you). Though many children of your Army come to live in our town, you were the one I worried the most for. Your mother, she is not a bad woman, though what I saw of her, she treated you poorly. I was always sorry that I did not hear from you again, my dear. I suppose Estelle threw my letters away. I knew by the way she avoided me at the end she regretted confiding in me. I suppose you may know all of this by now, but I will repeat anyway, if only to release myself from the sadness of this story. Know that I wish only the best for you, and I hope you have remained the sweet Alexandra that I knew.

Alex couldn't help but be enthralled by Helena's beautiful Italian accent, laboring over the translation. Helena read a few sentences in Italian, translated to English afterwards. Her eyes moved from the paper while she was reading, to Alex's face while she translated, silently gauging Alex's reaction to each statement.

This is what I was told: Henry, your birth father, and Estelle met when they were only teenagers. Young. He was their paper boy. I am sure you know that he married her at seventeen, that he joined the army, and took her with him to Alaska. After he died, the army took care of you all until your mother married Clive, who had been friends with your father.

You likely know all of this, but you may never have learned how, as a teenager, Estelle lived in fear of her stepfather.

Helena faltered in her translating here, fumbling to find the word "stepfather," as if she detected reluctance from Alex. "Are you sure you want to hear this?" she asked.

Bubbie, Alex thought. *What about Bubbie?* "Go on."

Helena hesitated for only a moment before she continued.

The poor child hid in the bathroom at night, with the door locked, afraid that he would find her, that he would take for himself what no man has the right to do to a child.

Estelle could not leave any of this history behind. She wanted to pretend, for your sake, that none of those filthy things happened, that he had not touched her in the night like a man touches a woman. She did not want to remember how he had entered her room while she was sleeping. How he laid in her bed, forced himself on top of her body. Estelle was very mad at me because I suggested she tell you, that you were old enough—not for the details, but for the understanding that your mother had been hurt. For this reason, we did not part friends.

Alexandra, you may now understand how the shame of the past, even shame that is not our own, can permeate everything we do. There is more I would like to share. All these years, I continue to worry. You might not want advice from this old woman, but I, for one, would like to see your face again.

With all the love in the world,

Abriana Rizzieri

* * *

Alex walked slowly back to the rental house, over cobbled streets, past old men sitting by the statue in the center of town; she remembered in a flash the feel of her thumb in her grandfather's wrinkled mouth. She stopped halfway there and rubbed her thumb clean as if she might wipe away the memory.

She unfolded the letter, staring at Mrs. Rizzieri's loopy, decorative writing. Strained to read the Italian, only understanding *know, children, army,* a few other words here and there. But she remembered clearly every sentence Helena translated, as if each word was the driving of hail against her skin. She felt a moment of irrational relief that her own stepfather had been so strict and distant, more like a figurehead than a parent. Alex wondered if perhaps her mother had purposely kept both of her children isolated from the adults. Estelle had never hinted at previous sexual abuse, though if Alex reflected on her mother's reserve, her inability to trust (a lack of eye contact her therapist had mentioned), her near-paralysis regarding emotion, she might have guessed.

As she held the letter, another memory came clear, an earlier time Bubbie had taken both she and her brother to Monkey Jungle on a visit to Florida. She had been left alone, staring at the baboons, their red bottoms so garish, so unseemly, while Bubbie took Junior to the bathroom. She waited and waited, pacing up and down in front of the cage until a park ranger asked where her parents were. Alex pointed to the bathroom just as her brother came out, walking stiffly towards her. He threw his arm around his sister, his face streaked as if he had been crying. They stood, motionless, watching the baboons circle, in a rare moment of quiet until Bubbie eventually joined them. Their grandfather lit a pipe and announced that the two of them were no fun. They were going home.

By the time Alex returned to the rental house, hastily tucking the letter in her back pocket, the clock had closed in on nine, and Kat leaned impatiently against the hood of the car. She tapped her foot and shook her head. The three of them waited, Lily in the back seat, bags stowed, until Brooke poked her head out the front door. "Lacking a bellhop, I'm in need of both strength and courtesy."

Alex marched toward the house, intent, her thoughts on her mother, on what she now understood about her grandfather. Step-grandfather.

"You don't have to carry her shit around," Kat grumbled.

"I don't mind." Lugging heavy gear was second nature to Alex—

should be to all of them at this point on tour. What was a few extra suitcases, she figured, since her strength was finally beginning to return after the miscarriage?

Kat called after Alex. "You're just encouraging her to act more helpless."

The house was silent and chilly, empty, ready for the next occupants. "You're driving Kat insane, you know," Alex said and grabbed two bags.

"No doubt." Brooke tucked a last hairbrush into her shoulder bag, disappeared for a moment, and returned with a cardboard box of food. "What exactly would Kat get up to if she didn't have me to complain about? Kat lives to take the moral high ground. Let her carp on about me being late; she's absolutely right. I concede to her self-righteousness, and that frees me up to be myself."

"Doesn't it ever bother you that you're never on time, that people see you as a pain in the ass?" Alex asked.

"That type of self-scrutiny isn't my bag." Brooke threw a strap over her shoulder and headed down the steps, without a glance back at the house. "If you go through life worrying about what other people think, you end up missing your own flow." She hoisted two bags into the trunk and settled into the front passenger seat.

As Alex crammed the trunk shut, she saw a woman across the street, a baby snuggled up close to her chest, swaddled in cloth. Suddenly, there were babies everywhere. The infant gave a powerful wail, and the mother bounced and cooed, soothed and swayed. Was Lily right? Was this another message she was supposed to hear?

The infant wore a tiny cloth cap, soft yellow like the one Alex purchased for her own baby—the only item she ever bought in anticipation. She wished she had buried it with the embryo, but the hat was still tucked in her underwear drawer, untouched, at her loft in Seattle.

Kat rolled down the car window. "Alex," she shouted. "Let's go."

Alex refocused on Kat's stern face. Dread came over her at the thought of returning to tour. She anticipated icy air pumping through the vents in her bunk, saw Tim's grin as he sent her up the truss, as he mutely, witheringly, reminded her that he had her job. The struggle to prove herself to those men, returning to the masculine world of dumping gear out of semis and hauling cable and bolting truss, seemed overwhelming now, when she considered how sad she felt, how much emotion was brewing in her chest. How she desired to hold a baby instead of a motor controller, how she wanted to sing lullabies instead of listening to Sadie's ridiculous songs.

"Pop the trunk, will you?" she shouted.

Kat sighed but pulled the lever anyway, as asked.

Her future unexpectedly wide with possibilities, Alex pushed Brooke's suitcases aside and yanked out her own; with the trunk open, she stuck her head in the rear window and addressed Lily. "Do you want to stay here?"

"Yes," Lily mouthed, startled out of what looked like a daydreaming stupor, an expression she seemed to have adopted here in Tuscany.

"Good," Alex said. "Me too. Come on, Lily."

Kat scrambled out of the car, hands on Alex's luggage to restrain her. "What are you talking about?"

Alex dragged Lily's bag from the trunk, plunked the wheels down into the soft gravel. "I'm not going." She slammed the lid shut and reached back, touching her fingertips to the letter, feeling the thick texture of the linen paper Mrs. Rizzieri used. If she stayed, Helena could translate for her again. Alex wanted to spend more time with her friend. She wanted to remember, to re-experience the contentment she felt here, in Italy, as a child. "Lily and I can stay here for a few more days, sort out our lives."

Kat blinked as confusion flickered across her face. Her eyes narrowed as she choked out, "I don't pretend to know what you're going through but quitting your job won't help."

"All those men blaming me," Alex said. "The testosterone. The attitudes. I don't need it."

Kat panned her head around to hunt for a response, as if the answer might have been a tangible object, as if it could have been sitting on the rock wall bordering the drive. "If you leave the tour this way, you'll have a hard time getting another gig. Word gets around."

"I'll get another job," Alex flatly announced, unperturbed. She couldn't stop thinking about what she had just learned about her mother. Her thoughts kept running back to the letter in her pocket, to the statement Mrs. Rizzieri made: *There is more I would like to share.*

Kat balled her fist in frustration. She looked like she might punch the car. "Is it because Tim is making you climb? I just haven't had a chance to tell Sadie about it yet. Let me talk to her. I'm positive she'll be on our side."

Alex shook her head and wondered if she could explain to Kat what was happening to her, how she thought, over fifteen years ago when she started touring, that her power lay in proving how strong she was, in subordinating her emotions to physical strength. And now, after the pregnancy, she had come to wonder if there was more to her femininity, if she could access a quieter, more subtle power. "That's not it."

Brooke got out of the car and watched their debate, strangely mute, as if she was planning a big scene with her own departure from the business someday, when it was her turn.

"I've already got a plan worked out to punk Tim. I'm gonna screw with his truck pack. You'll love it," Kat said and then, running out of arguments, sputtered, "Joe expects us to come back."

"He'll probably be glad I'm not there."

Kat's face quivered and looked softer, though not quite relaxed. "We'll probably never see each other again if you leave the tour."

"I'll keep in touch," Alex said, though they both knew it was unlikely. Alex was always happy to run into friends she'd toured with out there on the road, but she rarely searched any of them out.

"Sure you will." Kat, defeated, stormed back to the car, rigid and upright, her face hidden from the other women, who stared mutely. "Get in the car, Brooke," Kat said.

"What?" Brooke asked, dumbfounded.

"Get in," Kat roared and started the engine, breaking through the twitter of birds, the whoosh of a draft through the olive tree in the yard.

As the car door slammed, Lily jumped and backed away. Her soles crunched on the gravel.

"See you, Lily," Kat said without a glance in her direction. She rolled the window up to put a barrier between herself and the rest of the world, however transparent.

Alex soberly stepped around to the passenger side, falling into a memory of the day her stepfather loaded her hard, blue Samsonite into a taxi in Tirrenia, how she pulled against his firm grip, determined to resist their departure. She had no power then, no choice but to go with them. These men who came into their lives and took over, stepfathers who changed everything.

Brooke danced over to give Alex a squeeze. She teased and joked to draw out a smile.

"You want to stay too?" Alex asked.

"I doubt anyone ever made it big in Radicondoli," Brooke said with an exaggerated Italian accent. Kat, fed up with the wait, backed down the driveway. "I believe she'd leave me," Brooke yelled and chased after the car, heels falling between cobblestones.

Brooke caught up as Kat got out to close the gate, pulling the latch firmly across iron bars. The two women left behind stood in the driveway, uncertain of their own future, with only their suitcases between them.

Chapter 18

RAIN SPLATTERED THE kitchen windowpane; beads merged into little rivers that drained down, looking like a map of tears. Connor stared out at the sidewalk as if he anticipated company. No one had passed in an hour—the hammering rain had kept everyone inside. Seattleites were accustomed to drizzle, but the city was taken off guard by the heavy, steady downpour that caused the streets to flood. Connor watched the rain puddle on his lawn, drank his fourth cup of coffee.

Where was Alex right now? Soaking up Italian sunshine? Lounging around in a bathing suit? Drinking espresso in a café? The mystery of her life was killing him. He wondered, day after day, what she was doing, who she was with, what she was talking about. He missed her long, rambling emails full of the sights and smells and colors of the countries she traveled through. He missed her observations.

Connor moved through the house and picked up random socks, straightened magazines abandoned on a side table. He half had her in mind as he cleaned, offering up his tidying to her absent spirit. The rain fell so hard he heard it beat on the roof a story above. He glanced out the back window, checked to make sure the rain hadn't turned to hail, not an impossibility this time of year. The madrone tree in the corner of the yard absorbed the water stoically.

Connor had the urge to walk out into the deluge, to let the cold and the wet soak into his skin. He could have taken refuge under the hundred-year-old tree, gazed up at the branches, dense and wide, that spanned the breadth of the trunk. Its leaves would create a natural barrier as they curved up and out toward the gray sky. And below the branches was the ground that he and Alex dug into only a few short weeks ago.

Connor hadn't spent any time in his backyard since the morning Alex knelt out there, sobbing. He'd considered planting something in that spot for Alex—maybe a rhododendron or a lilac bush. Last spring, when he and Alex were walking through Seward Park, she mentioned lilac was probably her favorite smell in the world. Lilacs. She would love that.

Drops pounded continuously on the roof, as if they were after him, as if the rain itself had an agenda. Connor opened the back door and listened, but all he heard was the heavy, continuous drone. This rain, and his aloneness, reminded him of thirty years ago, the night he left his wife and Lucy. The memory created a chill so strong that Connor shivered now as he leaned against the doorway. When he drove away that night in his old beat-up Toyota, he felt a mixture of elation at being free and disgust with himself for seizing his freedom. With each passing landmark advertised—the exit for Belle Isle in Richmond, Edgar Allen Poe house in Baltimore, Brandywine Creek State Park in Delaware—with each Mars Bar unwrapped, each Coke bottle popped, he felt lighter, as if, like the car, he burned off fuel, eased his load. He drove all the way to New York that night. When he could no longer keep his eyes open, he finally stopped off at a dive masquerading as a hotel along I-95.

After his disastrous first attempt at fatherhood, his confidence in himself, in the type of man he imagined he was—responsible, loving, even noble—was shattered. This fear that had pecked away at his relationships for decades reared its head now as he considered how he could console Alex. For two and a half months, while Alex was pregnant, Connor did his best to pamper her—he brought her decaf coffee in the mornings, rubbed her feet, and laughed when she joked about ridiculous baby names like "D'Artagnan" or "Isis." But underneath his strained laughter was a thick knot that ran from his stomach to his throat, constricting any possible joy. Now, that dread was gone, but Alex was gone too. What if she didn't come back to him, to Seattle, to what he thought they were building, to what they might have had?

Connor mounted the stairs to his bedroom and took his brown leather aviator bag off the top shelf in the closet. When he was in his thirties and felt he needed to get out and see the world, this bag accompanied him across the globe. His heart gave a slight quaver when he pulled out the dusty valise again, as if his youth, too, had been tucked away in a dark corner of the house. His stomach rumbled, having only had coffee this morning. The milk had gone sour and there weren't enough Grape Nuts in the cupboard to feed a mouse. Connor placed the bag on the bed and stuffed two shirts, a pair of jeans, two pairs of underwear, and two pairs of socks inside. He tucked his shaving kit and a book about landfills into the side pocket.

On his way out, Connor knocked the one-by-six board beside his bed. The first time Alex spent the night with Connor, she tripped over the trim and cursed so loudly (as if he had planted it for just that reason), Connor thought she'd leave right then.

"Why is this board even here?" she asked. They had argued over the board's existence so consistently and fiercely, it became a point of pride for Connor not to move it.

He'd originally carried it into the bedroom for baseboard trim but had gotten distracted by another project. Eventually he'd begun setting his books and bedside lamp on it, rather than on a proper side table. He stopped to contemplate why it had become important for him to leave it there. He set down his bag, carefully removed his books, his lamp. Her lip balm. Why hadn't he just moved the trim board when she asked? Why did it take Alex leaving for him to bend? He leaned the board against the base of the wall across the room and stepped back to observe. Ten minutes. That's all it would take him to attach the board. Would ten minutes have made the difference in her staying? Connor walked to his workshop in the garage, chose a box of finishing nails, a hammer, a driver pin and went back to his bedroom to complete at least this one, simple action.

When the board was nailed in, permanent, Connor reached for the phone and considered who he might call. He flipped through Alex's tour book that arrived in a Fed Ex package only a week ago. Someone in there knew. Connor found the page with that day's date and dialed the number for the French promoter—maybe that man could find his girlfriend who had gone off-script.

After a five-minute chat in choppy English where he found himself speaking too loudly, over-enunciating as if this would help in translation, after two other calls—one to Brooke back in the Production office—he replaced the phone in the cradle, picked up his old leather bag and wandered out into the cool Seattle rain.

* * *

Suitcases in hand, Alex and Lily arrived on the stoop of 35 Via Sedice. Milo opened the door smiling, as if greeting guests at a party, unsurprised to see them. After Milo wrested their suitcases out of their hands and pulled the rolling bags into the hallway, he kissed each of them on both cheeks and escorted them down the hall, pointing out the kitchen, the bathroom, the linen closet.

"Of course, you've already seen the kitchen, Alex," Milo said and continued on. In a small bedroom, he told them to wait, then went back for the suitcases, talking the whole time, shouting from the hallway: "We are glad to have you, truly. Helena does not get too many visitors. Certainly not from so far away. Not Americans."

A velvety comforter was peeled back on the bed to reveal chocolate brown sheets. He pulled open a drawer in a plain wooden bureau and emptied out rolled up balls of socks and what looked like folded, black underwear that he quickly shoved into a bottom drawer.

"Do you live here too?" Alex asked.

"Only when I visit. I call the room mine, but this is Helena's guest room. I'm afraid you'll have to share." He finished his clothing shuffle. "You can have the top two drawers."

"What about you?" Lily asked.

"I have to go home. To Firenze. Helena is at work, if you need her—the dress shop over on *Via Tiberio Gazzei*."

"But what if we have to leave Radicondoli? We don't have a car." Alex turned to Lily. "I'm sorry. This was a rash decision. I wasn't thinking."

Milo placed his hand on Alex's shoulder and gave her a rough, brotherly shake. "You worry too much, my friend. You and Helena will have plenty to fill the time. Eat and drink, relax. You can talk about all the years between visits. I will only be gone a few days, I promise. Once I return, if you wish to go back to Firenze, I will drive you."

He steered them through the remainder of the apartment. Helena's home was not large, but Alex and Lily both immediately warmed to the space, both of them so appreciative of Helena's generosity. In the living room (the thin layer of dust on the mantel somehow making Alex feel at home, highlighting the fact that she was somewhere entirely less sterile than a hotel), they studied photographs hung in careful arrangements on the walls—black and white pictures of what looked to be grandparents, ancestors, people with pleasant expressions, innate joy. Candid shots showing Martina and Milo on a bright day in a park, playing with a large rubber ball. One of Milo as he held a newborn Martina. And formal, seated school pictures of Martina in uniform. The only shot with Helena was a group portrait at a large family gathering. The unscarred side of Helena's face was turned toward the photographer; a bulky, jovial-looking man had his arm wrapped protectively around Helena's waist.

Milo said goodbye, and headed off to Firenze, leaving them to themselves. Used to new spaces, the women kept their clothes in their suitcases, rather than bothering with the drawers. Lily stealthily opened the door to Martina's room, snooping. Alex watched from the hallway as Lily lifted an olive-skinned doll from the bed and sniffed at the head as if expecting that new-baby smell, fresh and milky.

Alex poked around in the kitchen, opening the old Frigidaire without any real intent to eat. She lifted the lids off dusty canisters, opened the thick-painted cupboards, assessing the contents, though she had no real purpose, was just killing time, familiarizing herself. Alex used the phone in the living room to ring Connor. He didn't pick up; Connor's outgoing voicemail message was brief and businesslike. Where was he today? Alex had lost all track of time, of the calendar. She left a message explaining where they were, slowly dictating Helena's international phone number. She considered calling Junior, trying to get some answers, but their last call was so stressful, so fruitless, she decided she would have better luck with Mrs. Rizzieri.

"I'm going to find Helena," Alex yelled down the hallway, just like her mother used to do, she realized, impersonal, informative. Feeling guilty, realizing there was a part of her that didn't want Lily (an energetic drain?) tagging along, she added, "Want to come with me?"

Lily appeared in the hallway. "Sure," she said, looking surprisingly like her old self, eyes clear; her face, if not ruddy, was not as pale and worn out as her complexion looked as she sat in the car just a half hour ago.

As they passed the school yard, Alex and Lily watched a handful of children—from six to fifteen—play a game with brightly colored, small round balls. "That must be *bocce*," Alex guessed. Martina spied them and waved enthusiastically. Her friends pointed and giggled as if Martina's American houseguests were celebrities.

Helena's shop was nestled between the florist's and a small post office that doubled as a library, the lobby lined with children's books and Italian novels, a couple of long-expired English language *National Geographic* and *Time* magazines on a shelf next to a boxy desktop computer. The dress shop was quaint, though not crowded. In the window a headless mannequin wore an elegant turquoise dress, a high-quality linen that would likely drape beautifully on real flesh as well as on a model.

"Brooke would have loved this shop," Alex said. "Too bad it was closed all last week." Helena was standing behind a wide stone counter surfaced with displays of hand-crafted silver and stone jewelry. Eight racks were sparsely hung with women's clothing, placed so that each article could be appreciated, just a single example of each dress, each shirt, each skirt.

"Come in, come in," Helena said heartily and gestured to the clothing. "So, you stayed after all! I am so pleased. Please, look around. What do you think?"

"Very lean," Lily said, her artist's eye appreciating the layout, two cerulean walls contrasting stark white walls—the space behind the counter demarcated with a larger-than life stencil of a woman's high heel in profile. The racks were mere wooden dowels suspended from the ceiling, creating a floaty, other-worldly perception. "Your shop reminds me of Massimo Vitali's photos. Have you ever seen his beach shots, taken from a distance, from above? His wide-angle shots of the beaches in the Mediterranean? Your walls look like that same ocean blue—and the clothes could be the umbrellas, the beach towels the bare skin of the sun bathers."

"What a delightful way to describe my shop," Helena said, "What an interesting artist you must be."

"Thank you," Lily said. "I used to think so."

"You will be again. As long as you can hold onto your camera, that is," Alex said, trying to rib Lily about her antics on the roof the other night, but the joke fell flat; Lily merely grimaced.

Helena came around the counter and gestured to a cream-colored sheer blouse and camisole. "Lily, try this combination. You have a darling figure. Anything we have to offer would look good on you. I have different sizes in the back. Tell me what you would like to try on. What are you? A size 36?" Helena moved across the room and held up a pair of hip-hugger pants, a slight flare at the base of the leg. "You, Alex, will look fabulous in these. Like we wore as children, but sexy, for your woman's body."

Alex held the pants up to her waist and moved over to a mirror against the blue wall. Turning sideways, imagining her hair swirled up into a bun, makeup and jewelry on, Alex could almost picture herself transformed, more sophisticated than the jeans and t-shirt wearing woman she'd been for years now. Alex laughed and handed the pants back to Helena. "Where in the world would I go in such feminine clothes?" she asked.

"Anywhere you'd like, darling," Helena said dramatically. "Anywhere you'd like."

Chapter 19

WHEN ALEX PASSED by Martina's room, she caught Lily teaching Martina pigeon pose, the first bit of yoga Alex had witnessed Lily doing here in Italy. Lily modeled the pose and then gently helped Marti adjust her hips forward. They had one of Alex's books of poetry between them, and it appeared that Martina was trying to help Lily learn a bit of Italian while they bent and stretched.

"*E la gioia nei miei piedi,*" Martina translated, shifting her hip so she could lean over the text. "Joy is *gioia*. Feet are *piedi*. And the joy in my feet."

Lily repeated the line slowly, "A la goya nee may pee-ed-ee."

Martina laughed at her accent. "Gioia, not goya."

Lily tried again, closer to the correct pronunciation of joy.

"*Io sono una donna,*" Martina continued. "I am a woman. Phenomenally. I do not know this word, phenomenally?"

"Incredibly, remarkably," Lily explained.

"*Va bene,*" Marti said. "*Io sono una donna. Incredibilmente. Donna incredibile.*"

Alex was tempted to join them, to talk about Maya Angelou's poem, about the history in that work, about the subject of women's self-confidence, unconventional beauty and independence, but knew her own tendency to be distracted by poetry.

Alex let the two of them, who had been nearly inseparable the last few days, continue on uninterrupted. Yesterday, Lily and Martina squeezed into the tiny bathroom to put on makeup, though

Helena forbid Marti to go out of the house with lipstick on. They'd chatted and giggled and played *Nomi, Città, Cose, Animali,* a word game, and for now, Lily seemed happy to regress back into childhood. Alex concentrated instead on surprising Helena by making dinner, an arena she certainly didn't feel comfortable inside.

"Thank you for taking Marti off my hands for a few hours," Helena said as she swept into the kitchen after work.

She threw a pile of mail on the kitchen counter, her tote bag and coat spilling out of her arms as Martina bounded in, threw her arms around Helena, pecked her cheek, and then ran back down the hallway.

"Martina's enthusiasm never wanes," Helena said with a smile, picking up her bag and neatly hanging it over a chair. "Maybe that's how all children are, I don't know, but she alternately wears me out and energizes me."

"I might say the same for you—I mean your enthusiasm," Alex said, standing at the farmhouse sink that was filled with plates and bowls, piled nearly to the faucet. Tomato seeds and juice ran off a cutting board. A container of breadcrumbs spilled onto the counter. Looking around at the disaster in the kitchen, Helena laughed.

Smoke wafted from a pan on the stove and Alex rushed to turn down the flame, though she was too late: the pan had begun to blacken on the sides. She grabbed a potholder, her tacky hands covered with flecks of cheese, and moved the pan of singed onions to a cold burner.

"Shoot," Alex said, "I was hoping to have dinner nearly finished by now." She'd found a recipe for chicken cacciatore in one of Helena's cookbooks, though it was in Italian and she had only understood pieces of the directions.

"Let me help you." Helena washed her hands in the sink, nearly toppling the stack, before she threw her apron over her head.

Alex insisted that Helena sit down. "I'm trying to learn to

cook! Who comes to Italy and doesn't cook? You can translate the recipe for me if you want. I've been guessing, mostly. I usually take pride in being a quick study, though the evidence is to the contrary. I grew up on Velveeta cheese, canned wax beans, and Vienna sausages."

Helena looked slightly confused by the list of processed foods but certainly understood that Alex was reared without the kind of effervescent approach to food Italians had, understood that Alex grew up in a household where cooking was considered a chore.

A line of ants had found a pile of spilled sugar on the counter. Alex squashed them with a towel, swiped the sugar into the trash can. She took the chicken from the fridge and unfurled the white butcher paper. Helena directed her to a sharp filleting knife. "Would you like me to debone the chicken?"

"I can do it," Alex said, though she wasn't quite sure how to go about the task. She pulled her shoulders back to indicate full confidence—an attitude that had gotten her through many years of touring. Alex refused to ask for help, though they both knew she was bluffing. "It's only a chicken," she muttered, facing down the carcass.

Helena poured two glasses of Tuscan Viognier and sat on a stool near the stove. "How long do you think you might stay with us?"

"Not sure," Alex said.

"My grandmother always said, '*Lascia che la vita ti mostri il suo piano.*': 'Let life show its plan to you.'"

Alex reached for wine. "Sounds like good advice. But I have to admit, I'm fully American. I like a good plan. Efficiency. In fact, I've had a hard time working with the slow pace of stagehands in Europe. Makes me think of a Rita Dove poem, about how she doesn't know how to sit still."

Helena held her glass of white wine up. "To sitting still. My grandmother gave me the same advice after my husband died. Tomas grew up here. He was supposed to take over for old Mr.

Tomboli, the baker, when he retired. After Tomas was gone, I thought, 'What in Christ's name am I going to do up in this tiny little village by myself?' I was all set to leave, return to Tirrenia."

"What about Martina?" Alex asked.

"That is a big story," Helena said, "almost as big as this story." She ran her hand down the length of the scar on her face. She walked to the doorway to peer down the hallway, then dropped her voice. "Here is the truth: Martina is not my daughter. I did not give birth to her, anyway."

Alex let the chicken flop back onto the cutting board with a thwack. "But she looks just like you. I just assumed."

"*Si*, we have mostly encouraged that belief—well, we haven't denied it anyway. She is Milo's daughter. I am her aunt. Now, as she gets older, I wonder if we have made a mistake, letting her call me *Mamma*," Helena said.

Alex realized how little she knew about Helena—how little they knew about each other—and how life had thrown them roadblocks and hurdles and how much they had each been wounded. They were children the last time they met, children whose problems ranged from too much schoolwork to an insufficient allotment of cookies.

Of course, it wasn't completely true that the girls had only frivolous concerns. Even at eight-years-old, Helena would listen intently as Alex complained of Estelle, a woman who withheld affection from her daughter as if she were the overseer of an orphanage, purposefully detached.

"The secrets we live with," Alex said. "We don't know how they affect us until much later. Your mother's letter explains a lot, for me. About Estelle. How she wasn't affectionate. I suppose she didn't know how to love—doesn't know."

Helena raised her eyebrows in response.

"I would love to see your mother. I can almost guess what else she's going to tell me. It may be hard, but I have to hear it face to face. I'd rather talk to her than try my family again."

"We will make that happen for you, *amica*," Helena said, easy in all her responses.

In the other room, the girls fell into a fit of laughter. Alex stood the raw chicken on end and hacked at the breast until pieces tore off. Helena winced. Alex glanced away from the chicken, thinking how good it was to hear Lily laugh, how much lighter they both felt here in Italy, with this family.

As she turned her attention back to the cutting board, the knife slipped on a piece of cartilage and sliced into her left index finger. At first, there was only a slight tingle and Alex thought the skin was just grazed, until a long thin streak of blood surfaced from the outside edge of the nail to the knuckle.

"Oh, damn," she said, as the pain began. She grabbed for a towel and wrapped it quickly around her finger.

Helena was on her feet. She peered over Alex's shoulder. "Is it bad?"

"Could be," Alex said and held her hands up, almost enjoying the physical sting, a sudden crisis that took her away from thoughts of her family. She stood with her arms raised, surrendering to the throbbing sensation, conceding to the ache.

"Keep the pressure on," Helena suggested and headed for the bathroom. When she returned with bandages and hydrogen peroxide, together they peeled back the towel and ran cold water over the cut. The wound was deep and gaping. "I think you will survive without stitches," Helena said. "We do not call the ambulance except for emergencies here. The closest hospital is nearly an hour."

They sat at the table, and Helena bandaged her up as blood seeped immediately through the gauze. Helena wrapped the tape tighter, doubled up the pad. The image was enough to bring Alex back, swiftly and intensely, into the night of her miscarriage. She let out a quick sob, just one, startling and loud.

Helena looked up but didn't comment as Alex breathed deeply and blinked back tears. It seemed as if the loss of the baby had taken away all of her poise; the physical grace of impending motherhood that made her feel so proud. She considered telling Helena about the miscarriage, but how did you start a conversation like that? She was exhausted just from telling Kat and Brooke and Lily.

Alex was relieved when Helena said, "I went to the hospital this time." Helena turned her face so that Alex could see her scar. "Fifty-two stitches. But then, I did not live here, in this remote place. I was in Firenze."

Alex, sobered by this change of subject, dry-eyed with interest about both the scar and Martina, held her wrapped finger above her head to let the blood drain back toward her heart.

"I was a student at Polimoda, so excited to be there. See? I *was* following my childhood dream—the school is famous for fashion design. I was most interested in shoes. You should have seen the heels I created, one made out of Plexiglas, another, tall on bamboo stalks. I loved to be eccentric."

At seventeen years old, Helena was driving home from her early morning classes on a Tuesday. She remembered only that she circled the roundabout on SS67, having just come over the *Ponte alla Vittoria*. The brake pedal hit the floor, no pressure, no resistance. The car wouldn't slow. Helena clutched the steering wheel and looked frantically for a clear path away from the crowd. The Arno flashed into her sight, and the car struck the brick guard wall at 40 miles per hour, enough force to throw Helena up and over the steering wheel. She was unconscious, halfway through the windshield, by the time a produce truck driver was able to reach her.

Recovery from the accident proved to be slow and arduous. Besides the painful facial cut, six ribs were broken, and her shoulder was dislocated. The doctors were certain she had a severe concussion as well. She spent three weeks in the hospital, four months in rehab. Helena's parents insisted she come home for therapy, and Helena relented, quietly relieved for the respite from the pressures and competition of the Institute.

"I had every intention of going back to school in the fall," Helena told Alex. "But I never did. The accident tainted all of life for me—Firenze and cars and even fashion, for a time. How could I be involved in a world of beauty, I thought, with such an ugly scar down my face?" Helena said. "For years after, I would only wear flats—no heels or strappy shoes, as if footwear were somehow to blame."

Alex looked around the disaster she'd made in the kitchen and thought of her own morphed goals. All the dreams of her childhood eventually dissipated: husband, children, even career. Though she had an early knack for electronics and design, Alex clearly recalled her mother flatly stating that girls should not aspire to be engineers. "You can be an interior designer," Estelle had said. "Women have a much better eye for color."

Those constant digs must have stayed with her, must have influenced her choices. Not daring to study math or science, Alex entered college as an English major. There, she found the Beat poets and learned about Elise Cowen's unconventional existence, her usual mention as a mere footnote to Allen Ginsberg's life. Alex was hooked when she read about the poet's struggle with her mother. Through the years, Alex had continued to seek and to discover poets who were able to voice what she couldn't, who were in touch with emotions she was unable to tap.

"It's too bad that we didn't have more confidence as young women," Alex said. "We might have accomplished a lot more." What relief Alex had felt when she took an elective in the drama department at the University of Washington and found she was allowed to work backstage, to use her technical skills, to train her attention on the equipment that made shows happen.

"I think we've done pretty well," Helena said, tidying up the medical supplies, re-stuffing gauze and antiseptic into a red, zippered pouch. "After all, like my poor, reliable husband—who, by the way, behaved as he was supposed to—we could be dead."

"That's what I always think," Lily said from the hallway, having joined them inaudibly, in a ghostly, detached way. "We could be dead."

Lily walked in with a blanket wrapped around her shoulders, though the preheating oven and half-successful preparations for dinner had made the kitchen warm, nearly steamy. Alex had the sudden idea that Lily had been listening from the hallway. She pictured Lily crouched down on her haunches, head against the wall.

"A somewhat morbid, if apt, reminder to live fully," Helena added, eyeing Lily.

Lily shivered under her blanket. "I heard you talking about shoes," she said. "I like shoes, too."

Alex offered up her chair to Lily and tried to pull the half-prepped ingredients into a passable dinner. She reattempted carving the chicken, carefully this time, holding her bandaged finger away from the meat. Helena looked up now and then and gently suggested that Alex turn the burner down, that she pound the chicken before she breaded it.

Lily, with a pained expression, told Helena stories about her own current tragedies: her photographs of feet and ground and shoes, her unfinished project. She quietly described the box of photos she might never get back from Sadie.

"If my foot had been hurt in the accident rather than my face, maybe I would have thought to design shoes to help with injuries, to save the feet. But instead, I ended up with this thing." Helena gestured to her scar, bringing Lily into the conversation. "Which only kept me hiding up here, made me feel like I didn't want to try to be a woman in the world."

"A beautiful place to hide, though," Lily said.

"Well, now I'm adjusted. I don't really feel like I'm hiding anymore. Martina has reminded me every day that real beauty is devotion, not the face you put forward."

"But not blind devotion," Lily said. "Blind devotion is dangerous."

Helena gave Lily a measured look, sizing her up. "Not to a child.

Children require both love and devotion."

"I wouldn't know anything about that," Lily said quietly.

The chicken sizzled in the fry pan and made small spatters that dotted the stove and countertop. As Alex listened to Lily's comments (what she could only assume was about Lily's devotion to Sadie), it occurred to Alex that both she and Lily would soon have to go back to the U.S. and clean up their lives. Suddenly, Alex wanted to see Connor.

* * *

Milo returned early Thursday afternoon, bearing gifts: a bouquet of flowers for his sister, a beaded purse for Martina. He gave Alex a thick bar of chocolate, which she hugged like a good friend. He presented Lily with a gray scarf of fine, soft wool, wrapping it gently around her neck.

"He doesn't bring us gifts very often. His visits are too frequent to make a big deal of each one. He must be trying to make a good impression," Helena explained as they all crowded in the hallway, each keen to greet Milo on his return to Radicondoli.

Waiting on the stoop behind Milo was the beaming, patient figure of Helena's mother, wearing stylish, chunky low-heeled black shoes, with a shawl wrapped around her short frame. Mrs. Rizzieri's hair was swept up into a tall bun, which seemed to draw attention to, rather than enhance her diminutive size.

"*Mia cara, mia cara,*" she said, hands on Alex's cheeks, only after she had squeezed her daughter and granddaughter in a similar matter. "*Come mi è mancato mancato questo viso dolce.*"

"She has missed your sweet face," Helena translated. "*Mamma,* let her go. *Lasciala andare.*"

Alex nearly melted into her, into the warm, cooked-pepper smell of her, into the sweet rhythm of her voice and her touch. "I've missed her too. *Anch'io, Mamma,*" Alex said, the Italian slipping off her tongue, so easily this time. Only this phrase. Me too, *Mamma.* "*Anch'io.*"

Chapter 20

ALEX INSISTED ON sitting next to Mrs. Rizzieri during dinner, wanting to absorb her presence the way she inhaled a favorite smell, deeply and hungrily. Alex felt a joy she'd almost forgotten could exist, a trilling energy in her chest that forced a near-constant smile. They all laughed at the matron's stumbling English, her amusing mix of languages. "You *due ragazze* such together *diavoletta*," she commented, speaking of Alex and Helena when they were young.

Lily talked very little during the dinner, though she blushed when Milo's hand touched hers as they passed around a plate of perfectly cooked green beans with garlic. Even Alex, rapt with watching Mrs. Rizzieri, understood in this moment that Milo, in his rough-edged and pretty spontaneous way, was wooing Lily. "Milo likes the fragile ones," Helena whispered in Alex's ear later, while the two of them cleared dishes.

Martina was tucked straight into bed after a plum tart was served— "too early!" Marti reminded them, so Lily offered to do the honors, lessening Martina's irritation. In the living room, there were only adults, finally. Helena and Milo settled into chairs while Alex sat next to the matron, their hands clasped as they looked into each other's faces, feeling safer than she had in years. Mrs. Rizzieri did not just tell a story: her lilting voice transported them to the frigid north, twenty years ago atop the frozen mass of water that would take Alex's grandfather's life.

"This is what Estelle told me," she said. "In a moment of trust. This is what her son did for her, what your brother Junior did," she said, looking pointedly at Alex. "Justice, Estelle called it. Justice."

* * *

Junior had eavesdropped on the fight between Bubbie and Estelle. "Keep your filthy hands off Alexandra," Estelle had whispered viciously. Through his mother's rage about catching Bubbie with Alex's thumb in his mouth, Junior put together his memory of the day in the restroom at Monkey Jungle and the visceral cringe he always felt around his grandfather. He confirmed that Bubbie was not just old grandpa, but a disgusting, lecherous man.

The next morning, the air in the ice shack was so cold, each time someone spoke they could see their breath. Junior gave a grunt, barely acknowledging his grandfather when Bubbie said he was going outside to "take a piss," as he described it. Junior too, had to go to the bathroom, but he didn't want to do such a bonding, brotherly act with Bubbie. Junior waited until his grandfather left, then walked out and around the ice shack in the opposite direction—Bubbie toward the bank, Junior toward the deep center of the river. The cracking sound was subtle, just a shifting of the ice; for a moment, Junior wondered where the sound had come from. Then he heard his grandfather's call, a quick yelp. He turned in time to watch Bubbie disappear.

There was a moment of disbelief, a second when Junior's brain denied that it was happening. Some people freeze in an unexpected tragedy. Others react immediately. Junior reacted.

Estelle, still inside the ice fishing shack, hadn't heard the break, hadn't registered the faint call. Junior walked calmly and carefully over the ice. He knew that if he moved too swiftly, he might break the ice, go under too. The space where he had just seen Bubbie was 100 or so yards away, but from there, he saw his grandfather's arms as he tried to grip the sides of the ice; he could make out his dark jacket and knit hat. Bubbie cried for help, but weakly, as if the cold had made his mouth hard to operate, his lips too heavy to move. Junior did not hurry. He let the idea roll through his mind that he would not intervene. He would not help this man. But still Junior slid across the ice, watching, considering, as adrenaline ran through his blood.

Junior moved up to within thirty feet. Bubbie had slipped back down into the frigid water, his hands beneath the surface. He locked eyes with Junior and managed to raise a hand, though the rest of him had grown still. His mouth moved, but there was not a word Junior could make out. His eyes, though, his eyes said everything: *I am afraid. I am afraid to die. I need your help. Please save me. We are family. We are humans, together. Please save me, help me live.*

"I know what you did," Junior shouted. And the eyes changed, just a flicker. "I know what you did to my mother."

Junior didn't know how he kept himself from reaching out. He was not a killer (though in the military he would learn to kill). It was not in his nature to be cold-hearted. Junior learned, in that moment, exactly how fragile human existence is. He watched life drain from his grandfather. This was the moment to change his mind, to save the man he had known as his Bubbie.

"I hope you're thinking, right now, about what you did to her," he shouted, then added, "what you tried to do to me."

He thought about his troubled mother, how he had never understood her detachment, her rigidity. How he had practically begged her to love him as a young child, clung to her as she entered the room. How she refused to hold him, over and over, shutting the door behind her.

"You fucked her up, you know." Junior had never used that word around a grown-up before, and it made him feel powerful. Scared, but powerful. "And you tried to fuck me up too, but I wouldn't let you! I remember. I wouldn't let you!"

As his mother appeared in the doorway of the shack, Junior turned to look at her, and Bubbie slipped under the water. When Junior turned back around, there was only the dark form of his winter coat sinking, sinking. The choice had been made. Perhaps he had a few seconds left. He could spread his body across the ice and reach for him, but Junior didn't. He walked slowly and deliberately toward his mother until he saw his stepfather's headlights break into the blue of dawn.

* * *

"Why didn't you tell me Bu..." Alex started to ask her brother, the name "Bubbie" catching in her throat, this name that she'd used with affection all of her life forever sullied by the knowledge that he was a predator. Alex tried again. "Why didn't you tell me our grandfather abused mom?"

"Jesus Christ, Alex," Junior said and cut the engine. "Way to ruin my boating day."

Alex imagined her brother in his sleek, racing-striped boat, sunglasses and flip flops on, despite a chilling gust. His Northwest pasty white chest, the beginnings of a beer gut expanding over the edge of his bathing suit. "You've known all of these years, right, since we were kids? When we were at Monkey Jungle," she said. "Didn't you think I might be affected? What if he had tried it with me?"

There were voices behind him, laughter, and the sound of waves lapping at the sides of the boat. "That old bastard."

"Why didn't anyone tell me?" Alex kept pressing, twisting the phone cord around her fingers as she gazed at family photos in Helena's living room—pictures where everyone smiled and hugged and laughed.

On the other side of the world, Junior took a drink, a swilling, swooshing sound. "Alex, can you please just let it be? You were a child;

we both were. I've worked hard, haven't I? I want to enjoy my life. Mom and Dad have moved on from all of that business, and I suggest you follow their lead. It has nothing to do with you. We all kept you protected."

Alex dropped her voice, taking the strain, the pleading out of her questioning. She asked him straight up. "Junior, please tell me: Did you watch that man die? Did you let him drown?"

"Damn right I did," Junior said without the slightest tremor in his voice.

Alex let the full force of this admission hit her, swallowed the fact that everything Mrs. Rizzieri had told her was true.

"And I'd do it again," Junior added. "He deserved it."

Chapter 21

ALEX SAID GOODBYE to Mrs. Rizzieri on the front stoop Friday afternoon, arms around the older woman's plump form, inhaling her earthy, garlicky scent. "Thank you for telling me what you remember of my mother," Alex said, her eyes tear-filled. "Though it's awful; somehow, it's also a relief."

"Your family did what they thought right. They meant to protect." Mrs. Rizzieri kissed Alex on each cheek and hugged her heartily before ducking into Milo's car with a spryness that belied her stout body and age.

Alex watched the Fiat until the car rounded the corner, out of sight, feeling a sudden sense of loss. A group of children yelled a few streets over, all gaiety and mirth. She recalled her childhood here in Italy, the warm smells of Italian kitchens, the large, extended families with scores of children playing ball in the street. How had she gotten so far from her desire for a large family? Up until now, she believed that if she kept moving, she wouldn't need someone to return to. She thought that if she was constantly busy, surrounded by people, she wouldn't need a family or a home of her own. And now, that long-dormant desire had resurfaced.

A swallow, a bird she recognized, whistled from the tiled rooftop. The bird appeared to be eyeing her specifically, his head cocked, as if he was judging her, as if the damn chirper could read her thoughts and expected a better explanation.

"I don't see you hanging out with anyone," she yelled.

The swallow squawked back at her with a flap of its wings.

"That's what I thought."

After her grandmother had said goodbye, Martina opened Helena's trunk full of delicate, musty shirts and linens. She hauled out quilts and a couple of leather-bound books. There was a photo of a thin woman in a polka-dotted dress and summer hat who leaned on an old car—maybe an Aston Martin, but Lily was unsure why that name came into her head; she didn't know cars. Ideas popped into her mind lately, words out of nowhere.

Lily fondled an old teddy bear while Marti opened the journal. She read until tears formed in her eyes, until her shoulders convulsed and she let out a sob. Lily reached over to rub Martina's slight shoulder, lightly patting in a way that even to Lily seemed ineffective, not enough. What could she say to this grieving girl? "It's okay?" "There, there now?" "You'll be okay?" All empty words. Martina's bluntly cut dark hair laid like a shroud across her cheek. Lily imagined observing the two of them from behind the lens of a camera, capturing the contrast in skin tones, and age, and vitality.

Lily's fingers touched the edge of the journal, but she didn't ask the crying child to translate from Italian. This would have to be a wordless exchange. She felt a surge of tenderness for the girl, for whatever made her cry. Unsure how to comfort her, unwilling to use rote phrases, Lily gathered Martina up in her arms—experiencing the bittersweet pleasure of consoling a weeping child.

Marti clung to Lily's shoulder and then finally pulled away and wiped at her tears. She held up the photograph. "*Mia madre,*" she said. "My mother."

"Your mother?" Lily studied the woman in the photograph more closely. Her pumps were caked with mud on the sides. Her eyes were half-closed in a squint, but still Lily could see that Martina got her bubbly smile, her bright eyes from this woman. Her mother was young, maybe in her early twenties in the photo, happy and grinning, captured as her hand reached up to hold onto her wide-brimmed beach hat.

"She died when I was a baby," Martina said. "My father couldn't take care of me alone, so I came to live with Aunt Helena. I don't remember my mother at all."

"Helena is your aunt?" Lily asked, surprised.

"I call her *Mamma*." Martina used her sleeve to wipe her nose. "Milo is my father, but I don't even call him *papa*. He is not like my friends' fathers—all strict and bossy. Milo is a lot more fun. He only comes to visit. He never yells at me."

"Milo is your father?" Lily was stymied, unsure why this information astounded, almost troubled her.

"They don't tell me about my mother. I read in Helena's journal." Martina flipped the pages back and began to read, her voice shaky and high as she translated each line:

I told my brother from beginning that she will not be easy. I hear it with her laugh, so strong-sounding, like she was hidden a secret. Like she flips her hair over shoulder with lots of people, but then I find her alone, looks like she has a knife pointed at her throat. She sees me and try to cover that scared look, but I saw. I saw it in months before she was pregnant.

Martina stopped reading and shut the journal. "I used to ask about my mother, but I could tell it made Aunt Helena feel bad." Martina's hands quivered with emotion. "I wish they would talk about her. I don't even know how she died." Martina's tears began anew, and the sobs escalated, so Lily pulled Martina close.

Lily had handled Sadie's hysterics for years now. She considered herself an expert in dealing with other people's pain. When it seemed Martina wouldn't stop crying, Lily got up and patted her hair. "I'll be right back."

In her room, Lily dug in her suitcase, as if she might find some soothing element, an answer to Martina's—or her own—stress, but she came up empty-handed. Finally, Lily grabbed the sedatives her doctor prescribed. She looked over the bottle, rotated it, looked for instructions, but it only said her name, the dose. They always made her feel better—and they had helped Sadie for years. She shook the bottle, broke up the tiny pill, and headed to Helena's room.

"What are you giving her?" Alex asked from the doorway, appearing out of the blue like an apparition in the middle of Lily's warped and weakened judgement.

"Just a half an Ativan. I take these to help me sleep."

Alex snatched the pill from Lily's palm with startling ferocity. "You can't give a child sleeping pills."

"It's a sedative," Lily argued.

"What are you thinking?"

Lily only knew that nothing else had helped her: not yoga, not deep breathing or meditation or prayer. "She's upset. They help me when I'm upset."

Martina, who followed their exchange closely, said "Helena," when the front door opened. There was panic in her eyes, a pleading look on her face.

"Martina?" Helena called. "Alex? Anyone home?"

The three of them worked together silently to shovel the contents back inside the trunk: books and clothes, old hats, and stuffed animals.

"There you are," Helena said when she'd worked her way down the hallway. "What are you all up to?"

Lily's heart raced and she knew, because of Alex's reaction, that she'd made an error, but there was too much going on for her to think clearly. *Assurance.* The word settled into her brain and confounded her further.

"I showed them your silk scarf from Milano," Martina fibbed, her eyes downcast. "Lily looks pretty in that color." She tugged on Lily's hand. "C'mon. You were going to teach me the warrior pose."

The two of them headed toward Martina's room while Alex palmed the bottle of Ativan, hoping the rattle of the pills didn't give her friend away.

* * *

Lily was already in bed, her back to the door, dark covers pulled up over her shoulders by the time Alex joined her that evening in their shared bedroom. Lily laid still and stiff as Alex slowly opened the dresser.

"I'm awake," Lily said quietly.

"Oh, good," Alex said and pulled Lily's bottle of Ativan from the drawer. "I wanted to tell you: I'm worried about you, Lily." Alex sat on the edge of the bed, toes curling around a soft yarn throw rug. "What the hell were you thinking, offering these to Martina? She's a child. Who knows what would have happened? What's going on with you?"

Lily listened quietly. When she spoke, her explanation was nearly as confounding as her actions. "I can't sleep without them," she said, hands still tucked under the covers so that Alex could only see her neck and her head. "All the while I'm lying here, images come up in my head. Words too. I can't slow down my thoughts— all of these scenes from some pretty bad times in my life."

"Are you talking about..." Alex wanted to be delicate here—she wanted to be sensitive to Lily's feelings, but also to her own. Alex wasn't sure she was ready to talk about babies and the lack the two of them felt. "Is this about what you mentioned the other day, about losing a baby?"

Lily squeezed her eyes shut, and a tear trickled across the bridge of her nose. "Don't," Lily said. "Please."

Alex fought the urge to cry herself, took a deep breath, and put her hand on Lily's shoulder, feeling like she didn't have any more room for sorrow. "I can't hang out here much longer," Alex said softly. "I have to go back to Seattle soon. I've got to see Connor. I will eventually have to see my family and talk about what I remembered. You should come back to the States with me."

"You don't have to worry," Lily said opening her eyes and smiling dreamily. "I've got Milo. He'll take care of me."

Every feminist bone in Alex's body reared up at the idea that Lily needed taking care of by a man, but that was another, deeper philosophical argument. The Lily she used to know never would have suggested such a thing. The truth was, this Lily likely did need someone to look after her.

"What makes you think Milo is going to take care of you?" Alex asked.

Lily reached out from under the covers and took the bottle of pills from Alex. She sat up, unscrewed the cap, and swallowed a pill without water. "Milo and I, we have a connection. I know it's hard to understand, but I can tell that fate brought me to him, a photographer, just when I had lost my lens. It's a sign."

Alex didn't know how to open Lily's eyes, didn't know how to bring her back to reality. She could argue or point out the fact that she and Milo just met, that Lily was in no shape to start a relationship, but Lily seemed out beyond the realm of reason.

Alex clicked off the lamp, bringing the room to a deep gray. "Good night, Lily." She decided to let the drugs take over and coax her friend into slumber. "So be it," Alex whispered into the dark.

Chapter 22

ALEX AND LILY HADN'T yet thought to visit any of the four churches that spattered the small village during their stay. They had stopped to admire the clock tower, but they never walked into any of the hushed and cavernous apses of Radicondoli's many vaunted churches. Almost alarmed, Helena said that no one should visit Radicondoli without seeing the paintings at *La Collegiata dei Santi Simone e Giuda*.

"People come for 'Our Lady of Mercy' by Naddo Ceccarelli," Helena said, "but look for di Domenico's *Assunzione*. You will notice, Lily, in that painting, the only two figures—in any of the church's paintings—who wear shoes. I believe those two are the educated men. You go see, decide if you have different thoughts on the footwear."

The Collegiate Church's marble façade stood flat and straight, austere, worn to the same gray color as the adjacent brick. A simple iron cross rose atop the roof, above two carved triangle porticos, next to two plain, round balls at the eaves.

"I haven't been inside a church in a long time," Lily said and took a breath before Alex heaved open the heavy mahogany door. It had taken some convincing for Lily to come along at all. "The Catholics," Lily muttered. "Some of the worst offenders."

In contrast to the unadorned exterior of the building, the inside was startling white and intricately carved. Lily blinked against the unexpected brilliance of the walls. She scanned the upper portico where small red curtains were flung aside, emitting a wan light. The pews, however, were simple planks carved of dark wood. Alex and Lily walked over brick-colored tiles, past a large tri-fold stand that held a bible, open to Psalms, a green silk ribbon placed across the page as a marker.

"Stunning," Alex said, just like Lily's mother when she stared up at the altar of Bethel church in Redding, California. The similarity hit Lily like a jolt, and unexpectedly, her mother was holding Lily's hand, squeezing too hard during an Easter service amid thousands of believers. There were lights in her eyes and pain in her knuckles.

This church was similar only in color to the Pentecostal church Lily grew up in—bright white, with dark, simple pews. The quiet emptiness, the haunting stillness was enough to throw Lily back into the past as they approached a marble and gold altar.

As they stood under a crystal chandelier, Alex turned and studied a painting of the Madonna high on the wall. Lily remained paralyzed. She'd never told a soul, other than her mother, what that elder in her parents' church did to her when she was sixteen.

Lily's footsteps rang out on the hard marble as she wrested herself away from that memory, which was never far from her self-loathing, and walked toward the painting to the right of the altar. She looked closely at the feet of each figure—at the pregnant woman, at Mary and Jesus and the cherubs. At the men in clusters. Lily scanned the rest of the paintings in the church. She turned her head in circles as she searched. It seemed Helena was right: only the two figures in the *Assunzione* wore footwear—one of them clad in something more like stockings than shoes, his toes bare. Lily twisted and grabbed a long taper candle from a stand in front of the altar. She lunged toward the painting and tapped the wick at the shoes, in a rash movement that brought Alex to her feet.

"Look!" Lily exclaimed and took another swipe. "Helena said they're wearing shoes. Educated men. She's right. The men, Alex, only the men."

The candle tip made a dent in the canvas as Lily pushed at the image. "The pregnant woman you see, is, of course, barefoot." She scraped the wick to the bottom right and across to the top, where Mary had risen into heaven. "This is what brings you to this." Tiny slivers of wax rubbed off onto her hand.

Alex grabbed her wrist and yanked her away from the painting. "What are you doing?"

Lily dropped the candle, and the taper broke in three places, shattering on the brittle tile.

"These paintings are valuable, Lily." Alex bent and picked up the candle, cradled the stick in her palm. "You could get arrested for vandalism."

Lily fought at the rage that had arisen powerfully in her body. The potency of this memory, the sensation of standing in a church, had invited a fury that hadn't surfaced in years. Her hand still shook with the force of needing to *do something*. She looked at Alex, utterly confused, completely lost. "I don't know, Alex. I don't know what I'm doing."

They moved slowly over to the first pew and sat in silence. Ever since Lily left home, she had worked to get the memory of that calm, practiced rapist out of her mind. She had never been successful, though she had always fought the images and the sensations when they came back with such force. *Opaque*. The word floated out of nowhere, circled her brain.

"I made a mistake," Lily finally whispered, though they were the only people in the church. "When you're young you imagine—not that there won't be any consequences to your actions—but that you will be able to handle the consequences. That you won't mind thinking about your mistakes. But your mistakes stay with you. Your new mistakes conjoin with the old mistakes, and eventually, you're just haunted by how badly you've screwed up your life.

"Even now, years later, I still haven't learned." Lily lifted up the back of her shirt and turned to Alex. "Look at this tattoo. One afternoon, a split decision. I was coerced into it—or at least wasn't strong enough to say 'no'—and now here it is, for the rest of my life."

Lily rubbed awkwardly at her skin with her forefinger, as if she was trying to erase the cherry blossoms. Alex put her hand over the top of Lily's to still her.

"It's a beautiful mistake."

Lily dropped the back of her shirt and looked up to the vaulted arches. "Not everyone's mistakes have a huge price. My mistakes have cost me and cost me."

Her voice was shaky as she told Alex about the rape, about how five weeks later she drove herself to a clinic, a squat white building in the middle of an industrial park in Reno—hours away, in another state. The nurse, kind but distant, asked several times, "Are you sure?" Lily never wavered. She bled for weeks—unusually long, just like Alex—and only discovered later that she'd been torn and scarred. Damaged.

"After you told us about your miscarriage," Lily said, "all I could think about is what I did. I killed that baby." Lily looked down at her hands. Her voice was high-pitched and weak at once. "I always thought I'd have children, lots of them. Maybe a farm somewhere. I imagined I'd make quilts for my babies, bake cakes." *Placenta*, Lily thought. Buried in the garden. "But the truth is, no matter what happens, I'll never live that life. I'll never experience birth."

A muffled sound came from the back of the church—a startled bird, the flapping of wings. They turned to see a pigeon fly up to the high windows. But they didn't see who or what startled the bird. No one was in sight.

"Another bird for you. Another sign," Lily said. "Have a baby, Alex. Before it's too late."

Sunday morning brought church bells. A fog hung high on the mountain, obscuring numbers on the clock tower in the center of town. The hazy mist encouraged Alex to think of romance and beauty and of love that lasted forever. Old couples held hands on their way to church. Mr. Tomboli stood in the doorway of his bakery. He nodded as people passed and remembered the woman he left behind in the Philippines forty years ago; her flushed cheeks, how she smelled so beautifully of frangipani.

Helena's small kitchen table, usually set to accommodate two—or three at the most—was crammed with empty plates, ramekins filled with condiments, bowls of shredded parmesan and olives, glasses ready to be filled with wine. Bright colored napkins sat under tarnished silver flatware. A crystal vase of chrysanthemum was placed on a gold-embroidered runner. In what seemed like just a few minutes to Lily, Helena managed to throw together an abundant midday meal of tagliatelle with small strips of steak in a wine and butter sauce, braised asparagus splayed on a platter, and a green salad drizzled with balsamic.

The talk turned to love at the table as Milo, back from Tirrenia, told the story of an ex-girlfriend, what he described as love at first sight. "She bent over a dead warbler in biology class, scalpel in hand, and I thought, as she sliced the flesh open without wincing, 'I'm going to marry that girl.'" Milo shrugged and swallowed a bite of pasta. "Unfortunately, not every story ends like they do in the movies, no? I didn't marry her. I think we had, what, three good months together? She began dating her physics professor."

Lily watched Milo intently and waited for him to say more, but he shoved a forkful of pasta in his mouth straight off the serving plate and chomped animatedly. "Alex says she has to leave soon," Lily said quietly. "I was thinking I might stay on for a while."

Milo stopped mid-chew and raised his eyebrows, gestured to his mouth. Helena quickly grabbed a crusty loaf of bread and shoved it under her brother's nose. "Mr. Tomboli makes this bread every afternoon, isn't that true, Milo? A second batch so that it is fresh for dinner," Helena said. "He delivers to my work every day as I am leaving. He has taken this on as his duty, though Tomas has been gone for many years now."

Squeezed in between Martina and Lily, Milo spooned heaps of pasta first on his plate, then on Martina's, still ignoring Lily's suggestion she stay. The stool he perched on nearly toppled as he reached for the salad. As if Lily, too, was a child, he ladled out food for her and filled her plate. Lily stared in horror at the quantity.

"*Basta*," she said.

"We are not afraid of food here," Milo said with a smile and dug into his plate.

Lily picked at the salad and wondered at the flush that had risen to her face, the heat that made her ears burn. Milo's enthusiasm was almost enough to make her join in. His exuberance for photography—for life—had re-energized her, made her long to get her photographs back from Sadie so she could continue with her collages.

Lily pierced a piece of spinach and ran each moment she had spent alone with Milo through her head, remembering, treasuring. Milo tore off a piece of bread and held it to Lily's mouth. He did so casually, almost automatically. Lily, startled at first, gently took the piece from his fingers into her mouth. Her lips grazed his fingernail, rough and sharp. The bread became slowly saturated in her mouth and the grains broke down until the morsel was soft and gooey on her tongue. *Communion,* she thought, and nearly spit out the bread. She looked to Milo's face and swallowed with his encouragement. He would want her to stay.

"Tomas was so young, his death was shocking," Helena said, after explaining the accident that injured her husband. "A simple concussion led to a coma. Even then, it never occurred to me that he wouldn't recover."

Lily felt somewhat embarrassed that their presence had caused Helena to recount this morbid story about a slip on an icy truck ramp, and from so long ago. Even Alex ate quietly, listening while Milo fed Lily again, like he would a bird, in small, torn-off chunks. He eyed Lily intently, as if he suspected that she might spew up.

She swallowed dutifully, mesmerized by his attention, until he offered a piece of steak. She shook her head and pulled away but he held it up insistently between his fingers. Again, she refused. Martina leaned into Milo and followed the exchange with interest. Helena, though, had not seemed to notice and continued to tell Alex her story.

"I met Tomas at a wedding in Pisa. His second cousin married my great-aunt's husband's sister's daughter." Helena rolled the string of relationships off her tongue with a sly smile. "It was only a year after my accident, and I was very shy to be seen with my face—caked-on makeup only seemed to highlight the scar. I wore my hair down that side of my face."

Helena made a feathery motion across her temple.

"Tomas asked me to dance. He was curious, but I was not offended. Other people looked horrified or showed such pity in their eyes, it made me sick. Tomas, so tall and handsome and confident, never looked disgusted, not once."

Milo had not given up on his insistence that Lily eat more of the food. He had, however, dropped the steak and moved on to a piece of pasta, the whole while managing to shovel forkfuls into his own mouth. Lily cringed but took the pasta between her teeth. The doughy texture was rife with the flavor of meat that nearly made her, a ten-year vegetarian, gag. Milo had already scooped up yet more food—asparagus this time. As he flitted his gaze back to his own plate for a moment, Lily turned her face and spit the pasta into her napkin. When she looked up, she saw Martina staring at her, laughter beginning to bubble up.

Helena paused in her story. "What's so funny?"

"*Allora*," Marti said. "*Niente.*"

Milo raised his eyebrows. "Yes, please tell us." He still pinched the asparagus between his fingers, the spear dripping dark vinegar off the tip.

Martina pointed to the splotches on the lace tablecloth.

"Ah," Helena complained and jumped up for a sponge. "That was *Nonna's.*"

"Why put covers on the table that you don't want to get dirty? We are eating. It is messy," Milo protested.

Helena elbowed him out of the way. "Just because life is messy, does that mean we should not strive for beauty?"

"I'll help," Alex said, leaping to her feet, her tendency to repair what had been broken, to clean up what had been stained. She grabbed a bottle of seltzer water at Helena's suggestion from the fridge.

"Milo has a point," Lily said quietly, placing her napkin over her plate to conceal the great mound of food she hadn't touched. "Maybe we shouldn't soil everything. Some things should be left pristine."

Helena rubbed at the stain with the sponge and seltzer water. Alex and Helena eyed each other across the table, wondering exactly what Lily was referencing, wondering if somewhere underneath her ghostly pronouncement some real wisdom resided.

* * *

At the foot of Helena's bed, her old brass and leather steamer trunk stood open, a forest-green crate that had been passed down through generations from her great-grandmother who used the chest for dowry items. Helena's mother, too, used the trunk to store a variety of lace doilies and a silver tea service in preparation for marriage. For years, as the oldest girl in her family, Helena was given articles for the trunk: undergarments handed over with a wink from aunties, garters, and plush baby blankets.

She pulled out a pair of shoes now and showed Alex. "Lily would love these," Helena exclaimed as she turned the resin-covered toe in her hand. "I designed them at Polimoda. So tacky, really. Look—decoupage."

"Do you ever regret giving up fashion?"

"Who says I did?" Helena asked. She grabbed a package, folded in tissue paper, off her bureau and handed it to Alex. "I have a small clothing line I started after I was married, when we moved back here. I needed something to do, so I designed clothes for myself, then for friends back in the city. Other women do the sewing for me now, since I opened the shop here. There is a store in Tirrenia that sells my designs, and a few others in Livorno and Grosseto. My mother took a load back with her."

Alex opened the package and held up a blue long-sleeve, fitted shirt with frills and gray linen pants, two buckles on each side of the waist. "Why didn't you tell me that the shop was yours when we came in? That's exciting."

Helena waved her off. "Old news," she said. "Speaking of news, my friend, why didn't you tell me about losing a child? Lily mentioned it—perhaps by mistake. I told you all of those stories about when Tomas died, about my scar, about Martina."

Tags hung from the clothes, bearing a stamped logo of a high-heeled shoe with Helena's married name, *Amatteis*. "They're beautiful," Alex said, ignoring Helena's more pressing question. "But they're not really my style."

"They will fit you exactly. As if I was thinking of you when I made them. Your clothing is too much like a man's. You will be fantastic in these, feminine," Helena said, pointedly looking at Alex, awaiting the real response.

Alex ran her hand over the silky fabric, imagining herself dressed as a professional woman, confident, non-road crew. "The more I talk about the miscarriage, the sadder I get."

"All you can do is sit in that sorrow for a while," Helena suggested. "Nothing else really works, I found." Helena dug into the trunk and pulled out a pair of leather high-heeled boots, dusted them off. "You wear a 38-39? See if these boots fit? Not so garish as the others." Helena had decided to let her friend off the hook.

A loud squeal and then ringing laughter came from the living room, where Martina played *nascondino*, a card game, with Milo and Lily on the last night of the women's stay. Helena fingered each item as she returned them to the trunk. When she lifted her journal, the photo of Martina's mother slid out and fell to the floor, landing face down, a stark white square on warm sienna tile. Alex almost couldn't help but reach for it, but Helena peeled it up with her painted fingernails and stared, for a moment, at the happy scene. "Martina's mother," Helena said, and turned the photo toward Alex. "Such a waif."

"What happened to her?" Alex asked.

Helena checked the doorway and lowered her voice. "She took her own life when Martina was only five months old. I have to say I was not completely surprised, but to see my brother so affected, so devastated, was hard. Milo seems to have been born with an instinct to save what I call his weak, little birds—your Lily being his latest project, of course."

She shifted her eyes to the door again.

"When Martina's mother died, our whole family rallied around Milo, taking care of Martina. In the end, we agreed it would be best if I raised her—I think they could all see that I needed it, with Tomas gone only one year before, and no children of my own. Quite a pair, my brother and I, both widowed in our twenties, like some kind of family curse."

"Why did she do it?" Alex asked.

"Depression, I suppose. She left no note. Just the other day, I saw an American actress on the Oprah show talking about this. They call it post-partum now. I thought Martina's mother only selfish at the time."

Alex was slightly amused to hear Helena quoting the Oprah show, couldn't imagine her friend sitting down to watch celebrities—a world away—talk sincerely about their beliefs.

Helena continued to narrate her possessions: on the dresser, a jewelry box made of olive wood that a great-uncle carved, while he waited for his Red Cross troop to deploy to Korea. In each corner of the room, on each surface, was a piece of the past. Helena's family was all around them, imbedded in objects, in memory.

"You've got so many stories, Helena. So much history. I love it here—I love your family, but they're not mine," Alex said. "I need to go home. I can't hide here."

"Why not?" Helena said with a smile. "Move to Italy. We would have such fun. We can adopt you into the Amatteis and Rizzieri clans, into these crazy families. Maybe we'll both meet new men, start again."

Alex shifted to her knees and handed the photo back to Helena. "Be careful, I might take you seriously."

"But I am serious. Think about it." Helena knelt and hugged her friend, grasping onto Alex as if trying to hold her there in Italy.

* * *

As Alex prepared to leave, plopping her suitcase down in the foyer in a practiced, automatic motion—another departure, another car ride to a plane ride to a taxi and then home—Helena whispered, "I am sorry that I cannot host Lily without you—the truth is, I am not prepared to watch over her. Her nerves look to be on the outside of her skin."

"Well put," Alex said just as there was a sharp knock on the door.

"Why do you knock? Just come in!" Helena shouted, imagining it was Milo at the door, there to deliver Alex and Lily back to Florence. Retreating down the hallway to get Lily's bags, Helena hollered again. "*Entra qui.*"

The door opened slowly, as if revealing a prize. When Alex unfolded from tucking a book into her luggage, she startled. It was not Milo who stood there on the stoop, come to take them home, but Connor.

"What are you...?" she began, then faltered. "How did you...?"

Alex laughed nervously, as if she didn't know this man at all, this man who might have been the father of her child.

Connor smiled with relief when he saw Alex, though he still looked unsure he'd gotten the right place, eyebrows furrowed, his stance slightly cowed and awkward like a child asking for paper route money. She'd never seen Connor look shy before, and she found this insecurity extremely charming. She reached for him but pulled back just as he was about to put his arms around her, their timing off, as if they'd forgotten each other's rhythms; she bumped awkwardly into his chest, trying to settle her jangly nerves.

Finally, as his warm hands wrapped her torso, she leaned her head against his shoulder, remembering the feeling of him, the humid straw smell. He kissed the top of her head, nuzzled his face into her neck.

"You came," Alex marveled, "all the way."

Connor gave a low groan, almost a hum, which she'd always found disarming. "I didn't know how else to get you back."

Alex hardly knew where to start—with her rekindled friendship with Helena and her family? With her grandfather's death in the icy stream and her brother's complicity?

"Well," Helena said from the far end of the hallway, arms crossed over her chest, a teasing smile on her lips. "I suppose you know this person?"

Milo arrived on the heels of Connor just as Martina popped out from the bedroom, crowding the foyer, creating the kind of bustling chaos that made Italy and this family so attractive to Alex.

"Sorry you came back up here for nothing." Alex said to Milo after introductions were made. "I guess Connor can drive us now."

Milo nodded towards the back where Lily was still packing up. "It was not for nothing," he said with a sly smile.

Arrangements were discussed. Plans were made for departure, for someday a return. They were all surprised when Milo returned quickly from the back bedroom, muttering that he had to get back to Firenze. He gave Alex a quick hug, Connor a handshake, and walked out, leaving the door ajar.

"Martina, come to the shop after they leave," Helena said, looking confounded by her brother's behavior. "I have to go meet my seamstress."

Alex clung to her friend, wanting to keep her there, wanting to linger. "We won't lose touch this time. I promise."

Outside, Connor commented on the beauty of the scenery and glanced around him, first down the hill and then up the street. "What now?" There was an uncomfortable minute as they watched Milo accelerate into the distance, watched Helena march determinedly off in the opposite direction. "Let's take a walk," he suggested, gently urging Alex forward with his hand on her lower back.

Alex led him toward the park. The wife of the restaurateur across the road wiped at an outside table. She resettled napkin holders on wrought iron and swept a few crumbs to the sidewalk. She called over her shoulder to her husband to come out, his interest peaked twenty minutes ago when he pointed Connor towards Helena's house. Half of the town had been speculating on the American women's love interests, particularly since Alex and Lily came to live with the Amatteises. They made no effort to hide their curiosity, staring openly.

"That Alitalia flight was amazing—what a difference from flying in the U.S.—leg room, decent food. They even offered free wine when we had to wait an hour on the tarmac in La Guardia," Connor began, narrating his journey, as if trying to fill the silence between them. "Long trip, though. Had to stop at this little store along the way for directions. Barely slept in two days."

As Connor and Alex meandered along the path, their footsteps crunched on the gravel. The birds seemed to have taken a break, the only other sound a soft breeze that rustled through the trees. Connor walked a half step behind her on a narrow section of path and she intuited his presence more than saw him. His shadow, long and thin, was thrown out in front of him. Alex wished she could address his shadow, tell the flat shape all she had been thinking: how she wanted a family, how lonely she'd been, how she was getting sick of show business, how betrayed she felt by his *sleeping* while she miscarried.

Alex might have remained silent if Connor hadn't come even with her and broken through her thoughts by clearing his throat. "I want us to talk about the miscarriage," he said.

"That's abrupt," she answered, even though she was just thinking about the same tragedy. Nice that they were on the same page, for once, but she didn't say so.

"I've had enough of not getting to the point," he said.

"You weren't there for me," she said, nearly blurted.

"When?"

Could he actually not know what she meant? She summoned her courage as even the wind seemed to have died. The tension bowed her and she squatted down on the path, head in her hands. "That night," she answered bluntly, challenging him to react. "The night it happened."

Connor spoke in a strangled voice. "Fair enough."

"Why weren't you?" Alex said into her hands.

She felt Connor study the top of her head. His voice was low and filled with emotion, none of the defensive attitude she heard over the phone. "I didn't know how to help."

"I was in serious pain," she said, sitting down on the gravel, ignoring the cold that seeped through the seat of her pants. She wiped her hands over her eyes, shielding them as if from the glare of the sun, though only a diffracted, soft glow lit the path; she forced herself to look up at him.

"Honey, I feel awful about not being helpful to you." Connor squatted down next to her, took his weight on one knee as if he was about to propose. "I wish I had been able to heal you. Believe me, I tried. I rubbed your back. I sat with you. What more could I have done?"

Alex's body twitched with the urge to run, but she forced herself to answer. "You could have stayed awake. I shouldn't have had to go through that alone." Alex's voice rose. Her throat tightened up, and she strove to bring the tone back down to her chest, to lower the register. "The baby we lost was yours too."

Connor urged her to get up, lifted her by the elbow. "That's just it, Alex." His voice was even, unemotional. "For you, it was a child. I get that. You felt the baby—it was inside of you. For me, this pregnancy was just a concept, an event that was maybe going to happen."

"It wasn't a concept," she choked out. "Our child died."

Connor cleared his throat. "I have a hard time seeing it that way."

"That's the truth, though," Alex sobbed. Her feet had a will of their own, and she continued on the path. She traveled hastily, nearly ran. Connor tried to hold her back, but she shook him off.

"Alex, please stop this," he insisted. "You're angry, I understand, but it's over. I'm sorry if I hurt you, I really am, but can't we get past this?"

"You walked away on the worst night of my life," she said over her shoulder.

"And I've apologized for that," Connor labored to keep up, fit as he was.

They reached the field beside the tower, the light in the meadow broken up by a low haze that hovered just beyond the crest of the hill. Alex halted in knee-high grass. He came up behind her and rested his hands on her shoulders. She stiffened from his touch, so intimate, so comforting. They stood this way for several minutes, hushed, until Alex relaxed and leaned back into him.

"I'm sorry, Lexi," he muttered into her hair.

She shivered as his lips touched the skin of her temple, the rough, unshaven stubble of his beard combined with the gentle sensation of his kisses. Her body melted into his despite her resistance, squashing her attempt at communication, muting for the moment her acute desire for him to understand her pain. She should have screamed that night, really vocalized what happened internally. Might he have reacted differently? Had she created this distance by keeping her feelings to herself?

Connor pulled the hair up off her nape; he drifted his lips across her sunflower tattoo and down her spine until she whimpered. He drew her body tighter against his until no air, not a hint of space was between them; firmly, confidently, he traced his hands up under her shirt. It had been so long since he touched her, since she had been open to his hands on her skin. She knew this was no answer to their problems. How easily those concerns were suppressed by layers of adrenaline. She couldn't help but want to stop her repetitive thoughts about the miscarriage and about her grandfather's abuse of her mother, about Junior's letting their grandfather drown. She followed Connor down into the grass, oblivious to the dirt and the bugs and the pieces of litter, overwhelmed with a need to feel pleasure, if only for a short while.

Alex's eyes were closed as they tumbled down in the tall grass where they would be cloaked from view. There was nothing now but his soft kiss on her collar bone, and she let out a sigh that caught in her throat. Grass tickled her neck where strands had crept up under the wave of her hair, each cell of her skin alive with sensation.

Connor understood her body, if little else about her. He moved his mouth over her skin, his hands crossed under her arched back. She let herself fall into the sensation of his caress, allowed him to arouse her. To her mind, his tender strokes, his generosity, were a form of apology, of trying to make up for his mistakes. She concentrated on his fingertips; she blocked the resistance that threatened to surface, allowed herself to feel the air across her chest—a draft too mild to be noticed against her cheek, but the sensitive pores of her exposed skin tautened, responded.

He looked into her eyes as he peeled her clothing down, hastily removed her shoes, a sock, one pant leg, not bothering with the other. She closed her eyes and took in his warm skin, felt Connor's weight on top of her, his hips as they moved into hers, a brief contact, back and forth, feeling all of the earth. She moved through pleasure, then calm, until the thought of how she bled all those weeks crept into her head. She kept in motion, worked to push the thoughts away, to brush them aside, but they were persistent, like a line of determined ants and she remembered the moment when Connor turned and trod up the stairs that night. She watched his back and had the sensation that she was alone in this world, truly and finally, with only her own body and the baby who had died inside her.

His eyes found hers, silently asked what was wrong. The sound of the nearby stream came loud and forceful, the sharpening of her senses robust. She smelled the loamy, punky odor of the earth, saw clear outlines of trees, heard the flit of little wings around them. Alex pulled her focus back, pushed the thoughts from her head and, to the sound of birdsong, climaxed, quickly, nearly unexpectedly. She opened her eyes and offered a conspiratorial grin then continued to move.

The sun was in Alex's eyes, and she searched the sky. The thought came over her like a revelation: she saw herself as she swayed in a hammock, her belly swollen with a newly formed life. A warm breeze pushed her back and forth, a gentle oscillation. A glass of lemonade on a side table sweated in the summer heat. She recognized the truth in her body, in her cells, and she knew she would forever remember this moment. She almost didn't speak, wanted to hold this incredible, earthy, sweet coupling as an idyllic memory; she tried to encapsulate, hold on to, take a mental picture of this moment and felt the pleasure fading from the effort.

"Connor," she said quietly. "I want a baby."

Alex sensed his reaction before she saw it. The pause in his breath, the tense of his shoulders; she prayed that she was wrong. When Connor didn't answer, Alex rolled over, reached for her underwear, and wrenched them on. She sat up in the dirt, grass scratching her lower back. Her fears were confirmed. Connor's brow was wrinkled into a deep furrow, and his chest heaved as if he'd been hit.

"You really do?" His arms cradled his chin on a bare patch of earth and he spoke casually, as if he had just come out of a dream, a stray leaf stuck to his forearm. "I thought the pregnancy was a mistake."

Alex let those words sink in. Yes, there they were. No way to retreat now. She leapt up and regarded Connor as if he was fading into the ether, as if his presence would soon become less than solid. Would her sweet memory of this day fade now too, or distort like some dark twist in a dream? "I didn't get pregnant on purpose, if that's what you mean."

Connor protested. "That's not what I said—"

"But I loved being pregnant. I loved having a life inside me. Our little baby." She didn't think Connor had ever seen her cry, other than the night of the miscarriage, when the force of her emotion drove him back to bed. Did he want to sleep now, too? Was that how he dealt with stress? Alex wiped at her face with the bottom of her t-shirt, unable to hold back the tears. "God, it's good to finally say that to you."

Connor dressed in stiff, automatic motions while he processed Alex's confession. "What about your career?"

"I guess that'll have to change. You wanted me to stop touring, right?"

No words came out of Connor's mouth; he shared none of his thoughts as he contemplated the grass.

"I'm going to do this, Connor," she said, "with or without you."

He closed the short distance between them and picked up her hands, rough against smooth, small inside large. "I didn't come all this way to turn my back on you, Alex. I love you."

Alex couldn't reconcile her disappointment with the joy of hearing that he loved her, a complexity that sent her running back to the simplest truth, bringing to mind a line from Jane Kenyon's poem, 'Happiness': *And how can you not forgive? You make a feast in honor of what was lost.* The cheerful sun, the optimistic birds that had moments ago been the backdrop of her idyllic scene now seemed an affront to her roiling emotions. She finally said, "You didn't want our baby."

"But I want you," he pleaded.

"You don't ever see yourself being a father again?"

Connor drew in his lower lip; his hazy eyes searched hers. "I don't think so, Lexi. I messed it up so badly last time."

Part of Alex wanted to dissolve into him, to relieve herself of all of her hurt, and all of her hope. Must she have everything? Here was a good man, a man who traveled thousands of miles to be with her. And he loved her. Why couldn't that be enough?

Alex stared over at the blinking lights of the radio tower. She longed to read a message in the rhythm of the pulses. Alex scanned his face, the rough, rugged skin of his cheeks, his solid forearms, his crooked bottom tooth, his intelligent eyes. She had spent her life running from place to place, from man to man but, finally, she had divined what she wanted her future to hold.

"A baby," she said firmly. "I want a family, one that doesn't tear itself apart with silence."

Connor reeled as if he'd been dealt a blow. "So that's it?"

Alex held firm to the one certainty she had. "Unless there's room for negotiation."

"I can't believe you're willing to end our relationship here, now." He was angry. "You might have given me some hint of what you were thinking."

"My reaction to the miscarriage—to the pregnancy—wasn't clear enough?"

"Maybe," he said, "but I couldn't see past my own feelings."

Alex almost blurted: "you had feelings?" but prevented herself from rehashing the same issues. She was aware, from many breakups before, that it was easy to get mired in blame. Comments like that were only delay tactics. An abrupt rip was better than the clinging, redundant, gut-punched recollection of the last few years. Why did people stomp around in the muck of a dead relationship?

"Alex, please," Connor begged. "Give us a chance. Maybe you'll change your mind once some time has passed."

"Time is the problem, Connor. I haven't got any time." A chipmunk made a sharp chirp, as if to emphasize her decision. In the high clouds, an airplane rumbled over their heads.

Connor shifted his feet and yanked at his jacket. Alex pretended for his sake that she didn't notice his eyes beginning to water. "I guess you've made up your mind," he said, his voice steady after he cleared his throat.

"I have."

She watched him withdraw from her, saw him put up the barriers a broken heart required. He winced and gave her a look of pity as she knocked a cigarette out of the pack and lit the tip. At a loss for what to do, embarrassed by her rebellious desire to smoke, Alex finally asked, "Can you at least bring Lily and me as far as Florence? I can make my way back from there."

Connor paused before he answered, as if the absolute last thing he wanted to do was give them a ride, as if he imagined an awkward two hours in the car, unable to talk freely, or cry, or whatever it was that he would do to deal with his sorrow. Finally, Connor gave his quiet consent. They remained mute all the way back through the park, down the long dirt path, past the rental house and out into town. With a minimum of dialogue, they walked back to Helena's, where they felt the locals' eyes on them, curious, wondering who this man was with the blond American.

* * *

Martina searched up and down the street, undecided and panicky outside the apartment; her face was a pale mask though the sun still shone. Clouds sat overhead, far off over distant vineyards, waiting, waiting.

When Alex and Connor entered the street, tense and silent, Martina ran to them and yanked on Alex's arm with surprising force. Out of her mouth came a stream of rapid Italian, solid and serious. A bead of sweat formed into a rivulet and rolled down her temple.

"What's wrong?" Alex asked, letting herself be hurried along. "*In Inglese, per favore.*"

Martina did not stop to explain. "Miss Lily," she cried, "she sleeps. Miss Lily. Come."

Alex and Connor rushed to the door, flung it open, and thundered down the hallway with Martina, into the guest bedroom. Lily was atop the chocolate-colored covers, her skin paler than even Martina's wan face, nearly gray. Her arm was bent to the side like bird's broken wing. She looked more than asleep. She looked dead.

Chapter 24

NO IMAGININGS OR books or movies could prepare Alex for watching a body as it edged close to death. Odors and mess are the partners of illness: the fetid stench of emptied bowels, mucus, and urine all mixed with the stringent scent of alcohol. Lily's body gave off a hint of that rotten odor, an aura of waning existence, as if her very being might hiss out of a slow leak.

"Oh God." Alex ran to her and shook Lily's shoulders like she was a broken toy. Lily didn't stir. Her head wagged from side to side with no resistance. Alex combed the room for pills or some type of poison. She scanned for blood, for a cut. She tried to find a pulse while Connor escorted Martina from the room. Martina would not cooperate, fought him, pushed up against Alex as she searched.

"Call an ambulance," Alex directed Martina. "Is there an ambulance? A medic?" Martina suddenly seemed unable to understand English.

Connor found the phone on a small, marble side table. "I'll dial an operator," he nearly shouted.

Finally, Lily made a small chirp as Alex prodded and slapped at her. "What did you take? Lily! Listen to me. What did you take? The Ativan?"

Lily moaned.

"I can't get anyone. 'o' doesn't work. Neither does 911," Connor yelled.

"Martina," Alex turned to the girl, who hadn't left her side. "*Telefono. Dottore.*"

Martina blinked several times and then ran to Connor. Her patent leather shoes clicked on the tile floor. She dialed the number and gave her address rapidly into the phone. Alex prayed an ambulance would come; Helena had said the hospital was an hour away.

Alex moved Lily's limbs in a poor attempt to keep her awake, up and down like a physical therapist might exercise a paraplegic. Another moan. Her skin was the ashen color of a cold fire pit. Even a wet face cloth against Lily's forehead failed to make her stir.

At a loss, Alex glanced over her shoulder at Connor in the doorway. His eyes moved across the solid oak headboard, over the dark sheets with Lily's frail body nearly lifeless on top. "Let's take her into the shower," he said.

Spurred into motion, Alex ran ahead to the bathroom while Connor lifted Lily like a child. Martina followed close behind. She darted between the bathroom and the front window, yanked back wispy chiffon curtains, on alert for the ambulance. Connor placed Lily, fully clothed, in the claw-foot tub and they turned on the cold water, a scene that brought to Alex's mind a Curious George book she read while in a children's store, while she shopped for baby clothes.

Lily sputtered when the water hit her skin, but her eyes remained shut. She groaned and tried to shrink away from the cold, rolled her body over, instinctively hiding her face. Alex reached in and pulled her back over, trying to fully rouse her. Lily's lids fluttered open for only an instant. The water thundered down onto her body until it was obvious she wouldn't wake. Connor leaned over Alex and spun the valve, yanked a dark towel off the rack to wipe Lily's face. Alex stripped Lily of her wet clothes while Connor grabbed a blanket from the bed. Even though Alex had no time to reflect, in the recesses of her mind, she couldn't help but notice their teamwork.

Connor bundled Lily and carried her to the front room, laid her on a patterned couch, the blue and pink and orange paisleys swimming with motion behind Lily's limp body. As they waited for the medics, Connor took Alex's hand in his, and she was tempted to lay her head on his shoulder as they stood looking out the window, together in this moment charged with disquiet, with the recognition of human fragility. She was glad he didn't offer any platitudes, didn't tell her, without knowing, that everything would turn out alright, that Lily would survive.

After a brutal half hour, sirens finally ripped through the air, tires rumbled down the cobblestone road before coming to a halt in front of their apartment. The townspeople emerged from their houses and shops. Alex tried to cover Lily's face as the emergency team carried her out on a stretcher, naked under the swaddling.

Helena came thundering up the street, frantically yelling for Martina, whom she found hovering just inside the door to their apartment, just as the medics loaded Lily into the ambulance. Helena enfolded her daughter in her arms as if dragging Martina back from the edge of a cliff, hugged her tightly, then pulled back to check her face, kissing the girl's cheeks, crying in relief that the ambulance was not there for Martina.

"*Ospedale dell'Alta Val D'Elsa,*" Helena told Alex through tight lips. Not until she and Connor were halfway up the street, heading for the car, did Alex realize she should have begged Helena's forgiveness: for leaving Lily at the house with Martina, for letting Martina witness her new friend's plunge toward death. For bringing Lily's personal tragedy into their lives.

The emergency room doors opened and closed, admitting bursts of cold air each time. The hospital was busy, but not disturbingly crowded. A man with a bloody arm was immediately admitted, a sweaty child was taken to the back, supported by two adults. There were no appalling injuries, no gunshot wounds, though a loud, belligerent woman shouted in dense Italian. People circled the lobby, most of them looking exhausted and uneasy. Alex stopped glancing up each time the door opened, in an attempt to calm her nerves. Just as in the States, the receptionist seemed coolly unconcerned. The room smelled of bleach and recirculated air.

Alex held the clipboard on her lap and had to admit to herself that she couldn't answer most of the health questions important to Lily's treatment. She couldn't help but think that those intimate details could only be known about a spouse, or a child. Alex forced herself to concentrate, to fill out what she could. She struggled not to be daunted by the Italian words and phrases: she marked what she could understand, *Nome*: LILY ANDREWS; *Nationalito/a*: AMERICANO; *Servizio militare:* X NON. But, she didn't have any emergency contacts for Lily. She had no clue about Lily's medical history and couldn't even decide what to write for her permanent address. In fact, all she knew was Lily's age, that she grew up in California (which the intake form did not ask) and that she couldn't have children.

In frustration, Alex dug through her bag and pulled out the book of lies; she flipped through the tour book for contact information. Feeling a sense of justice, she wrote down Joe's cell number under *contatto primario*, the office in New York as a secondary number. If anyone should take responsibility for Lily, it was Sadie. She noticed the tour would be in Florence tonight, not fifty miles away.

Alex subtracted Lily's age from 2005, and wrote 1975 in clear, round numbers, though she was unsure of her exact birth date. She remembered celebrating last spring—in March or April—a party at the Drake Hotel's rooftop bar in Toronto. She kept re-reading the other questions over and over again, slaved doggedly, persisting through the translations.

Though Alex was acutely conscious of the break-up, she was also comforted by Connor's warm, solid, quiet presence. She couldn't decide whether he was just better in a light-of-day, out-of-country emergency, or whether he had learned a lesson from the night Alex suffered. She glanced over and caught Connor staring at her, eyes rife with concern, and she wondered if Lily's misfortune had spurred in him thoughts of longevity, of progeny.

An uncomfortable and much too silent three hours passed before they heard a word. Alex and Connor counted out lire to buy a strange mixture of snacks from a vending machine: pineapple juice, chocolate Bueno bars, and dried salami. Alex considered heading to the car for a toothbrush just as a doctor—a short, wiry woman with a nervous tic in her right shoulder and a bright orange stethoscope around her neck—came out and explained in clear, deliberate English about Lily's condition.

She pushed a pair of red-framed glasses up onto her head to address them. "You are with the American girl?"

Connor and Alex rose—looking unified—from their padded chairs. "Yes."

"The evidence indicates that she took over twelve mg of Lorazepam, also known as Ativan or Temesta. Ingestions in this amount are not usually fatal, but we took the precaution of performing a gastric lavage. If she does not stabilize in the next two hours, we will consider intravenous flumazenil."

Alex listened stoically to the woman, unsure how to take the news, realizing she had only a vague idea of what the procedures meant. Alex focused, revisited what she'd been told: gastric, intravenous, stabilize, those were all words she understood. The doctor went on to say that because of the amount of Lorazepam in her system, she could not consider this overdose accidental. No surprise to Alex, but the pronouncement was still hard to hear. The doctor continued to talk medicine: reasoning, procedures, plans. Connor grasped Alex's arm, gently, but with enough pressure to prop her up if necessary and Alex wondered if she looked woozy. She wondered whether she looked as if she might fall.

"When she awakes," the doctor said, "we will screen her for psychiatric evaluation. We most likely will transfer her from emergency to the psychiatric ward." After a pause during which the doctor looked at each one of them pointedly, she continued. "I suggest you fortify yourselves. Go have a meal," she said. "It will be a good while before the patient is ready to see you."

Just as the doctor finished with her careful English commentary, Alex saw Milo and Helena tear through the emergency room doors. They did not hesitate but rushed over, easily spotting Connor and Alex who huddled together in that nearly haughty, yet somewhat perplexed manner Americans tend to display—more edgy than Europeans, less elegantly dressed. Helena embraced her friend, looking directly and deeply into Alex's eyes; she placed her hand on Alex's cheek. Milo's expression was pained, and he too reached for Alex.

"How is she?" Milo asked. Alex clung to him longer than she intended, taking in the bright, soft smell of his leather jacket. Over Milo's shoulder, she saw Connor listening half-heartedly to Helena. He wore his dinner party look—combined tolerance and impatience. She and Connor never developed a silent signal as a long-married couple might have: a lift of the eyebrows, the tap of a cheek signaling need of rescue from an insufferable conversation, but still Alex could see his head wasn't with Helena. She had the urge to tell Connor to trust Helena, to get to know her as a dear friend.

"I shouldn't have left her alone," Alex said. "I gave her the pills back. I didn't think she'd hurt herself."

Milo dipped his head reverently. "I have a confession as well." Around them, people spoke in Italian; they chattered about their conditions, about their suffering. "I'm sorry to say that Lily asked if she could live with me in Firenze—and I suggested it was not a good idea."

Alex reeled back. "When?"

"This morning, after Connor arrived." Milo laid his hand on her shoulder, either to comfort Alex, or to steady himself. "I like Lily very much, but I am in no place... no position to take care of her. She may have taken this refusal very hard."

"It's not your fault," Alex said.

"*Ne anche il tuo,*" Milo said with a gentle smile. "You either." Milo reached into his jacket and removed a packet of photographs. "Lily asked me to develop these for her. For you."

Alex glanced briefly, distractedly, into the packet before she turned her attention to Helena. "I'm so sorry about Martina. I didn't think about them being alone together when we went to the park."

"I know that much about you," Helena said. "Martina is with neighbors now. She wanted to join us, of course—she is concerned for her new friend, and I believe she has figured out it was not an accident. Tell me, was Lily trying to take her own life?"

Alex sat, clumsily, almost dropping into the seat, as if her body misjudged the height of the chair. "I don't think it was an accident," Alex said as Helena wrapped her arm around her friend. Connor crowded in on the other side, close enough that their legs made contact.

Milo stood, as if he was about to give a presentation to the three of them. His leather jacket, his stout frame, made him look like an aging Marlon Brando in *On the Waterfront*. "I have not been a very good father to Martina," he announced. "I should be with her more, there when she needs me. *Grazie*, Alex. You have made me see this."

As if embarrassed by his pronouncement, Milo grabbed the questionnaire off the chair, which Alex had still not handed in, and headed across the room. Connor's hand moved to Alex's thigh, a practiced, caring motion. She looked up at his face and saw, unmasked, his regret about not being a good father. It occurred to her that Connor's reluctance about her pregnancy had not been about her, but about his fear of failure, about his shame around his daughter, Lucy. If he would be willing to talk about his fear, willing to admit his feelings, was this a hurdle they could work around, work through together? Could she convince him that even if they were terrified, they should take this exceptional journey together?

Helena leaned in closer to Alex. "All of this raises the issue of Martina's mother, of course. Now, I think, would be a good time to talk about what happened. She wants to know, but it's hard for me and for Milo. There's been so much tragedy in both of our lives; neither of us likes to dwell on the hard times. Maybe now, we have to tell her."

At the reception desk, Milo conversed heatedly with the nurse. He gestured and raised his voice and returned a moment later, having gathered no further information. "*Non possono dirci nulla.* Nothing," he growled through his teeth. "We cannot see her, maybe even until tomorrow."

Milo and Helena had a rapid exchange in Italian and finally announced that they would come back the next day.

"We will keep our eyes on Lily," Milo said. "We will help you get her home."

Connor stood close to Alex after they said goodbye. Before he came to Italy, he wasn't even convinced Alex was angry with him. He thought she was enraged at the world, at God, maybe, for the whole experience. But because he loved her—because she loved him, he (mistakenly) felt separate from her frustration or her wrath.

"I find it disorienting," he finally said, "to be in a place where you don't understand the language, like a child listening in on adult conversations."

Across the room a man consoled a small girl—only a few years old—cuddling her close to his chest. Both of his arms were wrapped around the girl's tiny body, and he whispered to her, his brow furrowed with worry, his voice drowned in her wails. Connor remembered a moment—one of the few he was present for—with his daughter in an emergency room, possibly the only time he was present at a medical event involving Lucy. In that instance, he was still living in his in-laws' basement and had been up all night trying to console his daughter, who had an ear infection. Lucy clung to her mother in just the same way as this hospital child clung to her father, as if she was afraid of being torn away into the large, frightening world. That one hospital night when Connor was there, Lucy forbade her father to touch her.

He set his heart aside that day, realizing he had never been a comfort to Lucy. It wasn't difficult, at twenty, to leave them. Who was to say he wasn't capable of taking off again? The same old fear reared its head. It ate at his gut. He'd never even allowed himself the possibility. When playing sports if he found himself hanging back, timid, he forced himself to hustle harder. The same at work. Why was he so reticent in his personal life?

"You get used to it," Alex said.

Connor stared at Alex, though his head was still in the past. "I don't know if I would," he acknowledged. "But I've never really tried." Could he try?

An ambulance wailed in behind them, another life at risk. Alex followed the van's trajectory, watched the medics quickly unload a stretcher. She wondered how long Connor would stick around. Now, with Lily in the hospital, had their feelings shifted? She had the fleeting thought, again, almost too painful to unearth, that maybe he'd change his mind about a baby, that maybe he loved her enough.

"Should we go?" Connor asked. "Get some dinner?"

"There's something I need to do first," Alex said.

Chapter 25

SUITCASES WERE STACKED neatly under the bays of the bus, doors pulled down with a thwamping sound followed by the click of the latch. Inside the bus, the driver had started coffee brewing, its nutty aroma filling the front lounge. A random plastic room key sat on the table, its owner too lazy or unconcerned to walk it back to the front desk of the hotel.

"Whose key is that?" Kat asked, more out of a sense of propriety than concern for the amount of plastic that was thrown in landfills. "You should return it." No one dared claim the key.

At seven a.m., the whole crew had climbed onto the bus, including Brooke, who was early for once.

"A guest appearance from Miss Brown," the stage manager joked, jump-starting a string of comments from the rest of the crew about Brooke's perpetual failure to be early.

"Where's Alex?" Joe asked.

"No sense delaying," Brooke said. "Alex has jumped ship. Defected. Gone A.W.O.L."

Touring crews loved a good drama. They longed for it, dying for an event to shake up their lives, to make one day different from the day before. They craved rumors, speculated like gossiping office workers. When Brooke announced that Alex wasn't coming back, you could've heard a Sharpie fall. The whole crew, to a man, turned and stared at Brooke.

"We know where she is, Brooke. She's not A.W.O.L.," Kat corrected.

"Alex isn't with you?" Ethan asked, confused.

"Nope," Brooke announced. "She stayed in Italy with Lily."

Everyone fired off questions: "Lily's not here? What happened to Alex? They quit? Neither one of them is coming back? Where are they?"

They quieted down when Joe hurled his radio toward the door of the bus. The battery flew off and narrowly missed the stage manager, who ducked, hands over his head as he stood on the bottom step.

"No fucking way," Joe spit. "Why didn't one of you tell me?"

"You didn't ask," Kat said, deadpan. Brooke couldn't do as well and grinned heartily.

Stepping over his radio, Joe marched out into the parking lot, cursing aloud, waving his hands, looking like a madman. He paced the length of the bus a couple of times, sucked air back into his lungs. His short legs marched up and down, even stomped on the pavement. The whole crew watched him out the windows until he finally re-boarded and told the driver to get a move-on. He glared at Brooke. He shifted his cold eyes to Kat, and for a second, she thought maybe they'd made a mistake. Maybe Joe would retaliate—what could he do to her? Not much unless Sadie turned on her. But Brooke? Joe knew how much she wanted to get out on stage with Sadie. He might make up some fake contractual clause that wouldn't allow her to perform. He might put her on some awful task like counting an inventory of the thousands of backstage passes. You couldn't count on loyalty with a hot shot like Joe.

"Fuck Alex," Joe declared. "We've got Tim."

No one protested. Joe was just stating another version of the basic touring mantra: "Everyone's replaceable." But half the people on the bus disagreed. This time it wasn't true, Kat thought; they *did* need Alex: for what she knew about putting the rig together. For stability. For the important balance of girl power in this throw-your-radio, super-macho, blame-someone-else showbiz crew.

The first load-in without Alex did not happen smoothly. The men who believed they didn't need Alex finally got the rig up after long hours and some real disorganization. During sound check, Sadie, too, was scattered. When Kat carried the Gibson onstage, Sadie complained, "You should've tuned it to B. We're doing 'All That You Aren't.'" Kat wouldn't even entertain the idea that she misheard; she knew Sadie most definitely asked for a D tuning so they could rehearse "Shake it Down." The last straw for Kat was when Sadie complained she didn't have any picks, though Kat already lined up three on her mic stand. Kat sauntered out on stage and pointed to the picks, then left the stage without a word.

The arena was dark, and the rig had been up for just over an hour, the sound and lighting systems finally flown and all the issues wrung out.

"Hey Kat," Ethan yelled, the two of them the only crew on stage right. Clip-on bulbs created isolated pools of light over their work cases. Everyone else had retired to the crew room. They were playing on Gameboys or shooting the shit, falling back into the patterns of touring as if they'd had no break at all, as if nothing had changed. "Come try out this cool site."

Kat was reluctant to leave the cable she was soldering, the connector perfectly poised in the vise, the solder gun just to temperature. "Maybe later."

"Come on," Ethan cajoled. "This is about the future of human relations. It'll blow your mind."

"I doubt it," Kat grumbled, but put down her roll of flux, flipped up her standing magnifying glass. Her eyes needed a break.

Ethan scrolled around the front page of the website on his laptop. He typed in his name. "Look at this, Kat. You can get hooked up with anyone, all over the world. People put in stuff about themselves: what they're doing, what they see, who they're with, what they're thinking about." To show Kat what he meant, he added a photo of himself and Lily to the page in just a few seconds, with a few clicks on the mousepad.

"I'd call it a waste of time," Kat said.

"It's for fun," Ethan explained. "So people can meet each other— expand their worlds."

"More like an invasion of privacy. Why not type, 'Hello stalker. Here's where you can find me today.'"

"You're so suspicious, Kat. Mark my words: you'll end up with an account someday. You should start playing around. You like technology. This could change your whole experience of downtime on tour. No more having to look at *Enquirer* magazines left in the crew room. No more bad television as your only option for entertainment."

"You know what it looks like to me? A huge vanity podium. The last thing this world needs is yet another stage for narcissists to parade themselves around on. Don't we have enough of that?" Kat gestured to the physical stage in front of them. "Why does everyone want to draw attention to themselves? What's wrong with being private?"

Ethan laughed openly at Kat. Over her head, in the upmost tier of seating, a janitor cleaned, swabbing his mop back and forth. "It's not just about showboating. You can look for and *find* people you haven't seen in years. Reconnect. Maybe we can even convince Alex to get an account; then we don't have to lose touch with her."

Kat crossed her arms and reconsidered, felt the blood pulse up behind her ears. "You can find anyone?"

"As long as they are signed up. And *a lot* of people are jumping in. I just found this girl I went to high school with. She was the star of the track team; I mean, this girl could *run*. She didn't even know my name back then, but she's friends with me now, online, kind of flirty, even. All of the drama of high school. None of the trauma."

Kat's mind raced immediately to afternoons on the horse farm, to those first stirrings of attraction: maple seed pods that fell in Jessica's hair, chills when Jessica's fingertips touched her. Did she dare try to find Jessica again? Even a 'hello' or a current photo would help.

Kat detected a whiff of clean, light perfume and heard the tinkle of jewelry before a hand grasped her arm. "Are you two looking at porn?" Sadie joked, interrupting.

"What?" Kat asked, shocked and annoyed. But then Lily had reported on Sadie's game of picking women she'd like to sleep with. Kat nearly blurted a joke about girl-on-girl porn, but she couldn't think fast enough, or wasn't brave enough, or didn't feel comfortable enough with Sadie anymore.

"Facebook," Ethan said, sitting up, almost defensively.

"Oh, I heard about that." Sadie nodded. "Let me look. I can't sign up. Too public."

"You could make up a different name. Post anonymously," Ethan suggested.

Sadie gave a wicked smile, always on stage, always performing. "Oh, but what am I without my name?" she asked and patted his hair like a puppy's. "I actually came over to have a little tête-à-tête with you, Kat. Here goes." She looked off at the distant scoreboard and bit her lip. "I just want to tell you that I value you. You are a great guitar tech. You understand my stage setup. You bring me what I need before I ask. Sometimes when I think you haven't done something, you have. I can't imagine anyone else doing as good a job as you. Thank you." Sadie finished with a dramatic curtsy before she strutted away, job done, lines executed. Bullet point checked.

Kat watched her retreat, stupefied. "She's never—" Kat said. "Holy shit."

Ethan returned to the computer screen and the photo of Lily—a glowing picture Ethan had taken early on, when Lily still shone like a beacon. "I guess Sadie finally figured out what she lost."

* * *

Sadie lounged alone on a faux leather couch in her dressing room, staring obliquely at the exposed pipes. White-painted steel.

A thick layer of dust and grime coated the tops of the pipes. The brocade pillow under her head was stiff and scratchy. *This is what I get to see of Paris? This is what I've come back to tour for?* Used to be—not so very long ago—Sadie would spend her days shopping or sightseeing. Maybe answer an invite from another celebrity or some new and fabulous friend. Lily used to set those things up for her, but today Joe just sent a town car (not even a limo!) from the hotel to the venue. No interesting side trips, no lunch in a café. *I should've stayed in New York with Jules.*

Last week, during the break, she and Jules bombed around the City together at night, but during the day, she would lie in bed and think about Lily, trying to get up the motivation to do a little yoga. Another assistant gone. Was she really so impossible to work with?

Looking for inspiration, Sadie even once lay on the floor in Lily's bedroom that still smelled like patchouli and sage and also a faint whiff of mustiness, almost like an old bookstore. She dropped her head to the side to investigate, and there, under the bed, was an old cigar box, a thick layer of dust across the green and gold patterned top. Sadie rolled into a seated position and pulled the box onto her lap. She wiped her hands on her pants as she exhumed the heaping stack of Lily's photos. She had the impression she'd nosed into Lily's personal thoughts, as if she'd read her diary. Those photos of feet and shoes narrated a story of Lily's days in New York. When did Lily find the time? Over the break, Sadie again and again thumbed through the box of Lily's photos like a trove of relics, like prized mementos.

She even managed to line up a show for Lily next winter at the little gallery down in SoHo. The curator seemed excited about the photos, truly excited; he didn't just pander to Sadie's celebrity status. She could tell the difference—by whether people looked her in the eye, by their fluttery hands. Surely Lily would come back when she heard the news. When they found her.

Jules rapped his knuckles on the dressing room door, a syncopated rhythm. "I've had a brainstorm," he said as he entered.

"Really?" Sadie answered. "Educate me."

Jules sat on the comfy, opulent chair across the room, and her heart leapt with the intensity of his stare. There was a moment last week, after they watched an off-off-Broadway production of some dreary Beckett play he'd chosen, when Sadie wondered whether he would make a pass at her. He gave her that look over cocktails in the back room of Bungalow 8, like he was thinking about sticking his tongue in her mouth, but they were interrupted. Since that night, she wondered what his hands might feel like on her body. He was a good guitar player. Precise, rhythmic.

Jules stroked his goatee. His expression morphed into a wry, almost conspiratorial grin. "You need a new assistant," he said.

Sadie's heart quickly settled into its regular pace. "I'm hoping Joe will track Lily down. I had him email Alex—who must be feeling a mound of guilt over nearly killing me. Why else wouldn't she have come back? I can only assume they are together."

"Well, if Joe doesn't find them—" Jules started.

Sadie interrupted. "Joe *will* find her. He has to find her."

"Well, just on the off chance he doesn't," Jules said, "I've got the perfect person."

"You?"

"Don't be silly. Brooke, of course."

"Oh, her." Sadie frowned. A cart rattled and clanged down the hall. The sound reminded her of the noisy *Fiesta de la Vendimia* parade floats rumbling by her grandparents' house in Chile. As a child, Sadie stood on the stoop, munching on empanadas and watching the Queen of the Grape Harvest on her float, lit with foot candles that flickered and cast shadows in the oncoming dusk.

Jules ignored Sadie's displeasure. "Brooke's already a part of this tour; she gets you. There'd be no adjustment period."

Sadie imagined herself as queen, Brooke as one of the fawning princesses, a basket of rose petals in her hand. Sadie had a hard enough time figuring out from day to day who was on her side, who actually cared about her. Lily was one of the few who had appreciated her. "I don't like it," she finally said.

Jules leaned back and a pout filled in his thin lips. "It could work."

There was no doubt Brooke would make a lousy assistant—she certainly didn't do yoga—but there was just over a month left on tour. She could manage that long, at least until Lily came back. She shrugged, as close as she'd get to a true assent.

"I'd rather have you." Sadie swung her legs around the edge of the couch and crossed over to sit on the edge of Jules's chair. "We make a good team."

Jules wasn't really her type, she thought, kind of mousy and intellectual; she usually went for tight, built bodies, chiseled faces, but he was here, and he was reliable. Over the break, he doted on her like she was his own child, made her wonder if it was time to try out a new variety. They'd been friends forever. Weren't friends supposed to be the best lovers?

"Just what are we talking about here?" Jules asked.

Sadie leaned down close to Jules's face, his breath warm on her cheek. She moved in and gave Jules a light kiss on the mouth, lingering for just a heartbeat, her lips millimeters from his. She guessed that he'd fantasized about pinning her down on the dressing room couch, as her lacy lingerie slipped to the floor. He'd probably even imagined three-ways with her and Brooke, as the two of them covered him with food and licked syrup off his chest.

"At your service," Jules said. His lip trembled in anticipation as he reached up and drew Sadie into his lap. Together they sank into the relative comfort of the overstuffed chair. "Whatever you want."

Chapter 26

IN THE CAR, Alex dug in her suitcase and found the clothes Helena gave her. She changed out of her worn t-shirt and cargo pants, kicked off beat-up old Skechers in the bathroom of the emergency room, and emerged a new woman, a shift that caused Connor to do a doubletake as she approached the car. He nodded in appreciation at her soft, draping shirt, at the well-cut pants that hugged her hips, accented by high heels (that Alex clearly wasn't one hundred percent comfortable walking in).

"Wow," he said. Connor climbed behind the wheel wearing a smile, despite the heavy events of the afternoon, despite the possibility that they made love for the last time just a few short hours ago.

They drove the hour from the hospital to the Mandela Forum in Florence where Sadie would play that night. The security guard nodded when Alex flashed her badge at the backstage gate. They walked by the buses, up short cement stairs, and through a heavy door. Alex scanned the dark corridor for a sign that pointed the way to Production. She was surprised to find she was nervous, the same sickening sense that came over her before a load-in, that emptiness in her gut, when she steeled herself to face forty-plus stagehands, mostly men, looking at her with skepticism and wonder.

Alex asked Connor to wait in the hallway—she had to do this part alone—and entered the production office feeling overdressed, as if she was somehow vulnerable without the anonymity of her stage blacks.

"You came back," Brooke yelled and jumped up to hug Alex. "Your clothes are fabulous. You won't believe what's been happening. I have so much to tell you." She lowered her voice. "I'm Sadie's assistant now."

Joe wheeled around in his chair and leaned back with casual ease, as if he had only seen her a few moments ago. "Look what the cat dragged in."

Alex had an impulse to cross her arms over her chest.

"I suppose you've come crawling back now, hoping we'll take you in like some lonely hitchhiker." He smiled. This was fun for him.

Alex bristled, ready to mount her defense as Brooke crinkled up a piece of paper, tossed the ball at Joe. "Now stop that. You said, quote: 'Our lives would be easier if Alex were here.'"

"Easier or not, you're too late, Alex. Your replacement's already boarded a plane in LaGuardia. Snooze you lose—that sort of thing."

Alex struggled to keep her ego at bay. "I'm not rejoining the tour."

"You're not?" Brooke was disappointed.

Joe flicked his pencil onto his desk. "Then why the hell are you here?"

Brooke boogied out the door to round up some of the other crew members when Alex asked (and before Joe could order her not to). The fluorescents hummed overhead, and Alex smelled the oily, bunker-like odor of the locker room. A faint whiff of urinal cakes lingered in the air. Despite the cold, desolate setting, Alex guessed she was likely to miss the passion and personalities of show business. Unease was, after all, the most familiar sensation to her, a relaxed discomfort, like an old pair of shoes with the heel worn down so far that her foot hit the pavement. This uncomfortable place was where she'd spent so many years. It was the only home she'd known.

Kat was the first person in the door. "I heard you were back." She gave Alex a quick hug while she took in her frilly, feminine outfit, the soft linen such a contrast to her own limp cotton and coarse jeans.

Ethan hugged Alex enthusiastically, though when he pulled back, he looked pained, his face strewn with hurt.

Red said, "Hey little mama." And Tim, entering last, looked her up and down and smiled widely. She thought he might be about to embrace her, so she immediately began to speak, trying not to lose her nerve.

"First of all, Lily's in the hospital. She's in *Val d'Elsa*, not far. I didn't have any emergency contact information for her. You must have that somewhere."

"Hospital?" Ethan looked panicked, maybe imagining a car accident or gunshot wound. "Where's the hospital? Why's she there?"

"She climb that tower again?" Kat asked.

Alex shook her head. "Pills."

"Oh God, my poor little girl," Brooke exclaimed. "Where is she? I'll send flowers."

"The tour should at least buy her a ticket home," Alex said. "She's stranded here. She had a breakdown because of how she was treated."

"I'll go see her," Ethan offered.

"No, you won't," Joe barked. "As I understand it, she quit. Just like you, Alex."

"You know why?" Alex said, unburdened, free of the need to swallow her rage and her sadness. She wasn't on the tour anymore; she didn't have anything else to prove to those men. "I quit because I had a miscarriage."

The room was as quiet as a courtroom waiting for a verdict. Ethan stood next to her and held on to her arm, offered his silent support.

Alex sniffed. "I'm tired of hiding it, pretending I'm not sad." She let the tears come without restraint. Her nose ran and she permitted that to flow too, tasted the salt on her lips. With no thought of dignity or composure, Alex finally released all the emotion she had shoved down for years—not only about the miscarriage, but from every time she'd been hurt or stunted or denied. Each emotion she was taught to bury by her family. The men looked shocked, uncomfortable with the news. Brooke's eyes were wild with excitement. She handed over a Dove Bar, which Alex opened on the spot.

Her mouth deliciously full, Alex turned and addressed Red. "I know that you don't give a damn about what I've been through, but I also came here because I have proof that I didn't cause that chain to fall. I'm not going out with that on my conscience and with people I work with thinking I was that careless."

"Here we go." Joe's body was rigid, his words sharp. He responded as if to some outrageous statement, a personal and tragic insult.

"Just let that shit rest, mama," Red warned, "nobody cares."

"I care," Alex insisted. No one else challenged her. She wiped at her face, gathered courage. "The riggers are responsible for checking the chain bags."

Red crossed his arms over his massive chest. "Better pack yourself on home, you and your fancy poetry and your family plans."

"Watch it," Kat growled at Red.

Alex grabbed the stack of photos from her bag and threw them on Joe's desk. "Lily took photos. That day, she took pictures of me in the truss. I never got near the chain bag."

Joe thumbed through the photos while Red, looking at them over Joe's shoulder, grimaced. "This could be from any day," Joe said, but the furrows around his brow grew deeper, his mouth a tense line. "Who's to say these pictures are from the day the chain fell?"

Alex pointed to the downstage truss in the photos, reminding him how in Barcelona they had to bring the wings in at a shallower angle, which forced them to flatten out the rig.

"She's right," Tim admitted and gave Alex a wink. "Barcelona."

Joe threw the photos down. "She probably took one of the photos out, the one that shows her stomping on the chain."

"Maybe you'd act like that, Joe," Kat said, "but that ain't Alex's style. First of all, she's as graceful as they come up there in the rig—Alex doesn't do any 'stomping' across the truss, and secondly, she would never take one of the photos out, wouldn't come all the way back here to trick everybody."

"Alex wouldn't lie," Brooke added. "She doesn't do that. If you paid attention, you would know."

"What is this?" Joe surveyed the room, "some kind of women's lib act you worked up over break? You're always going on about women this and women that," Joe spit.

"What about Red? Or Tim?" Alex asked. "Why do they get off without taking responsibility?"

"Are you trying to throw me under the bus?" Red complained.

"If that's the only way to clear my name I will," Alex said.

Tim's ever-present smile faded to a wan grin, and she read in his expression a hint of regret.

Finally, Ethan, who had been quiet the whole time, spoke up. "The accident wasn't Alex's fault."

The men all focused on him, each looking as if they'd like to institute a gag order for him, and Alex realized that Ethan was about to make his own life hard by defending her. If he didn't join in with the boys' club, his life for the rest of the tour might be difficult. The stage manager might not assign him enough stagehands. Ethan wouldn't be invited to play golf with the promoters on their days off. The guys would be reluctant to go for a drink with him. His cases wouldn't come off the truck until the end. Maybe they'd even be smashed up. Who could guess how far Joe would go?

"Ethan, don't," Alex warned.

"No, I saw you that day. Tim saw too. You never went near that chain bag." Ethan swallowed hard. "Alex didn't kick the bag or shake the truss. In fact, I saw the assistant rigger settling the chain bags that morning—check with your own guy, Red."

Red glared, but Ethan held his ground, unblinking, until Alex moved closer and patted him on the shoulder. "Thank you," she whispered. "I don't deserve you."

"So what?" Joe spit. "Like Red said, nobody cares. It's history. Sadie sure as hell doesn't want to talk about that day. And neither do I." He turned his back to the door and to Alex.

There was nothing more to say, nothing more that Alex wanted here, so she jotted the name and address of the hospital on the back of a yellow packing slip.

"I'll go visit Lily, one way or the other," Ethan leaned in and whispered, close enough that Alex was pricked by the stubble on his chin.

Ethan would, in fact, manage to rent a car on the tour's next day off in Pisa, drive the hour and a half to the ward where (with Helena and Milo's help) Lily would have been admitted. Ethan would spend the day with Lily, making her smile for the first time since her overdose as they sat in the hospital rose garden, the castle-like stone building at their backs. Ethan would promise to return at the end of tour, to help Lily figure out where to go next, how to rebuild her life. Ethan would make Lily laugh, even, when he recalled the first time he asked her out. "How awkward," she'd said. "I'd be a female Humbert Humbert. How old are you? Sixteen?" though Ethan was actually twenty-two at the time, not so very far from her twenty-eight.

In the few weeks between visits, Lily would have grown stronger, more hopeful with each day she had spent away from Sadie. Milo, too, would pay Lily regular visits, bringing her yoga magazines and bags of chocolates and nuts and dried fruit she rarely touched. With time, with therapy, Lily would begin to understand how the drugs, exhaustion, and constant berating piled up and caused her to break. She would also begin to understand that though she could let her friends help, really, she must do the work herself.

"You, I'll miss," Alex whispered to Ethan.

In the dim hallway, Alex, Kat, and Brooke huddled. Gray cement closed in on them like a bomb shelter. Lights from the stage leaked through a crack in the curtain. Out front, the board op programmed his moving lights, streaking from blue to white to purple. The cracked oil of a hazer filled the air and a Latin beat blared for ten seconds, one last test of the monitors before sound check. Rhythms of the backstage schedule sank into Alex's bones: the particular quiet of afternoons when most of the stagehands had gone home. The smells and the sounds she'd taken in for a decade. Alex wondered how long she would remember the sensations, wondered what other memories would rise up after she walked away.

The adrenaline rush of load-outs, when they were finished, and her face was covered with grease, when she loaded a truck stacked to the roof and sweat dripped down her temples. When the locals were amazed to see her take charge of the dismantling, of the equipment getting so quickly folded away—that satisfaction couldn't be beat. And beyond all else, touring had offered her the option to travel—no—to keep running. Now, if she really wanted to have a family, if she really wanted to build a life of truth and interdependence with Connor or anyone else, she would have to learn how to settle down; she would have to learn how to tap into that feeling of contentment she had in Tuscany, with Helena and her family.

Alex was glad that at least she'd been able to experience touring with other women before she retired, a rare chance, though she suspected that would change. If women like Brooke could survive out here, then who knew?

Brooke, as if she'd read her thoughts, took Alex's hand. She grabbed at Kat's as well, but Kat jerked it away, disgusted.

"Oh Kat." Brooke laughed. "You're so butch sometimes. Give the tough guy act a rest."

Kat sucked in her bottom lip as if she was tempted to either run away or to slug Brooke.

"Anyway, I have so much to tell you about Jules and Sadie and me." Brooke jumped in, practically about to bubble over. "Jules and I broke up—big surprise, right? He's such a slimeball, really. He probably figures he's going to be a big star, too, just because he's boinking Sadie. Every time I walk in her dressing room, I have to see them together, but I'll tell you what; Sadie's a lot nicer to me now." Brooke halted her rambling tirade and lowered her voice. "Of course, I can see she's faking it, lording it over me that she's got Jules. But I plan to milk it, get out on stage with her because I bet somewhere deep down, she feels guilty." Brooke finally took a breath. "Oh, and what about Lily?"

Alex—confounded by Brooke's dizzying, rattling report—looked to Kat, who only shrugged and gave Brooke a look of revulsion, as if she was watching a badly-produced soap opera. Alex was sure these two remaining women on the tour would be lighting up the hallways of arenas and theatres all over Europe, arguing over how soon Brooke sent out a runner for a guitar part (which Kat, of course, believed should be everyone's number one priority). Lacking a better argument, they might conjure up a fight over what kind of snacks to stock the bus with, or where to pull over for a rest stop on the highway (not that either one of them had a say in that decision). Alex imagined, underneath Kat's criticism and distain, under Brooke's frivolity and dismissal, there was some true affection.

"Do you think Lily would come back to tour?" Brooke asked with a worried look. "I mean, Lily's moving on, right? Besides, Sadie's got an opportunity at a gallery brewing that's much more suited to her personality. Lily will love it."

"I doubt she'll come back." Alex explained how they found Lily on top of the bed, the depth of her trouble. "I thought she was dead," Alex said.

There was a moment when all three women were silent, recognizing the severity, where the only sound was the crackle of the PA in the arena. Alex planted a kiss on Brooke's cheek. "I'll keep in touch, I promise, and I'll find out more about how Lily is faring. Email me, and tell me all about what happens with Sadie, too."

"You know it, sister. Your amazing fellow may have wandered outside," Brooke said. "I saw him heading that way. I knew Connor was coming to Italy, by the way. He called to ask where he could find you. What a guy. I'm jealous. I recommend you hang on to that one—I mean, someone willing to fly across the country in search of you? They're not all so chivalrous. Believe me, I know."

Alex realized that this might be the last time she was backstage at a concert, the last time she would wear a coveted all access pass. Alex felt the decision she'd quietly made: it was time for her life to change. At the loading dock, she stopped by the tour's empty semi-trailers. She dug in her bag for her pack of cigarettes and tossed them with determination into a metal drum by the entrance.

She pushed the heavy door open, the blinding light harsh on her eyes. Transitioning from hours and hours in dark arenas to outdoors was always a shock to her body, a sensory overload of sunshine, fresh air (even when peppered with the odor of diesel or smoke), wind or rain on her skin. With one hand, she shaded her eyes and searched for Connor. Had he gone? Dread gripped her chest when she thought for a moment that she was totally alone, and she panicked. But no, there he was, leaning patiently against the fence that separated the cavernous, closed arena from the city beyond. She lifted her hand in a wave and let the huge steel door clang shut behind her.

"Too dark in there," Connor said when she caught up with him. He put his hand on the small of her back and guided her to the austere-looking brown sedan parked on the far side of the tour buses. She didn't shake him off, didn't make any comment at all, but was reminded of what a gentleman he could be when he opened the door for her. Jane Kenyon's poem occupied her thinking with the ease and welcome of a breeze, the idea that there was no accounting for how happiness just shows up, and that it shouldn't be squandered when it arrived at your doorstep.

This was a brand-new moment in their lives; she had gained a new perspective, down here on the ground, below the hanging trusses, outside the arena. She considered that she must not squander. Alex settled in and waited for Connor to come around and drive them away, waited for her future to begin.

Acknowledgements

Through many years and many drafts, I have felt the love of the following people: Cindy Hoyt, Kathy Ostrom, Mary Paradise and Joan Sells, thank you for all your shrewd comments. Alice Bloch, you went above and beyond what anyone could reasonably expect from a friend, repeatedly correcting my confused tenses. A special thanks to the MISers: Tracy Isaacs, Christine Junge, Megan Doney and Robyn Bradley. Without your inspiration, I may have faltered. Mandy Davis and Elicia Johnson, I wish I'd had your counsel years earlier. To Bonnie Darby, Susan Tower, Jesse Johnson, Peggy Rubens-Ellis and Sharon Huizinga, a huge thank you for reading and being honest. Ture Brusletten, *grazie* for the last-minute Italian lesson. Rob Hamilton, your writer's cabin was a true gift. Vickie Black-Vigue and Tom Vigue, your belief in me and logistical support remains essential. To A.J. Verdelle, my mentor, my wise guide who taught that clarity is non-negotiable, my deepest gratitude. Philip Elliot, your confidence in this book reencouraged me. To the women who originally inspired this story, Kim Karston Bush, Mia Adams, Kelly Macaulay, keep on shining your lights. The world needs women like you. Hannah Green, you're my biggest cheerleader. To my touring families past and present, you continue to teach me about humanity. Lisa Schettino, I'm devastated you're not here to celebrate with me. Thank you to my Vashon Island community of friends and artists and yogis and moms, too numerous to name. Kimberly Coghlan, you made the editing process a breeze. Thank you to TouchPoint Press for believing in this book. And to my loves Dorsey Davis and Zelda Davis, nothing is possible without you. I am grateful every day.

Permissions

Made in United States
North Haven, CT
21 June 2022

20478811R00157